英汉对照·中国文学宝库·现代文学系列
English-Chinese·Gems of Chinese Literature·*Modern*

孙犁小说选
Selected Stories by Sun Li

孙 犁 著
Sun Li

中国文学出版社
Chinese Literature Press
外语教学与研究出版社
Foreign Language Teaching and Research Press

图书在版编目(CIP)数据

孙犁小说选:英、汉对照/孙犁著.—北京:中国文学出版社;外语教学与研究出版社,1999.8
(中国文学宝库·现代文学系列)
ISBN 7-5071-0574-1

Ⅰ.孙… Ⅱ.孙… Ⅲ.小说-中国-现代-对照读物-英、汉 Ⅳ.H319.4:I

中国版本图书馆 CIP 数据核字(1999)第 29631 号

中文责编：邓锦辉
英文责编：殷 雯

英汉对照 中国文学宝库·现代文学系列
孙犁小说选
孙 犁著

中国文学出版社
(北京百万庄路24号)
外语教学与研究出版社 出版发行
(北京西三环北路19号)

北京市鑫鑫印刷厂印刷
新华书店总店北京发行所经销

开本 850×1168 1/32 10印张
1999年8月第1版 1999年8月第1次印刷
字数:150千 印数:1—5000册

ISBN 7-5071-0574-1/I·517
定价:12.90元

总编辑 杨宪益 戴乃迭

总策划 野 莽 蔡剑峰

编委会（以姓氏笔划为序）

吕 华

李朋义

赵文炎

凌 原

野 莽

蔡剑峰

目 录
CONTENTS

大学生读书计划 ················· 编 者（ I ）
　　——中国文学宝库出版呼吁
Lotus Creek ························ （ 2 ）
荷花淀 ···························· （ 3 ）
The Marshes ······················· （ 22 ）
芦花荡 ···························· （ 23 ）
Parting Advice ····················· （ 36 ）
嘱　咐 ···························· （ 37 ）
Honour ···························· （ 62 ）
光　荣 ···························· （ 63 ）
Recollections of the Hill Country ······ （102）
山地回忆 ·························· （103）
Little Sheng ······················· （120）
小胜儿 ···························· （121）
The Blacksmith and the Carpenter ····· （142）
铁木前传 ·························· （143）

大学生读书计划
—— 中国文学宝库出版呼吁

在即将开机印刷这第一批50本名为中国文学宝库的英汉对照读本时,我们的心情竟然忧多于喜。因为我们只能以保守的5000册印数,去面对全国400万在校大学生。

虽然我们并非市场经济的局外者,若仅为印数(销售量)计,大可奋起而去生产诸如TOFEL应试指南,或者英语四六级模拟试题集一类的教辅图书,但我们还是决定宁可冒着债台高筑的风险,也有责任对大学生同胞发出一声亲切的呼唤:请亲近我们的中国文学。

身为向世界译介中国文学和向国内出版外语读物的,具有双重责任的出版社,我们得知目前大学生往往仅注重外语的学习而偏废了母语的提高,以及忽视了中国文学的阅读,放弃了人文知识的训练。有统计表明,某理工院校57%的同学不曾读过《红楼梦》等四大名著,以致校园内外流行着"样子像研究生,说话像大学生,作文像中学生,写字像小学生"的幽默。还有一副这样的对联,说大学生的文章是"无错不成文,病句错句破残句,句句不堪入目;有误方为篇,别字错字自造字,字字触目惊心",横批"斯文扫地"。作为未来社会中坚和整个社会发展关键力量的大学生,这种"文弃"现象的流行,势必导致一场人文精神危机的爆发。对照以科学与人文精神追求为主题的五四新文化运动,八十年的历程告诉我们,以上提醒绝非危言耸听。

我们已经迈入知识经济时代,在追求科学知识的同时,创新精神已成为关键;而创新的源泉其实有赖于多学科多领域知识的交融,依靠的是新型的复合型人才,所以,文学对于新一代的大学生来说绝非装点,而是沟通自然科学与人文科学的桥梁,使我们在汲取知识的同时更能获得智慧,于创造物质的同时还进一步丰富和完善着精神;无怪乎爱因斯坦认为自己受影响最大的竟是陀思妥耶夫斯基。由此证明,一个真正的科学家应该拥有丰富的文学和文化知识以及完整的人格。十年前,七十五位诺贝尔奖得主聚会巴黎,当时他们所发表的宣言开篇就是,"如果人类要在 21 世纪生存下去,必须回首 2500 年去吸收孔子的智慧。"确实,十年的时间让我们有目共睹,现代经济科技的飞速发展何尝不是一柄双刃的剑?只有文化的力量才能抵消随之而来的负面后果。可见,知识的获取与技能的训练对于大学生来说固然重要,但文化与修养却尤需关切。正因为大学生代表着社会先知先觉的知识力量,置身当前的文化现实,就应有一分责任感与使命感,力求对知识技能以外许多带有根本性质的精神追求形成明确的意识,从而具备一种对生命意义进行探索与追问的精神,一种以人文精神为背景的生存勇气和人格力量。那么,能够引导我们探索前行的一盏明灯,不就是闪烁着理想光芒的不朽的文学名著吗?

一个人乃至一个民族,从其对文学的亲疏态度,可以衡量出其文化素质的程度。文学应是从人类文化中升华出的理想的结晶,她"使人的心灵变得高尚,使人的勇气、荣誉感、希望、尊严、同情心、怜悯心和牺牲精神复活起来"(威廉·福克纳);无疑,只有文学才能从更高的层次上提升人的文化素质和整体素质,充实人的内心世界,焕发人的精神风貌,带给人们真善美。而亲近文学,特别是热爱祖国灿烂的文学以及文化,正是当代中国大学生加强文化修养,弘扬人文精神的有力脚步。

"越是民族的,就越是世界的",中国文学属于中国,也属于世界。和平是人类的共同愿望,交流与共享则是新世纪的潮流。

中国当代大学生的血液里流动着数千年的文化积淀,没有理由在让世界了解中国大学生聪明才智的同时,却无缘分享我们的骄傲——中国大学生不但能够读懂英语的莎士比亚,而且能让世界感动于中国文学的伟大。

这是我们作为出版者的理想。我们原有一个世纪礼物的构想,是同大学生一起做一个"读书计划"。这一次将中国文学的最新荟萃配设高水平的英语译文,是其中推荐给新世纪大学生的第一批读物。盼望着您——我们无数知音中的5000名先来者,给我们鼓励,也给我们意见和批评。

编者
一九九九年五月三十日

只有文学才能从更高的层次上提升人的文化素质和整体素质,充实人的内心世界,焕发人的精神风貌,带给人们真善美。而亲近文学,特别是热爱祖国灿烂的文学以及文化,正是当代中国大学生加强文化修养,弘扬人文精神的有力脚步。

Lotus Creek

It was a summer night in the year 1940. The moon had risen and the little courtyard was delightfully fresh and clean. The rushes split during the day were damp and supple, just waiting to be woven into mats. A woman was sitting in the yard plaiting the long soft rushes with nimble fingers. The thin, fine strands leaped and twisted in her arms.

Baiyangdian lies in the middle of the province of Hebei and is known all over China for its reeds and rushes. I can't tell you the exact area grown with them nor the yearly output. All I know is that each year when the rush flowers blow in the breeze and the leaves turn yellow, the whole crop is cut and stacked in the squares round Baiyangdian like a Great Wall of reeds. The women plait mats in their threshing-fields or courtyards, vast quantities of silvery, snow-white mats. And in June, when the water in the creek is high, countless boats ship them away, until soon towns and villages in all parts of the country have these finely woven mats with their lovely designs.

"Baiyangdian mats are best," is quite an axiom.

The young woman in the yard was plaiting a mat, seated on the long stretch of it already accomplished where she seemed enthroned on virgin snow or on a fleecy cloud. From time to time she strained her eyes towards the creek, another world of silver white. Light,

荷花淀
——白洋淀纪事之一

月亮升起来,院子里凉爽得很,干净得很,白天破好的苇眉子潮润润的,正好编席。女人坐在小院当中,手指上缠绞着柔滑修长的苇眉子。苇眉子又薄又细,在她怀里跳跃着。

要问白洋淀有多少苇地?不知道。每年出多少苇子?不知道。只晓得,每年芦花飘飞苇叶黄的时候,全淀的芦苇收割,垛起垛来,在白洋淀周围的广场上,就成了一条苇子的长城。女人们,在场里院里编着席。编成了多少席?六月里,淀水涨满,有无数的船只,运输银白雪亮的席子出口,不久,各地的城市村庄,就全有了花纹又密,又精致的席子用了。大家争着买:"好席子,白洋淀席!"

这女人编着席。不久在她的身子下面,就编成了一大片。她像坐在一片洁白的雪地上,也像坐在一片洁白的云彩上。她有时望望淀里,淀里也是一片银白世界。水面笼起一层薄

英汉对照
English-Chinese
中国文学宝库
Gems of Chinese Literature
现代文学系列
Modern Literature

translucent mist had risen over the water, and the breeze was laden with the scent of fresh lotus leaves.

The gate was still open — her husband wasn't home yet.

It was very late before her husband came home. He was twenty-five or twenty-six, a barefoot young fellow in a large straw hat, a spotless white shirt and black trousers rolled up over his knees. His name was Shuisheng and he was chief of the anti-Japanese guerrillas in Lesser Reed Village, as well as the leader of the Communist Party branch there. Today he had taken his men to the district town for a meeting. His wife looked up with a smile as he came in.

"What kept you so long today?"

She stood up to fetch him some food. Shuisheng sat on the steps.

"Never mind about that — I've eaten."

She sat down on the mat again. Her husband's face was rather flushed and he seemed out of breath.

"Where are the others?" she asked.

"Still in town. How's Dad?"

"Asleep."

"And Xiaohua?"

"He was out half the day with his grandad shrimping and went to bed hours ago. Why haven't the others come back?"

Shuisheng gave a forced laugh.

"What's wrong with you?"

"I'm joining the army tomorrow," he said softly.

His wife's hand twitched as if a reed had cut it, and she started

薄透明的雾,风吹过来,带着新鲜的荷叶荷花香。

但是大门还没关,丈夫还没回来。

很晚丈夫才回来了。这年轻人不过二十五六岁,头戴一顶大草帽,上身穿一件洁白的小褂,黑单裤卷过了膝盖,光着脚。他叫水生,小苇庄的游击组长,党的负责人。今天领着游击组到区上开会去来。女人抬头笑着问:

"今天怎么回来的这么晚?"站起来要去端饭。水生坐在台阶上说:

"吃过饭了,你不要去拿。"

女人就又坐在席子上。她望着丈夫的脸,她看出他的脸有些红涨,说话也有些气喘。她问:

"他们几个哩?"

水生说:

"还在区上。爹哩?"

女人说:

"睡了。"

"小华哩?"

"和他爷爷去收了半天虾篓,早就睡了。他们几个为什么还不回来?"

水生笑了一下。女人看出他笑的不像平常。

"怎么了,你?"

水生水声说:

"明天我就到大部队上去了。"

女人的手指震动了一下,想是叫苇眉子划破了手,她把一个手指放在嘴里吮了一下。水

英汉对照
English-Chinese
中国文学宝库
Gems of Chinese Literature
现代文学系列
Modern Literature

sucking the finger.

"The district committee called this meeting today. Very soon now, they say, the Japanese devils are going to try to set up more bases. If they manage to get a base at Tongkou — which is only a few dozen *li* away — that will alter our position here completely. The meeting decided to form a district brigade to keep them out. I was the first to volunteer to go."

His wife lowered her head and muttered:

"Always a step ahead of the others, aren't you?"

"I'm chief of our village guerrillas and one of the cadres: of course I have to take the lead. The others volunteered too. They didn't dare come home, though, for fear their folk would try to hold them back. They chose me to come back and explain things for them to their families. Everyone felt you had more sense than most wives."

His wife digested this in silence.

"I won't try to stop you," she said presently. "But what about us?"

Shuisheng pointed to his father's room and told her to keep her voice down.

"You'll be taken care of, naturally. But our village is small and seven fellows are joining the army this time. That doesn't leave many young men at home. We can't look to others for everything: the main burden will fall on you. Dad's old and Xiaohua's too young to do much."

His wife felt a lump in her throat but held back the tears.

"So long as you know what we're up against, that's all."

生说:

"今天县委召集我们开会。假若敌人再在同口安上据点,那和端村就成了一条线,淀里的斗争形势就变了。会上决定成立一个地区队。我第一个举手报了名。"

女人低着头说:

"你总是很积极的。"

水生说:

"我是村里的游击组长,是干部,自然要站在头里,他们几个也报了名。他们不敢回来,怕家里的人拖尾巴。公推我代表,回来和家里人们说一说。他们全觉得你还开明一些。"

女人没有说话。过了一会,她才说:

"你走,我不拦你,家里怎么办?"

水生指着父亲的小房,叫她小声一些。说:

"家里,自然有别人照顾。可是咱的庄子小,这一次参军的就有七个。庄上青年人少了,也不能全靠别人,家里的事,你就多做些,爹老了,小华还不顶事。"

女人鼻子里有些酸,但她并没有哭。只说:

"你明白家里的难处就好了。"

水生想安慰她。因为要考虑准备的事情还

英汉对照
English-Chinese
中国文学宝库
Gems of Chinese Literature
现代文学系列
Modern Literature

7

Shuisheng wanted to comfort her but time was short. He still had many things to do before leaving.

"You shoulder the load while I'm away. When we've driven the Japs out and I come home, I'll make it up to you."

With this, Shuisheng set off for some neighbours' houses, promising to come back and explain matters to his father.

He didn't come back till cock-crow. His wife was still sitting like a statue in the yard, waiting.

"What instructions have you got for me?" she asked.

"Nothing really. Mind you go on making progress while I'm away. Work hard and learn to read and write."

"Uh-huh."

"Don't fall behind the others."

"Uh-huh. What else?"

"Don't let the Japanese devils or traitors take you alive. If you're caught, fight to the finish." This was the main thing he had to say, and his wife assented in tears.

When day broke she made a little bundle of a new cotton suit, a new towel, a new pair of cloth shoes. The other wives had similar bundles for Shuisheng to take. The whole family saw him off. His father, holding Xiaohua's hand, said:

"You're doing the right thing, Shuisheng, so I won't stop you. Go with an easy mind. I'll look after your wife and boy for you, don't worry."

The whole village, men and women, young and old, turned out to see him off. Shuisheng grinned at them all, stepped into a boat and rowed off.

太多,他只说了两句:

"千斤的担子你先担吧,打走了鬼子,我回来谢你。"

说罢,他就到别人家里去了,他说回来再和父亲谈。

鸡叫的时候,水生才回来。女人还是呆呆地坐在院子里等他,她说:

"你有什么话嘱咐我吧!"

"没有什么话了,我走了,你要不断进步,识字,生产。"

"嗯。"

"什么事也不要落在别人后面!"

"嗯,还有什么?"

"不要叫敌人汉奸捉活的。捉住了要和他拼命。"这才是那最重要的一句,女人流着眼泪答应了他。

第二天,女人给他打点好一个小小的包裹,里面包了一身新单衣,一条新毛巾,一双新鞋子。那几家也是这些东西,交水生带去。一家人送他出了门。父亲一手拉着小华,对他说:

"水生,你干的是光荣事情,我不拦你,你放心走吧。大人孩子我给你照顾,什么也不要惦记。"

全庄的男女老少也送他出来,水生对大家笑一笑,上船走了。

女人们到底有些藕断丝连。过了两天,四

But there must be something of the clinging vine about women. Two days after Shuisheng left, four young wives gathered in his house to talk things over.

"Apparently they're still here: they haven't gone yet. I don't want to cause problems, but there's a jacket I forgot to give him."

"I've something important to say to him."

Shuisheng's wife said:

"I heard that the Japanese devils want to set up a base at Tongkou...."

"There's not a chance of our running into them, not if we pay a flying visit."

"I didn't mean to go, but my mother-in-law insists that I ought to see him. What for, I'd like to know?"

Without breathing a word to anyone, the four of them took a small boat and paddled to Ma Village across the river.

They dared not look for their husbands openly there but went to a relative's house at one end of the village.

"You've just missed them," they were told. "They were still here yesterday evening but left some time in the night. No one knows where they've gone. You've no call to worry, though. I hear Shuisheng was made a vice-platoon leader straight off: they're all in tremendous spirits."

Shame-faced and blushing, the women took their leave and rowed off again. It was nearly noon, without a cloud in the sky, but on the river was a breeze from the paddy fields and rushes in the south. Theirs was the only boat afloat on this endless expanse of water like rippling quicksilver.

个青年妇女集在水生家里来,大家商量:

"听说他们还在这里没走。我不拖尾巴,可是忘下了一件衣裳。"

"我有句要紧的话得和他说说。"

水生的女人说:

"听他说鬼子要在同口安据点……"

"哪里就碰得那么巧,我们快去快回来。"

"我本来不想去,可是俺婆婆非叫我再去看看他,有什么看头啊!"

于是这几个女人偷偷坐在一只小船上,划到对面马庄去了。

到了马庄,她们不敢到街上去找,来到村头一个亲戚家里。亲戚说:你们来的不巧,昨天晚上他们还在这里,半夜里走了,谁也不知开到哪里去。你们不用惦记他们,听说水生一来就当了副排长,大家都是欢天喜地的……

几个女人羞红着脸告辞出来,摇开靠在岸边上的小船。现在已经快到晌午了,万里无云,可是因为在水上,还有些凉风。这风从南面吹过来,从稻秧苇尖上吹过来。水面没有一只船,水像无边的跳荡的水银。

几个女人有点失望,也有些伤心,各人在心

英汉对照
English-Chinese
中国文学宝库
Gems of Chinese Literature
现代文学系列
Modern Literature

Disappointed and rather upset, each woman was secretly laying the blame on her heartless brute of a husband. But young people are optimistic and women have a special knack of forgetting their troubles. Very soon they were laughing and chattering again.

"So they just up and left!"

"I'm sure they're having the time of their lives. This means more to them than New Year or getting married."

"They're like wild horses: they won't stay tied up in a stable."

"No, they all break away."

"Take it from me, that man of mine hasn't given one thought to his home since he joined the army."

"That's true. Some young soldiers once stayed in our house. Singing from dawn to dusk they were. We've never larked like that! I was fool enough to think that once they had nothing to do, they'd start looking glum. But what do you suppose? They painted a whole set of white circles on our courtyard wall, and squatted down one by one for target practice, still singing all the time!"

They paddled easily along while water gurgled on each side of the boat. One of them scooped up a water chestnut, still tiny and milky white. She threw it back into the river. The water chestnut floated placidly there, where it would grow.

"I wonder where they've gone."

"He can go to the end of the earth for all I care!"

"Look! A boat!"

They all raised their heads and gazed into the distance.

"Why, they're Japanese soldiers — see that uniform!"

"Quick!"

里骂着自己的狠心贼。可是青年人,永远朝着愉快的事情想,女人们尤其容易忘记那些不痛快。不久,她们就又说笑起来了。

"你看说走就走了。"

"可慌(高兴的意思)哩,比什么也慌,比过新年,娶新——也没见他这么慌过!"

"拴马桩也不顶事了。"

"不行了,脱了缰了!"

"一到军队里,他一准得忘了家里的人。"

"那是真的,我们家里住过一些年轻的队伍,一天到晚仰着脖子出来唱,进去唱,我们一辈子也没那么乐过。等他们闲下来没有事了,我就傻想:该低下头了吧。你猜人家干什么?用白粉子在我家影壁上画了许多圆圈圈,一个一个蹲在院子里,托着枪瞄那个,又唱起来了!"

她们轻轻划着船,船两边的水哗,哗,哗。顺手从水里捞上一棵菱角来,菱角还很嫩很小,乳白色。顺手又丢到水里去。那棵菱角就又安安稳稳浮在水面上生长去了。

"现在你知道他们到了哪里?"

"管他哩,也许跑到天边上去了!"

她们都抬起头往远处看了看。

"唉呀!那边过来一只船。"

"唉呀!日本,你看那衣裳!"

"快摇!"

小船拼命往前摇。她们心里也许有些后

英汉对照
English-Chinese
中国文学宝库
Gems of Chinese Literature
现代文学系列
Modern Literature

Lotus Creek

They rowed on for dear life. One started wishing they had never taken such a risk, another blaming the husbands who had deserted them. But in no time they put these thoughts out of their heads. They must row fast — the larger boat was coming after them.

The Japanese were going as swiftly as they could.

It was lucky that all these young wives had grown up by the river: their boat went like the wind. It shot forward like some flying fish, hardly skimming the water. They had been in and out of boats since they were children, and could paddle as fast as they could spin or sew.

If the enemy overtook them, they would drown themselves in the river.

The large boat was making quick headway. No doubt about it, those were Japanese. The young women clenched their teeth and fought down their panic. They did not let their hands tremble. The oars plashed loudly, steadily through the water.

"Head for Lotus Creek! It's too shallow for a boat that size."

They raced for the creek, a good many *mu* in extent, where as far as eye could see massed lotus leaves reached towards the genial sun like a solid wall of bronze. Their pink buds, thrust up like arrows, seemed sentinels watching over Baiyangdian.

They rowed for the creek and with one final effort drove their small craft in among the lotus. Some wild ducks flapped their wings and flew off with shrill cries, whirring low over the water. A volley of shots rang out!

Pandemonium broke loose. Sure that they had fallen into an enemy ambush with no hope of escape, they jumped all together into

悔,不该这么冒冒失失走来;也许有些怨恨那些走远了的人。但是立刻就想,什么也别想了,快摇,大船紧紧追过来了。

大船追的很紧。

幸亏是这些青年妇女,白洋淀长大的,她们摇的小船飞快。

小船活像离开了水皮的一条打跳的梭鱼。她们从小跟这小船打交道,驶起来,就像织布穿梭,缝衣透针一般快。

假如敌人追上了,就跳到水里去死吧!

后面大船来的飞快。那明明白白是鬼子!这几个青年妇女咬紧牙制止住心跳,摇橹的手并没有慌,水在两旁大声哗哗,哗哗,哗哗哗!

"往荷花淀里摇!那里水浅,大船过不去。"

她们奔着那不知道有几亩大小的荷花淀去,那一望无边际的密密层层的大荷叶,迎着阳光舒展开,就像铜墙铁壁一样。粉色荷花箭高高地挺出来,是监视白洋淀的哨兵吧!

她们向荷花淀里摇,最后,努力地一摇,小船窜进了荷花淀。几只野鸭扑楞楞飞起,尖声惊叫,掠着水面飞走了。就在她们的耳边响起一排枪!

整个荷花淀全震荡起来。她们想,陷在敌人的埋伏里了,一准要死了,一齐翻身跳到水里去。渐渐听清楚枪声只是向着外面,她们才又

英汉对照
English-Chinese
中国文学宝库
Gems of Chinese Literature
现代文学系列
Modern Literature

the water. But presently, realizing that all the shots were aimed towards the river, they caught hold of the boat's side and peered cautiously out. Not far away under a broad lotus leaf they saw a man's head — the rest of him was submerged. It was Shuisheng. Looking right and left, each soon discovered her husband — so this was where they were!

But the men under the lotus leaves were too busy aiming at the enemy to so much as glance at their wives. Quick shots rang out, and after four or five volleys they threw hand-grenades and rushed forward.

The grenades sank the enemy boat with everything on board, leaving nothing but smoke and fumes of saltpetre on the surface. With shouts and laughter, the men started salvaging trophies. They dived as if they were after fish. They raced to retrieve enemy rifles, cartridge belts, and sack after sack of dripping flour and rice. Shuisheng swam with a great splashing after a carton of biscuits bobbing on the waves.

Soaked to the skin, the wives climbed back into their boat.

Holding the biscuits high in one hand and paddling hard with the other, Shuisheng shouted towards them:

"Come out of that, you!"

He sounded angry.

They rowed out — what else could they do? Without warning a man popped up from under their bows, and Shuisheng's wife was the only one to recognize him. It was the captain of the district brigade. Wiping the water from his face, he demanded:

"What are you doing here?"

扒着船帮露出头来。她们看见不远的地方,那宽厚肥大的荷叶下面,有一个人的脸,下半截身子长在水里。荷花变成人了?那不是我们的水生吗?又往左右看去,不久各人就找到了各人丈夫的脸,啊!原来是他们!

但是那些隐蔽在大荷叶下面的战士们,正在聚精会神瞄着敌人射击,半眼也没有看她们。枪声清脆,三五排枪过后,他们投出了手榴弹,冲出了荷花淀。

手榴弹把敌人那只大船击沉,一切都沉下去了。水面上只剩下一团烟硝火药味。战士们就在那里大声欢笑着,打捞战利品。他们又开始了沉到水底捞出大鱼来的拿手戏。他们争着捞出敌人的枪支、子弹带,然后是一袋子一袋子叫水浸透了的面粉和大米。水生拍打着水去追赶一个在水波上滚动的东西,是一包用精致纸盒装着的饼干。

妇女们带着浑身水,又坐到她们的小船上去了。

水生追回那个纸盒,一只手高高举起,一只手用力拍打着水,好使自己不沉下去。对着荷花淀吆喝:

"出来吧,你们!"

好像带着很大的气。

她们只好摇着船出来。忽然从她们的船底下冒出一个人来,只有水生的女人认的那是区小队的队长。这个人抹一把脸上的水问她们:

"你们干什么去来呀?"

水生的女人说:

英汉对照
English-Chinese
中国文学宝库
Gems of Chinese Literature
现代文学系列
Modern Literature

Shuisheng's wife answered:

"We were taking them some more clothes."

The captain turned to Shuisheng:

"Are they all from your village?"

"That's right. A bunch of backward elements!" He hurled the biscuits into their boat and disappeared with a splash, reappearing some distance away.

The captain laughed.

"Well, your trip wasn't wasted. If not for you, our ambush wouldn't have been so successful. But now you've completed your mission, you'd better hurry home and dry your clothes. The situation is still pretty serious."

By now the men had loaded all their trophies on their boats and were ready to move on. Each of them had plastered a large lotus leaf on his head to keep off the midday sun. The women rescued their bundles which had fallen into the water and threw them over. Then the men's three boats made off quickly towards the southeast, to be swallowed up soon in the heat haze over the river.

The women lost no time in starting back, bedraggled as drowned rats. But all the excitement they had been through soon set them laughing and chattering again. The one in the stern made a face over her shoulder.

"Did you ever see the like? Just couldn't be bothered with us!"

"As if we'd lost face for them!"

They laughed, knowing that they hadn't exactly covered themselves with glory. Still:

"We haven't got rifles. If we had, we could take on the Japanese

"又给他们送了一些衣裳来!"

小队长回头对水生说:

"都是你村的?"

"不是她们是谁,一群落后分子!"说完把纸盒顺手丢在女人们船上,一泅,又沉到水底下去了,到很远的地方才钻出来。

小队长开了个玩笑,他说:

"你们也没有白来,不是你们,我们的伏击不会这么彻底。可是,任务已经完成,该回去晒晒衣裳了。情况还紧的很!"

战士们已经把打捞出来的战利品,全装在他们的小船上,准备转移。一人摘了一片大荷叶顶在头上,抵挡正午的太阳。几个青年妇女把掉在水里又捞出来的小包裹,丢给了他们,战士们的三只小船就奔着东南方向,箭一样飞去了。不久就消失在中午水面上的烟波里。

几个青年妇女划着她们的小船赶紧回家,一个个像落水鸡似的。一路走着,因过于刺激和兴奋,她们又说笑起来,坐在船头脸朝后的一个噘着嘴说:

"你看他们那个横样子,见了我们爱搭理不搭理的!"

"啊,好像我们给他们丢了什么人似的。"

她们自己也笑了,今天的事情不算光彩,可是:

"我们没枪,有枪就不往荷花淀里跑,在大淀里就和鬼子干起来!"

英汉对照
English-Chinese
中国文学宝库
Gems of Chinese Literature
现代文学系列
Modern Literature

devils without hiding in the creek."

"Well, so at last I've seen fighting! What's so wonderful about it? As long as you don't lose your head, anybody can squat there and let off a gun."

"When a boat sinks I can dive to collect stuff too. I promise you I'm a better swimmer than they are — I can go down deeper than that."

"Let's set up a unit when we go back, or we'll never be able to leave the village again."

"Looking down on us the moment they join the army! In another two years they won't think us worth talking to, but are they all that much better?"

That autumn they learned to fire rifles. When winter came and the time to catch fish in the ice, they took it in turn to take out the sleigh and whizz back and forth over the ice, patrolling the village. When the enemy attempted to "mop up" the marshlands, they worked hand in glove with the army, slipping fearlessly in and out of the sea of reeds.

1945
Translated by Gladys Yang

"我今天也算看见打仗了。打仗有什么出奇,只要你不着慌,谁还不会趴在那里放枪呀!"

"打沉了,我也会浮水捞东西,我管保比他们水式好,再深点我也不怕!"

"水生嫂,回去我们也成立队伍,不然以后还能出门吗!"

"刚当上兵就小看我们,过二年,更把我们看得一钱不值了,谁比谁落后多少呢!"

这一年秋季,她们学会了射击。冬天,打冰夹鱼的时候,她们一个个登在流星一样的冰船上,来回警戒。敌人围剿那百顷大苇塘的时候,她们配合子弟兵作战,出入在那芦苇的海里。

1945年于延安

The Marshes

At night the enemy peered through the slits of their gun towers across the dark, shadowy marshes while the stars seemed ready to drip from the liquid sky. Only after midnight could singing and the whirr of waterfowl's wings be heard among the rushes — by day the birds kept to their nests out of harm's way. Reeds kept thrusting fiercely up as if aiming at the sky.

The Japanese were blockading these marshes to stop fuel and rice from going in and the troops there from slipping out. As it happened, our forces had no intention of withdrawing. But on a still moonlit night sharp eyes could detect a small boat shaped like a rush-leaf nosing out of the marshes to speed away to the south-east. After midnight it would return laden with fuel, rice, oil and salt, and sometimes a couple of cadres from far away.

The small pointed craft was punted by an old wan of nearly sixty, wearing nothing but short, tattered blue pants, he stood in the stern with his bamboo pole.

He was lean and stringy as an old cormorant. But there was remarkable energy in his dark leathery face and short grey beard, remarkable brightness in his sunken eyes. Outside the lake, Baiyangdian, you seldom saw eyes so bright.

This old man plied back and forth on the lake night after night on errands of every kind: delivering messages, shipping grain and

芦花荡
——白洋淀纪事之二

夜晚,敌人从炮楼的小窗子里,呆望着这阴森黑暗的大苇塘,天空的星星也像浸在水里,而且要滴落下来的样子。到这样深夜,苇塘里才有水鸟飞动和唱歌的声音,白天它们是紧紧藏到窠里躲避炮火去了。苇子还是那么狠狠地往上钻,目标好像就是天上。

敌人监视着苇塘。他们提防有人给苇塘里的人送来柴米,也提防里面的队伍会跑了出去。我们的队伍还没有退却的意思。可是假如是月明风清的夜晚,人们的眼再尖利一些,就可以看见有一只小船从苇塘里撑出来,在淀里,像一片苇叶,奔着东南去了。半夜以后,小船又飘回来,船舱里装满了柴米油盐,有时还带来一两个从远方赶来的干部。

撑船的是一个将近六十岁的老头子,船是一只尖尖的小船。老头子只穿一件蓝色的破旧短裤,站在船尾巴上,手里着一根竹篙。

老头子浑身没有多少肉,干瘦得像老了的鱼鹰。可是那晒得干黑的脸,短短的花白胡子却特别精神,那一对深陷的眼睛却特别明亮。很少见到这样尖利明亮的眼睛,除非是在白洋淀上。

老头子每天夜里在水淀出入,他的工作范围广得很:里外交通,运输粮草,护送干部;而且

英汉对照
English-Chinese
中国文学宝库
Gems of Chinese Literature
现代文学系列
Modern Literature

The Marshes

fodder, or escorting cadres. And he never carried a gun. He told the men in charge in the marshes: "Whatever you want done, you can count on me. I can count on my skill on the lake, it'll never let me down."

The old man was almost too confident, too cocksure. Every night he punted calmly up and down on those waters so closely watched by the enemy. He punted happily, as carefree as if he were going out early and returning late to cast his nets and all the time thinking up ways to please himself and others.

Because of him, the enemy's scheme was foiled.

The songs which rose so clearly from the marshes at dusk didn't sound as if sung by men with empty stomachs, and the appetizing smell of rice and fish kept wafting out from the rushes. There was nothing the Japanese could do about it.

One night the old man came back from a long trip as the crescent moon was sailing down through a sky as limpid as water. He had two girls with him this time. For a month or more they had been under enemy fire and both were shivering with malaria. The previous day they had come here to find our troops, hoping for a good rest in the marshes, perhaps some injections.

The old man had taken a fancy to these girls, Big Ling and Little Ling. Helping them aboard, he assured them: "You've nothing to worry about now. Go ahead and have a good sleep. In the marshes you'll get a square meal of rice and fish."

But after the strain and tension of days of fighting, the girls' eyes opened at the slightest sound. In these novel surroundings they couldn't possibly sleep, not crossing the lake in a boat like this

不带一支枪。他对苇塘里的负责同志说:你什么也靠给我,我什么也靠给水上的能耐,一切保险。

老头子过于自信和自尊。每天夜里,在敌人紧紧封锁的水面上,就像一个没事人,他按照早出晚归捕鱼撒网那股悠闲的心情撑着船,编算着使自己高兴也使别人高兴的事情。

因为他,敌人的愿望就没有达到。

每到傍晚,苇塘里的歌声还是那么响,不像是饿肚子的人们唱的;稻米和肥鱼的香味,还是从苇塘里飘出来。敌人发了愁。

一天夜里,老头子从东边很远的地方回来。弯弯下垂的月亮,浮在水一样的天上。老头子载了两个女孩子回来。孩子们在炮火里滚了一个多月,都发着疟子,昨天跑到这里来找队伍,想在苇塘里休息休息,打打针。

老头子很喜欢这两个孩子:大的叫大菱,小的叫二菱。把她们接上船,老头子就叫她们睡一觉,他说,什么事也没有了,安心睡一觉吧,到苇塘里,咱们还有大米和鱼吃。

孩子们在炮火里一直没安静过,神经紧张得很。一点轻微的声音,闭上的眼就又睁开了。现在又是到了这么一个新鲜的地方,有水有船,荡悠悠的,夜晚的风吹得长期发烧的脸也清爽

英汉对照
English-Chinese
中国文学宝库
Gems of Chinese Literature
现代文学系列
Modern Literature

with the night wind fresh on their hot, fevered cheeks.

It was like a dream. Running away from the enemy, they had spent the night, wet through, in a sorghum field and had to cross endless roads, crawl past countless ditches. Shivering with fever, they had never stopped. Their one idea was to find the troops — then they would be all right!

The two sisters, one fifteen, the other thirteen, came from Hebei. Marching down the highways of their native province, they had fixed their eyes on the Dipper at the horizon. They saw wheat turn yellow in the early summer, the autumn sorghum in the last stage or ripening. Wild geese flew south over their heads and before long winged north again. The girls were growing up.

Little Ling leaned on the side of the boat to dabble in the lake. Her feverish hands found the water so cool and refreshing that she splashed some over her muddy, perspiring face. She was washing her face and short hair when Big Ling scolded softly:

"Is this a time to wash your face? What's made you so anxious to clean up all of a sudden?"

Little Ling looked up at the old man and said with a smile:

"A wash makes me feel good."

"Don't be afraid," he said. "Go ahead, there's a pretty lass."

A lurid yellow beam circling in the distance suddenly picked out their boat. Wringing out her hair, Little Ling gave a cry of dismay.

"Don't be afraid," said the old man. "That's the searchlight on the steamer. They can't see us."

He crouched down and made the boat veer to the north. The yellow light kept circling round, illumining the water one moment,

多了,就更睡不着。

眼前的环境好像是一个梦。在敌人的炮火里打滚,在高粱地里淋着雨过夜,一晚上不知道要过几条汽车路,爬几道沟。发高烧和打寒噤的时候,孩子们也没停下来。一心想:找队伍去呀,找到队伍就好了!

这是冀中区的女孩子,大的不过十五,小的才十三。她们在家乡的道路上行军,眼望着天边的北斗。她们看着初夏的小麦黄梢,看着中秋的高粱晒米。雁在她们的头顶往南飞去,不久又向北飞来。她们长大成人了。

小女孩子爬在船边,用两只小手淘着水玩。发烧的手浸在清凉的水里很舒服,她随手就掏了一把泼在脸上,那脸涂着厚厚的泥和汗。她痛痛快快地洗起来,连那短短的头发。大些的轻声吆喝她:

"看你,这时洗脸干什么?什么时候呵,还这么爱干净!"

小女孩子抬起头来,望一望老头子,笑着说:

"洗一洗就精神了!"

老头子说:

"不怕,洗一洗吧,多么俊的一个孩子呀!"

远远有一片阴惨的黄色的光,突然一转就转到她们的船上来。女孩子正在拧着水淋淋的头发,叫了一声。老头子说:

"不怕,小火轮上的探照灯,它照不见我们。"

他蹲下去,撑着船往北绕了一绕。黄色的光仍然向四下里探照,一下照在水面上,一下又

英汉对照
English-Chinese
中国文学宝库
Gems of Chinese Literature
现代文学系列
Modern Literature

the far-off woods the next.

"Don't talk now!" the old man whispered. "We're going to run the blockade!"

Noiselessly the little craft nosed swiftly forward. When it drew level with the steamboat, the searchlight suddenly caught it and stopped abruptly. The girls' faces gleamed white in its rays. The next moment a machine gun opened fire.

"Lie down!" cried the old man, jumping into the water to push the boat with both hands. Big Ling threw her arms around her sister and pulled her down, covering her with her own body.

Bullets ricocheted into the water by the boat, some of them exploding as they hit the lake.

One hit Big Ling. Not a cry or whimper escaped her, but her arms dropped slackly away and she fell back. Little Ling felt something warm and wet on her face. She sat up at once to put her arms round her sister, calling tearfully to the boatman:

"She's been hit!"

The old man, shoving furiously, didn't hear.

"Don't be afraid!" he called softly. 'They won't hit us!'

"She's been hit!"

"What!" He gave such a start that the boat wobbled violently. Strength ebbed from his legs and arms. Clinging to the stern he floated a little way before starting pushing again with all his might.

They were very near the reeds now. He clambered aboard, spots dancing before his old eyes. But parting the reeds with his pole he found the narrow entry to the marshes.

Once under cover he put down the pole and raised the elder

照到远处的树林里去了。

老头子小声说：

"不要说话,要过封锁线了!"

小船无声地,但是飞快地前进。当小船和那黑虎虎的小火轮站到一条横线上的时候,探照灯突然照向她们,不动了。两个女孩子的脸照得雪白,紧接着就扫射过一梭机枪。

老头子叫了一声"趴下",一抽身就跳进水里去,踏着水用两手推着小船前进。大女孩子把小女孩子抱在怀里,倒在船底上,用身子遮盖了她。

子弹吱吱地在她们的船边钻到水里去,有的一见水就爆炸了。

大女孩子负了伤,虽说她没有叫一声也没有哼一声,可是胳膊没有了力量,再也搂不住那个小的,她翻了下去。那小的觉得有一股热热的东西流到自己脸上来,连忙爬起来,把大的抱在自己怀里,带着哭声向老头子喊：

"她挂花了!"

老头子没听见,拚命地往前推着船,还是柔和地说：

"不怕。他打不着我们!"

"她挂了花!"

"谁?"老头子的身体往上窜了一窜,随着,那小船很厉害地仄歪了一下。老头子觉得自己的手脚顿时失去了力量,他用手扒着船尾,跟着浮了几步,才又拚命地往前推了一把。

她们已经离苇塘很近。老头子爬到船上去,他觉得两只老眼有些昏花。可是他到底用篙拨开外面一层芦苇,找到了那窄窄的入口。

英汉对照
English-Chinese
中国文学宝库
Gems of Chinese Literature
现代文学系列
Modern Literature

The Marshes

girl's head.

She opened her eyes with an effort and said feebly:

"It's all right. Just take us in as fast as you can."

He sat down limply, letting the boat stop. The moon had gone down, it would soon be dawn. A chilly wind was blowing. The old man sighed and after a long pause said:

"I can't take you in."

Little Ling stared:

"Why not?"

Gazing stonily ahead, he answered:

"I've lost face too badly."

She began to panic. They'd met guides like this before, who turned back halfway, leaving them in the lurch.

"Do take us in, Grandad!" she pleaded. "She's lost so much blood! We must find a doctor for her!"

He stood up then and started punting again. Turning this way and that they reached the heart of the marshes.

Only then did the wounded girl begin to whimper. Her younger sister tried to comfort her, but a note of indignation crept into her voice. They'd come through so many difficulties safely only to land in trouble here.... Every word she uttered pierced the old man's heart. In his time he had crossed great rivers, sailed the high seas; how could he have fallen down on this job today? Childless himself, he'd taken a special fancy to these girls. Yet now, after all his boasting, he was taking in a casualty. Would he ever live it down? He told Big Ling:

"They've spilled your blood. Tomorrow I'll make ten of them pay

一钻进苇塘,他就放下篙,扶起那大女孩子的头。

大女孩子微微睁了一下眼,吃力地说:

"我不要紧。快把我们送进苇塘里去吧!"

老头子无力地坐下来,船停在那里。月亮落了,半夜以后的苇塘,有些飒飒的风响。老头子叹了一口气,停了半天才说:

"我不能送你们进去了。"

小女孩子睁大眼睛问:

"为什么呀?"

老头子直直地望着前面说:

"我没脸见人。"

小女孩子有些发急。在路上也遇见过这样的带路人,带到半路上就不愿带了,叫人为难。她像央告那老头子:

"老同志,你快把我们送进去吧,你看她流了这么多血,我们要找医生给她裹伤呀!"

老头子站起来,拾起篙,撑了一下。那小船转弯抹角钻入了苇塘的深处。

这时那受伤的才痛苦地哼哼起来。小女孩子安慰她,又好像是抱怨,一路上多么紧张,也没怎么样,谁知到了这里,反倒……一声一声像连珠箭,射穿老头子的心。他没法解释:大江大海过了多少,为什么这一次的任务,偏偏没有完成?自己没儿没女,这两个多么叫人喜爱?自己平日夸下口,这一次带着挂花的人进去,怎么张嘴说话?这老脸呀!他叫着大菱说:

"他们打伤了你,流了这么多血,等明天我叫他们十个人流血!"

for this!"

Neither of the girls answered. The old man felt they must despise him. He said:

"All right, you don't believe me. It's my own fault for talking big. But tomorrow just wait and see!"

Little Ling asked doubtfully:

"Can you fight at your age?"

"Why not?" he retorted. "I won't fight with a gun, that's not my way. You can watch tomorrow if you like. I'll show you a trick or two tomorrow, Little Ling!"

Noon the next day was sweltering. A heat haze hung over the lake in the blazing sun. The steamer moved a little further away from the reeds and the Japanese soldiers slipped into the water to bathe. Ten or more of them, all good swimmers, were splashing about in the lake. No one else was in sight. Only a flock of silky white waterfowl flew off to the north away from the Japanese soldiers, alighting to rest in the shade of big lotus leaves. A small boat came gliding out from between the lotuses. It was lazily punted by a scrawny old man in shabby pants who was standing in the stern busily peeling fat juicy lotus seeds and popping them into his mouth.

Beside him lay a great pile of newly plucked lotus pods. Where but in Baiyangdian can you eat them so fresh? The Japanese soldiers had arrived a couple of days already but they could not get into the marshes. They yelled to the old man to come over.

After one glance he lowered his head again. He went on punting lazily and eating. His boat moved slowly towards them.

Not till he was within a stone's throw of the soldiers did the old

两个孩子全没有答言,老头子觉得受了轻视。他说:

"你们不信我的话,我也不和你们说。谁叫我丢人现眼,打牙跌嘴呢!可是,等到天明,你们看吧!"

小女孩子说:

"你这么大年纪了,还能打仗?"

老头子狠狠地说:

"为什么不能?我打他们不用枪,那不是我的本事。愿意看,明天来看吧!二菱,明天你跟我来看吧,有热闹哩!"

第二天,中午的时候,非常闷热。一轮红日当天,水面上浮着一层气。小火轮开的离苇塘远一些,鬼子们又偷偷地爬下来洗澡了。十几个鬼子在水里泅着,日本人的水式真不错。水淀里没有一个人影,有只一团白绸子样的水鸟,也躲开鬼子往北飞去,落到大荷叶下面歇凉去了。从荷花淀里却撑出一只小船来。一个干瘦的老头子,只穿一条破短裤,站在船尾巴上,有一篙没一篙地撑着,两只手却忙着剥那又肥又大的莲蓬,一个一个投进嘴里去。

他的船头上放着那样大的一捆莲蓬,是刚从荷花淀里摘下来的。不到白洋淀,哪里去吃这样新鲜的东西?来到白洋淀上几天了,鬼子们也还是望着荷花淀瞪眼。他们冲着那小船吆喝,叫他过来。

老头子向他们看了一眼,就又低下头去。还是有一篙没一篙地撑着船,剥着莲蓬。船却慢慢地冲着这里来了。

小船离鬼子还有一箭之地,好像老头子才

英汉对照
English-Chinese
中国文学宝库
Gems of Chinese Literature
现代文学系列
Modern Literature

The Marshes

man seem to realize who they were. With one shove on his pole he turned and started away. Flailing through the water, the Japanese gave chase.

The old man lost his head, his boat hardly seemed to move, the soldiers gained on it.

Just in front were some old logs driven into the lake long before for some obscure reason. The water was smooth as glass, blue as the sky, with only a few weeds floating idly on top. Just as the Japanese were reaching the boat, with a shove on his pole the old man circled round them — they could actually smell the fresh scent of the lotus seeds. As if playing hide-and-seek, they started grabbing for him.

Then with a yell one Japanese flopped down. Something had nipped him hard. A sharp hook was imbedded in his thigh. Before the others could scatter in alarm, each got a hook in his leg. They thrashed about, trying to free themselves. But the hooks to avenge Big Ling all found their mark — each soldier was caught by two or three of them. They bellowed and howled but could not get away.

Then the old man punted nearer and brought his pole down on their heads as hard as if beating the tough cobs of maize.

As he laid about him he glanced towards the reeds where clusters of lovely flowers, like purple velvet, were nodding in the breeze.

At the edge of the lake, under the flowers, was a girl. Hidden by the rushes she watched the whole glorious manoeuvre.

1945

Translated by Gladys Yang

看出洗澡的是鬼子,只一篙,小船溜溜转了一个圆圈,又回去了。鬼子们拍打着水追过去,老头子张惶失措,船却走不动,鬼子紧紧追上了他。

眼前是几根埋在水里的枯木桩子,日久天长,也许人们忘记这是为什么埋的了。这里的水却是镜一样平,蓝天一般清,拉长的水草在水底轻轻地浮动。鬼子们追上来,看看就抓上了船。老头子又是一篙,小船旋风一样绕着鬼子们转,莲蓬的清香,在他们的鼻尖上扫过。鬼子们像是玩着捉迷藏,乱转着身子,抓上抓下。

一个鬼子尖叫了一声,就蹲到水里去。他被什么东西狠狠咬了一口,是一只锋利的钩子穿透了他的大腿。别的鬼子吃惊地往四下里一散,每个人的腿肚子也就挂上了钩。他们挣扎着,想摆脱那毒蛇一样的钩子。那替女孩子报仇的钩子却全找到腿上来,有的两个,有的三个。鬼子们痛得鬼叫,可是再也不敢动弹了。

老头子把船一撑来到他们的身边,举起篙来砸着鬼子们的脑袋,像敲打顽固的老玉米一样。

他狠狠地敲打,向着苇塘望了一眼。在那里,鲜嫩的芦花,一片展开的紫色的丝绒,正在迎风飘撒。

在那苇塘的边缘,芦花下面,有一个女孩子,她用密密的苇叶遮掩着身子,看着这场英雄的行为。

1945年于延安

英汉对照
English-Chinese
中国文学宝库
Gems of Chinese Literature
现代文学系列
Modern Literature

Parting Advice

The day had just turned full light as Shuisheng, a Japanese fur-lined greatcoat draped over one shoulder, slipped across the Beiping-Wuhan Railway line. Although he hadn't been home in eight years, the plain still looked familiar. It was the last month of the lunar year. Gazing across the level ground to where the flaming red sun was rising, he straightened up and inhaled deeply of the cold air. The fatigue of more than ten days of marching vanished. His feet grew light, his eyes a trifle blurred. He seemed to float. These past eight years, he had travelled mostly in mountainous country. He had climbed all kinds of mountains — the great heights near Wutai, the precipitous slopes on both sides of the Yellow River, the big lumpy hills of Yan'an and the northwest. Wherever the enemy was, there he went. Eight years, his rifle always on his back or in his hands.

Shuisheng was a good soldier. Now he was also his battalion's assistant political instructor. But to tell the truth, during those eight years he often thought of home, especially between battles. That sort of thing could make a soldier miserable. Whenever he felt homesick, he would take up a book, or go out to the athletic field or the vegetable garden, and exercise or work or study, until he had shaken it off.

His ardent wish had been that they would fight on the Hebei

嘱 咐

水生斜背着一件日本皮大衣,偷过了平汉路,天刚大亮。家乡的平原景色,八年不见,并不生疏。这正是腊月天气,从平地上望过去,一直望到放射红光的太阳那里,他深深地吸了一口气。把身子一挺,十几天行军的疲劳完全跑净,脚下轻飘飘的,眼有些晕,身子要飘起来。这八年,他走的多半是山路,他走过各式各样的山路:五台附近的高山,黄河两岸的陡山,延安和塞北的大土圪瘩山。哪里有敌人就到哪里去,枪背在肩上、拿在手里八年了。

水生是一个好战士,现在已经是一个副教导员。可是不瞒人说,八年里他也常常想到家,特别是在休息时间,这种想念,很使一个战士苦恼。这样的时候,他就拿起书来或是到操场去,或是到菜园子里去,借游戏、劳动和学习,好把这些事情忘掉。

他也曾有过一种热望,能有个机会再打到

Parting Advice

plains again, so that he would have a chance to see his home.

Now that chance had come. He had asked for leave, and it had been granted. Because he knew the terrain well, he no longer worried about the enemy once he crossed the railway. Strolling along, he looked about him, feasting his eyes on the plain he hadn't seen in eight years. Some of the Japanese gun towers by the side of the railway were being torn down. Their broken walls were spattered with bird droppings. Willow trees, leaves yellowing, marched along the steel rails that stretched far to the north. A train rolled slowly from that direction, coughing white smoke and hooting mournfully.

Instantly, a powerful urge to fight surged up within him and old battles rose before his eyes. Then he laughed. "You ought to forget about such things for a while. Just concentrate on familiar sights and dear faces." He ambled on slowly, wanting to savour all the joy that high excitement brings. Shuisheng gazed at the wheat fields, at the sky, at the scattered villages that looked as if they had been painted on the plain in watercolours of deep blue and pale grey. He was less than ninety *li* from home — one day's walk. Tonight, he would be there.

But soon he felt that his emotions were a bit forced. He wasn't really so stimulated. When, as a child, he neared his village at dusk after an absence of half a month or so and saw the pale smoke rising from the chimney of his home, his heart grew intoxicated. Today, although he still loved and venerated his native place, he had that feeling no longer.

The streets of the villages he walked through were very familiar,

平原上去,到家看看就好了。

现在机会来了,他请了假,绕道家里看一下。因为地理熟,一过铁路他就不再把敌人放在心上。他悠闲地走着,四面八方观看着,为的是饱看一下八年不见的平原风景。铁路旁边并排的炮楼,有的已经拆毁,破墙上洒落了一片鸟粪。铁路两旁的柳树黄了叶子,随着铁轨伸展到远远的北方。一列火车正从那里慢慢地滚过来,惨叫,吐着白雾。

一时,强烈的战斗要求和八年的战斗景象涌到心里来。他笑了一笑,想,现在应该把这些事情暂时地忘记,集中精神看一看家乡的风土人情吧。他信步走着,想享受享受一个人在特别兴奋时候的愉快心情。他看看麦地,又看看天,看看周围那像深蓝淡墨涂成的村庄图画。这里离他的家不过九十里路,一天的路程。今天晚上,就可以到家了。

不久,他觉得这种感情有些做作。心里面并不那么激动。幼小的时候,离开家半月十天,当黄昏的时候走近了自己的村庄,望见自己家里烟囱上冒起的袅袅的轻烟,心里就醉了。现在虽然对自己的家乡还是这样爱好、崇拜,但是那样的一种感情没有了。

经过的村庄街道都很熟悉。这些村庄经过

英汉对照
English-Chinese
中国文学宝库
Gems of Chinese Literature
现代文学系列
Modern Literature

though after eight years of warfare, the villages were badly scarred. Many of the houses burned by the enemy had not been rebuilt. All the gun towers on the edges of the villages had been demolished, their bricks and tiles piled in heaps. In some places these materials had been used to build public toilets. But the villages did not seem any larger. No new compounds or houses had been added. Many tall buildings and big clan temples had been levelled to make way for gun towers. In several of the large family cemeteries which Shuisheng remembered from childhood, the tall poplars and cedars had been felled, revealing forlorn-looking grave mounds. But the lifeblood of the countryside, the hearts of the people, were healthy and thriving. The vitality so characteristic of the plains flourished more vigorously than ever.

Shuisheng's home was on the shore of the marshy Baiyang Lake. He reached the dyke that ran to his village when the sun was sinking in the west. Only fifteen more *li* to go.

The dyke had been breached and the shady willows which used to line its banks cut down. On the inner side, the fields were filled with water. Shuisheng wove through them on a small path. Because landmarks had changed, he couldn't tell exactly in which direction his village lay.

As the sun rested on the tops of trees on the western horizon, villages in the distance changed colour rapidly. Shuisheng recognized his village by its dense trees. Not far now. He soon would be entering his own home. Home didn't draw him, it only upset him. He thought of many things. He had forgotten how old his father was. Was the old man still alive? He had been suffering from asth-

八年战争,满身创伤,许多被敌人烧毁的房子,还没有重新盖起来。村边的炮楼全拆了,砖瓦还堆在那里,有的就近利用起来,垒了个厕所。在形式上,村庄没有发展,没有添新的庄院和房屋。许多高房,大的祠堂,全拆毁修了炮楼,幼时记忆里的几块大坟地,高大的杨树和柏树,也砍伐光了,坟墓曝露出来,显的特别荒凉。但是村庄的血液,人民的心却壮大发展了。一种平原上特有的勃勃生气,更是强烈扑人。

水生的家在白洋淀边上。太阳平西的时候,他走上了通到他家去的那条大堤,这里离他的村庄十五里路。

堤坡已经破坏,两岸成荫的柳树砍伐了,堤里面现在还满是水。水生从一条小道上穿过,地势一变化,使他不能正确地估计村庄的方向。

太阳落到西边远远的树林里去了,远处的村庄迅速地变化着颜色。水生望着树林的疏密,辨别自己的村庄,家近了,就进家了,家对他不是吸引,却是一阵心烦意乱。他想起许多事。父亲确实的年岁忘记了,是不是还活着?父亲

ma for years. Then Shuisheng thought of his wife. She had been in the flower of her youth when they parted eight years ago, and a child was growing in her womb. And what about the house — had it been burned down?

He felt none of the mixed sorrow and gladness usually experienced on homecoming. Instead he was consumed by a heavy sense of oppression. Trying to rid himself of it, he slackened his pace. He decided to sit down, to have a smoke and a rest.

Shuisheng lit his pipe. There wasn't a soul around. The wind was rather cold. He spread open the greatcoat and draped it over his shoulders. Gazing across a muddy expanse of rotting grass, he could see faintly the shore of Baiyang Lake.

He entered his village at dusk. His home was right at the entrance. No houses had been burned. The street was very peaceful. It was the hour of the day when people had finished their evening meal and were getting ready to bolt their doors.

Shuisheng saw his wife. She was quietly closing their compound gate.

"Hey!" he shouted warmly.

Startled, she stared at him, then she smiled. But the next moment she turned and burst into sobs. When Shuisheng saw the white cloth mourning shoes on her feet, he knew that his father was gone. The two simply stood there for several moments. In the end it was Shuisheng who bolted the compound gate and said: "Don't cry. Let's go inside." He walked ahead of her, but as they crossed the courtyard, she passed him quickly and went into the house to light the lamp. Shuisheng waited outside. He heard his wife strike

很早就是有痰喘的病。还有自己女人,正在青春,一别八年,分离时她肚子里正有一个小孩子。房子烧了吗?

不是什么悲喜交加的情绪,这是一种沉重的压迫,对战士的心的很大的消耗。他在心里驱逐这种思想感情,他走的很慢,他决定坐在这里,抽袋烟休息休息。

他坐下来打火抽烟,田野里没有一个人,风有些冷了,他打开大衣披在身上。他从积满泥水和腐草的水洼望过去,微微地可以看见白洋淀的边缘。

黄昏时候,他走到了自己的村边,他家就住在村边上。他看见房屋并没烧,街里很安静,这正是人们吃完晚饭,准备上门的时候了。

他在门口遇见了自己的女人。她正在那里悄悄地关闭那外面的梢门。水生热情地叫了一声:

"你!"

女人一怔,睁开大眼睛,咧开嘴笑了笑,就转过身子去抽抽嗒嗒地哭了。水生看见她脚上那白布封鞋,就知道父亲准是不在了。两个人在那里站了一会。还是水生把门掩好说:"不要哭了,家去吧!"他在前面走,女人在后面跟,走到院里,女人紧走两步赶到前面,到屋里去点灯。水生在院里停了停。他听着女人忙乱地打

a match, then lamplight glowed on the window. "Come in," she said. "You're not a guest."

As Shuisheng entered, she called to a little girl who had been asleep on the brick *kang* and pulled her up. Smiling with tears in her eyes, she said:

"This is your father. Complaining all the time that everyone else has a father and you have none. He's come back, hasn't he?" Her voice by then was almost inaudible. Shuisheng said:

"Let me hold her."

She passed the child to him. He hadn't realized that a little girl of eight or nine would be so heavy. Awakening from a sound sleep, the child gazed curiously at this stranger in the uniform of the Eighth Route Army. Shuisheng's wife put the things on the *kang* in order — the spinning wheel, the yarn....

After holding the child in his arms for a while, Shuisheng said: "Let her go back to sleep."

His wife put the little girl on the *kang* and covered her with a quilt, but the child continued to stare at him. Shuisheng paced about the room. He saw his reflection in the long mirror on the door of the clothes wardrobe that faced the entrance.

Picking up the lamp and starting for the next room to cook him some food, his wife looked at him and asked:

"Where have you come from?"

"Far away. A place you don't know."

"How many *li* did you walk today?"

"Ninety."

"Aren't you tired? What are you walking around for?"

火,灯光闪在窗户上了,女人喊:"进来吧!还做客吗?"

女人正在叫唤着一个孩子,他走进屋里,女人从炕上拖起一个孩子来,含着两眼泪水笑着说:

"来,这就是你爹,一天价看见人家有爹,自己没爹,这不现在回来了。"说着已经不成声音。水生说:

"来!我抱抱。"

老婆把孩子送到他怀里,他接过来,八九岁的女孩子竟有这么重。那孩子从睡梦里醒来,好奇地看着这个生人,这个"八路"。女人转身拾掇着炕上的纺车线子等等东西。

水生抱了孩子一会,说:

"还睡去吧。"

女人安排着孩子睡下,盖上被子,孩子却圆睁着两眼,再也睡不着。水生在屋里转着,在那扑满灰尘的迎门橱上的大镜子里照看自己。

女人要端着灯到外间屋里去烧水做饭,望着水生说:

"从哪里回来?"

"远了,你不知道的地方。"

"今天走了多少里?"

"九十。"

"不累吗?还在地下蹓跶?"

英汉对照
English-Chinese
中国文学宝库
Gems of Chinese Literature
现代文学系列
Modern Literature

Shuisheng sat down on the end of the *kang* and leaned against the wall. The wind was rising. It blew through the small locust tree in the courtyard. Moonlight shone on the paper panes of the window. The room seemed nice and warm. In the shadows, he asked the child:

"What's your name?"

"Little Ping."

"How old are you?"

His wife, working the stove bellows in the next room, called: "Don't tell him. He ought to remember."

"I'm eight," the child said.

"Did you think of me?"

"We thought of you," the child laughed. "We thought of you, but you didn't come."

"It's true," his wife, in the next room, also laughed. She asked him: "Did you think of us, too?"

"Yes," Shuisheng said.

"When?"

"When we weren't doing anything."

"When was that?"

"After a battle, or during halts on a march, or during rests when we were opening up new farmland."

"These last few years must have been hard on you."

"It hasn't been easy for you either."

"Me? It wasn't so bad for me," Shuisheng's wife said, almost angrily. She carried in the food and placed it on the *kang* table. "Pa had it worst of all. He didn't live to see you return...." She

水生靠在炕头上。外面起了风,风吹着院里那棵小槐树,月光射到窗纸上来。水生觉着这屋里是很暖和的,在黑影里问那孩子:

"你叫什么?"

"小平。"

"几岁了?"

女人在外边拉着风箱说:

"别告诉他,他不记的吗?"

孩子回答说:

"八岁。"

"想我吗?"

"想你。想你,你不来。"孩子笑着说。

女人在外边也笑了。说:

"真的!你也想过家吗?"

水生说:

"想过。"

"在什么时候?"

"闲着的时候。"

"什么时候闲着?……"

"打过仗以后,行军歇下来,开荒休息的时候。"

"你这几年不容易呀?"

"嗯,自然你们也不容易。"水生说。

"嗯?我容易,"她有些气愤地说着,把饭端上来,放在炕上。"爹是顶不容易的一个人,他不能看见你回来……"她坐在一边看着水生吃

sat down to one side and watched Shuisheng eat. She hadn't seen him eat for eight years. Shuisheng thought of his father. He forced himself to eat a little, then put his bowl down.

"What's the matter?" his wife smiled. "Isn't it as good as the millet you get in the army?"

Shuisheng didn't answer. He buttoned his tunic and went out.

When he came back, he bolted the door of the house. From time to time the chickens crowded in the coop in the courtyard stirred and fluttered. The little girl was asleep. How peacefully she slept. Her breath was like the bubbles of a freshet in the spring sunlight, merrily rising, happily sinking away.

His wife sat down beside her. She stared at the child's face as if she had never seen her before, as if it were someone else's child, not one that she herself had borne. As if this were not the little girl she had managed to raise while hiding from cruel Japanese "mop-up campaigns" in damp, muggy sorghum fields, darting breathlessly, running pell-mell. As if she had not pinned all her hopes on this child and breathed to her the prayer: "May the one who is far away return victorious soon and the family be united." As if she had not awakened many times in the still of the night and whispered to this innocent child the well-worn theme:

"Your pa, you know where he's gone? To fight the Japanese army.... He's carrying a big gun and riding a big horse.... He'll be home very soon, Precious, and let you ride on the horse's back. Won't that be fun!"

And suddenly he was here, as if he had dropped from the sky. She seemed to be thinking over all the things that had happened,

饭,看不见他吃饭的样子八年了。水生想起父亲,胡乱吃了一点,就放下了。

"怎么?"她笑着问,"不如你们那小米饭好吃?"

水生没答话。他拾掇了出去。

回来,插好了隔扇门。院子里那挤在窝里的鸡们,有时转动扑腾。孩子睡着了,睡的是那么安静,那呼吸就像泉水在春天的阳光里冒起的小水泡,愉快地升起,又幸福地降落。女人爬到孩子身边去,她一直呆望着孩子的脸。她好像从来没见过这个孩子,孩子好像是从别人家借来,好像不是她生出,不是她在那潮湿闷热的高粱地,在那残酷的"扫荡"里奔跑喘息,丢鞋甩袜抱养大的,她好像不曾在这孩子身上寄托了一切,并且在孩子的身上祝福了孩子的爹:"那走的远远的人,早一天胜利回来吧!一家团聚。"好像她并没有常常在深深的夜晚醒来,向着那不懂事的孩子,诉说着翻来复去的题目:

"你爹哩,他到哪里去了?打鬼子去了……他拿着大枪骑着大马……就要回来了,把宝贝放在马上……多好啊!"

现在,丈夫像从天上掉下来一样。她好像是想起了过去的一切,还编排那准备了好几年

arranging the words she had been preparing for years, to tell them to the husband who was now seated by her side.

Shuisheng looked at her. She hadn't aged much in eight years. She was twenty-nine this year. Though her hair was tousled, it was still very black. Her face was paler, but the light in her eyes was as strong as ever.

He looked at the cotton-padded tunic she was wearing — she had spun the thread and woven the cloth herself — and at the furnishings of the room. A profound determination, an ability to drive through innumerable hardships, was obvious both in her appearance and her manner.

"Don't you want to go to bed yet?" Shuisheng asked after a while.

"You go to bed if you're tired," she said slowly. "I can't sleep."

"I'm not sleepy either." Shuisheng covered himself with the greatcoat. "I'm a little cold."

She looked at the fur-lined Japanese coat and laughed.

"Tell the truth. Did you really think of me these past eight years?"

"Haven't I said so? Of course I did."

"What made you think of me?" she persisted.

"The night before I crossed the Beiping-Wuhan Railway, I stopped at a small inn. A fish pedlar from our village was staying there too. I bought some fish from him to go with my supper. When I ate them I thought of you."

"Pooh. Any other time?"

的话,要向现在已经坐到她身边的丈夫诉说了。

水生看着她。离别了八年,她好像并没有老多少。她今年二十九岁了,头发虽然乱些,可还是那么黑。脸孔苍白了一些,可是那两只眼睛里的光,还是那么强烈。

他望着她身上那自纺自织的棉衣和屋里的陈设。不论是人的身上,人的心里,都表现出是叫一种深藏的志气支撑,闯过了无数艰难的关口。

"还不睡吗?"过了一会,水生问。

"你困你睡吧,我睡不着。"女人慢慢地说。

"我也不困。"水生把大衣盖在身上,"我是有点冷。"

女人看着他那日本皮大衣,笑着问:

"说真的,这八九年,你想起过我吗?"

"不是说过了吗?想过。"

"怎么想法?"她逼着问。

"临过平汉路的那天夜里,我宿在一家小店,小店里有个鱼贩子是咱们乡亲。我买了一包小鱼下饭,吃着那鱼,就想起了你。"

"胡说。还有吗?"

英汉对照
English-Chinese
中国文学宝库
Gems of Chinese Literature
现代文学系列
Modern Literature

"That's all. I left home to fight, you know, not to moon over you."

"We thought of you always, day and night." She sat up. "Can you imagine how badly we missed you?"

"I can't," Shuisheng laughed.

"We missed you, but we didn't want to call you back. The Japanese were just outside our village then. At night I used to wake up thinking: If you were a star and I could see you shining in the sky, everything would be all right. But how could that be?"

Frost flowers were forming on the small pane of glass in the papered window frame. It was late. From the roof of a building on the main street, a man shouted an announcement:

"Attention militia defence corps. Assemble tomorrow at the third cock's crow. Bring your weapons and rations for one day."

The sound shifted as the man turned and repeated the announcement in different directions. In the chill frosty night, the voice boomed warmly through the big megaphone.

"Where are they going?" Prompted by habit ingrained in battle, Shuisheng rose alertly.

"Must be Shengfang. Things have been pretty tense these last two days," she retorted softly. She listened with care.

"Your militia knows our unit's come."

"Your whole unit? Where are you going?"

"We've been sent to protect the central Hebei plain, to beat back the enemy attack."

"How many days can you stay here at home?"

"Just tonight. I asked permission to leave the line of march and

"没有了。你知道我是出门打仗去了,不是专门想你去了。"

"我们可常常想你,黑夜白日。"她支着身子坐起来,"你能猜一猜我们想你的那段苦情吗?"

"猜不出来。"水生笑了笑。

"我们想你,我们可没有想叫你回来。那时候,日本人就在咱村边。可是在黑夜,一觉醒了,我就想:你如果能像天上的星星,在我眼前晃一晃就好了。可是能够吗?"

从窗户上那块小小的玻璃上结起来冰花,夜深了,大街的高房上有人高声广播:

"民兵自卫队注意!明天,鸡叫三遍集合。带好武器,和一天的干粮!"

那声音转动着,向四面八方有力地传送。在这样降落霜雪严寒的夜里,一只粗大的喇叭在热情地呼喊。

"他们要到哪里去?"水生照战争习惯,机警地直起身子来问。

"准是到胜芳。这两天,那里很紧!"女人一边细心听,一边小声地说。

"他们知道我们来了。"

"你们来了?你要上哪里去?"

"我们是调来保卫冀中平原,打退进攻的敌人的!"

"你能在家住几天?"

"就是这一晚上。我是请假绕道来看望你。"

英汉对照
English-Chinese
中国文学宝库
Gems of Chinese Literature
现代文学系列
Modern Literature

come to see you."

"Why didn't you say so before?"

"I hadn't the chance."

She was speechless. She lowered her head, then listlessly lay down on the *kang*. After a long pause, she said:

"Hurry up and come to bed. I'll take you back tomorrow on the sled."

At the third cock's crow she rose and cooked breakfast for him. There was a heavy fog that day, and the ground was covered with frost. Awakening the little girl, she dressed her warmly. Then, carrying the long narrow sled on her shoulders, she locked the compound gate and set out with Shuisheng. As they left the village, she wanted him to go and look at his father's grave. Shuisheng said there would be time for that when he returned. His wife insisted. She said:

"You must. Pa took care of us all his life. In eight years you've spent only one night at home. But Pa, after he sent you off to war, had to look after the whole family. We never had a moment's peace, running and hiding day after day. Because you weren't home, Pa felt he never could do enough for us. He was always afraid that something might happen to the wife or child or his son fighting the Japanese and he wouldn't be able to face you. If there was the least suspicious sound in the night, the old man would come across the courtyard and wake me. Get up, he'd say, dress the child. No matter what the weather — wind, rain, cold or hot — he ran with the baby on his back, wheezing and coughing from weariness. It was those bitter days, those days of hardship and ter-

"为什么不早些说?"

"还没顾着啊!"

女人呆了。她低下头去,又无力地仄在炕上。过了半天,她说:

"那么就赶快休息休息吧,明天我撑着冰床子去送你。"

鸡叫三遍,女人就先起来给水生做了饭吃。这是一个大雾天,地上堆满了霜雪。女人把孩子叫醒,穿的暖暖的,背上冰床,锁了门,送丈夫上路。出了村,她要丈夫到爹的坟上去看看。水生说等以后回来再说,女人不肯。她说:

"你去看看,爹一辈子为了我们。八年,你只在家里呆了一个晚上。爹叫你出去打仗了,是他一个老年人照顾了咱们全家。这是什么太平日子呀?整天价东逃西窜。因为你不在家,爹对我们娘俩,照顾的惟恐不到。只怕一差二错,对不起在外抗日的儿子。每逢夜里一有风声,他老人家就先在院里把我叫醒,说:水生家起来吧,给孩子穿上衣裳。不管是风里雨里,多么冷,多么热,他老人家背着孩子逃跑,累的痰喘咳嗽。是这个苦日子,遭难的日子,担惊受怕

英汉对照
English-Chinese
中国文学宝库
Gems of Chinese Literature
现代文学系列
Modern Literature

ror, that wore him out and killed him. We also had famine that year...."

At the edge of the frozen river, they got on the sled. Shuisheng sat in front, holding the child. He wrapped her in his greatcoat. His wife stood in the stern and took up the long-pointed pole. She was first-rate at punting on the ice.

"Just look at your pa," she said jestingly to the little girl. "Useless. Eight years in the Eighth Route Army and he can't get back unless I deliver him in our sled." She leaped lightly on the the tail end, like a dragonfly landing on a leaf after rain. She shoved back easily with the pointed pole and the sled moved forward. Heavy fog mantled the network of waterways. They couldn't see more than a few metres ahead. Flecks of frost from the dry reeds on the banks floated in the air. Their clothing soon turned a silvery white.

Her hair bound tightly by a strip of black cloth, she propelled the sled so rapidly that it seemed to fly above the ice. She drove directly into the wind, the two ends of her scarf fluttering behind her. After a number of quick thrusts, she straightened up and smiled at Shuisheng. Her face was rosy with cold. Hot breath steamed from her mouth. The small sled shot across the ice like an arrow from a bow, its runners throwing up clouds of frosty particles. Ahead was an open rivulet of fast running water. All she said was: "Careful." Her legs bore down a bit, and the sled raised its head like a startled snake and skimmed across.

"Slow down a little," Shuisheng cautioned. "Are you crazy?"

Wiping the frosty rime and sweat from her face, she laughed. "We're sending you back to your battlefield, comrade, and you tell

的日子,把他老人家累死。还有那年大饥荒……"

在河边,他们放下冰床。水生坐上去,抱着孩子,用大衣给她包好脚。女人站在床子后尾,撑起了竿。女人是撑冰床的好手,她逗着孩子说:

"看你爹没出息,当了八年八路军,还得叫我撑冰床子送他!"她轻轻地跳上冰床子后尾,像一只雨后的蜻蜓爬上草叶。轻轻用竿子向后一点,冰床子前进了。大雾笼罩着水淀,只有眼前几丈远的冰道可以望见。河两岸残留的芦苇上的霜花飒飒飘落,人的衣服上立时变成银白色。她用一块长的黑布紧紧把头发包住,冰床像飞一样前进,好像离开了冰面行走。她的围巾的两头飘到后面去,风正从她的前面吹来。她连撑几竿,然后直起身来向水生一笑。她的脸冻得通红,嘴里却冒着热气。小小的冰床像离开了强弩的箭,摧起的冰屑,在它前面打起团团的旋花。前面有一条窄窄的水沟,水在冰缝里汩汩地流,她只说了一声"小心",两脚轻轻地一用劲,冰床就像受了惊的小蛇一样,抬起头来,窜过去了。

水生警告她说:

"你慢一些,疯了?"

女人擦一擦脸上的冰雪和汗,笑着说:

"同志!我们送你到战场上去呀,你倒说慢

英汉对照
English-Chinese
中国文学宝库
Gems of Chinese Literature
现代文学系列
Modern Literature

us to go slower!"

"If you get your nose scraped you won't be so frisky."

"Impossible. I've been playing with these things since I was a kid. There's even less chance today. You don't know how many Eighth Routers I've delivered in this sled these past eight years."

Through the frosty mist, the sled flew on.

"Take me to Dingjia Landing," said Shuisheng. "I can find my unit from there."

She stared at him in silence for some time. Finally, she said:

"Cover Little Ping again. Can't you see she's pulled her hands out?" Panting slightly, she said: "I'm all upset. I haven't seen you in eight years, but you could only spend a few hours at home. Do you know why I'm rushing so fast? Why I'm in such a hurry to send you back to the battlefield? I keep thinking: The sooner you go, the sooner you'll beat back the enemy and come home to me again.

"We wives at home, you know, long for victory more than anyone. As we hide in tunnels, and out in the high sorghum, we're just waiting for that day. When it comes we'll be happier than words can tell.

"The Kuomintang troops attacking Shengfang have been flown in by plane. During the eight or nine years we were fighting the Japanese, they were resting comfortably in the rear with their wives. Their coming has shattered our happiness. It's broken our hearts. They are committing a terrible crime. You must destroy them!"

The sled raced on to the broad lake. Here the ice was a boundless expanse. Rising out of it, the sun split the fog, opening a

一些!"

"擦破了鼻子就不闹了。"

"不会。这是从小玩熟了的东西。今天更不会。在这八年里面,你知道我用这床子,送过多少次八路军?"

冰床在霜雾里,在冰上飞行。

"你把我送到丁家坞,"水生说,"到那里,我就可以找到队伍了。"

女人没有言语。她呆望着丈夫。停了一会,才说:

"你给孩子再盖一盖,你看她的手露着。"她轻轻地喘了两口气。又说:"你知道,我现在心里很乱。八年我才见到你,你只在家里呆了不到多半夜的工夫。我为什么撑的这么快?为什么着急把你送到战场上去?我是想,你快快去,快快打走了进攻我们的敌人,你才能快快地回来,和我见面。

"你知道,我们,我们这些留在家里当媳妇的,最盼望胜利。我们在地洞里,在高粱地里等着这一天。这一天来了,我们那高兴,是不能和别人说的。

"进攻胜芳的敌人,是坐飞机来的;他们躺在后方,和妻子团聚了八九年。他们来了,可把我们的幸福打破了,他们打破了我们的心。他们造的罪孽是多么重!一定要把他们完全消灭!"

冰床跑进水淀中央,这里是没有边际的冰场。太阳从冰面上升出来,冲开了雾,形成一条

crimson lane and splashing its colours on the sled.

"When Pa was alive," she continued, "he used to say: Shuisheng has gone to hack out a road to life. If he can do it, we'll live. If he can't, we'll die.... Eight years. The old man died of worry. The Kuomintang reactionaries are just like the Japanese. They want to drive us all to our graves.

"You ought to remember Pa's words. Keep moving forward. Don't let anything distract you. Fight well. Eight years have passed. They were pretty long. But if only you stay at the front, I'll wait for you till I die."

Dingjia Landing, surrounded by willows, was draped in mist when they arrived. Shuisheng got off the sled at the edge of the village. He gazed at his wife, standing motionless on the ice.

"You and Little Ping come into the village and warm up," he urged.

There were tears in her eyes. She smiled.

"Hurry along with you. We're not cold. Remember! Fight well and come back soon. We'll be waiting for news of your victory."

1946

Translated by Sidney Shapiro

红色的胡同,扑到这里来照在冰床上。女人说:

"爹活着的时候常说,水生出去是打开一条活路,打开了这条活路,我们就得活,不然我们就活不了。八年,他老人家焦愁死了。国民党反动派又要和日本一样,想来把我们活着的人完全逼死!

"你应该记着爹的话,向上长进,不要为别的事情分心,好好打仗。八年过去了,时间不算不长。只要你还在前方,我等你到死!"

在被大雾笼罩、杨柳树环绕的丁家坞村边,水生下了冰床。他望着呆呆站在冰上的女人说:

"你们也到村里去暖和暖和吧。"

女人忍着眼泪,笑着说:

"快去你的吧!我们不冷。记着,好好打仗,快回来,我们等着你的胜利消息。"

1946年河间

Honour

North of Raoyang County Town is a village with a good ferry service across the Hutuo River. In its upper reaches the Hutuo, hemmed in by hills, roars sullenly day and night; but once down on the plain it races wherever it will, veering north one year, south the next.

This river brought the peasants beside it a load of grief until they built dykes along its north and south banks. The flats between these dykes lie waste, but when the Hutuo dwindles in May willows, reeds and rushes spring up there. And as fuel is scarce thereabouts all the boys and girls swarm there with their crates and sickles. Fanned out over the flats, stooping and straightening up alternately as they cut the tall reeds under the blazing sun, they look like browsing flocks of sheep and cattle.

Late in May 1937, the first year of the War of Resistance against Japan, the reeds had grown high enough to cover the girls' bright head scarfs. With no work to be done in the arid fields, the village youngsters spent all their time on the flats.

Guns were booming to the north, east and west. The sound spread southeast and southwest as the Japanese advanced, and wave after wave of Kuomintang troops and officials crossed the Hutuo here in their flight south, harassing and looting the villages they passed.

光 荣

饶阳县城北有一个村庄,这村庄紧靠滹沱河,是个有名的摆渡口。大家知道,滹沱河在山里受着约束,昼夜不停地号叫,到了平原,就今年向南一滚,明年往北一冲,自由自在地奔流。

河两岸的居民,年年受害,就南北打起堤来,两条堤中间全是河滩荒地,到了五六月间,河里没水,河滩上长起一层水柳、红荆和深深的芦草。常常发水,柴禾很缺,这一带的男女青年孩子们,一到这个时候,就在炎炎的热天,背上一个草筐,拿上一把镰刀,散在河滩上,在日光草影里,割那长长的芦草,一低一仰,像一群群放牧的牛羊。

"七七"事变那一年,河滩上的芦草长的很好,五月底,那芦草已经能遮住那些孩子们的各色各样的头巾。地里很旱,没有活做,这村里的孩子们,就整天缠在河滩里。

那时候,东西北三面都有了炮声,渐渐东南面和西南面也响起炮来,证明敌人已经打过去了,这里已经亡了国。国民党的军队和官员,整天整夜从这条渡口往南逃,还不断骚扰抢劫老百姓。

英汉对照
English-Chinese
中国文学宝库
Gems of Chinese Literature
现代文学系列
Modern Literature

That was when the peasants realized they would have to take their defence into their own hands. People's defence corps were organized in Gaoyang and Suning and soon the movement was spreading like wildfire. The young men seized all the guns they could find, the rifles buried in the villages and those used by the landlords' thugs and police patrols. They went about with rifles over their shoulders.

Arms became a vital necessity, the peasants' most precious possession. And before long they hit on the scheme of holding up the retreating Kuomintang troops and relieving them of their guns. Their reasoning was simple. Soldiers are fed and trained to fight. If you run away from the enemy, all right, leave us your guns — we'll show you what we can do with them.

First they lured a squad or small unit into the village, often giving the soldiers a feast or some silver dollars before confiscating their rifles.

Then bolder spirits, unarmed, took to holding up soldiers on the highway. It was like taking cake from a child.

Now that the river was dry, a large ferry boat lay upturned to sun on the flats. Its owner Yin Tingyu was a man in his fifties who made a humble living as a boatman. He was helped when the river was full by his son Yuansheng, but at present the fifteen-year-old was out cutting reeds all day with the other youngsters.

Yuansheng had just filled his crate today as twilight fell and was picking it up to start home when his name was called.

He turned and saw Xiumei, a girl from the west of the village. In a shabby white short-sleeved tunic and patched cloth shoes, she

是从这时候激起了人们保家自卫的思想,北边,高阳肃宁已经有人民自卫军的组织。那时候,是一声雷响,风雨齐来,自卫的组织,比什么都传流的快,今天这村成立了大队部,明天那村也就安上了大锅。青年们把所有的枪支,把村中埋藏的、地主看家的、巡警局里抓赌的枪支,都弄了出来,背在肩上。

枪,成了最重要的、最必需的、人们最喜爱的物件。渐渐人们想起来:卡住这些逃跑的军队,留下他们的枪支。这意思很明白:养兵千日,用兵一时;大敌压境,你们不说打仗,反倒逃跑,好,留下枪支,交给我们,看我们的吧!

先是在村里设好圈套,卡一个班或是小队逃兵的枪;那常常是先摆下酒宴,送上洋钱,然后动手。

后来,有些勇敢的人,赤手空拳,站在大道边上就卡住了枪支,那办法就简单了。

这渡口上原有一只大船,现在河里没水,翻过船底,晒在河滩上。船主名叫尹廷玉,是个五十多的老头子,弄了一辈子船,落了个"车船店脚牙"的坏名儿,可也没置下产业。他有一个儿子刚刚十五岁,名叫原生,河里有水的时候,帮父亲弄弄船,现在船闲着,他也就整天跟着孩子们在河滩上看过逃兵,看过飞机,割芦苇草。

这一天,割满了草筐,天也晚了,刚刚要杀紧绳子往回里走,他听得背后有人叫了他一声。

"原生!"

他回头一看,是村西头的一个姑娘,叫秀梅的,穿着一件短袖破白褂,拖着一双破花鞋,提

英汉对照
English-Chinese
中国文学宝库
Gems of Chinese Literature
现代文学系列
Modern Literature

ran up to him swinging her sickle. Catching hold of his sleeve she pointed east to a clump of reeds ruffled by the evening wind.

"What's up?" demanded Yuansheng.

"There's a Kuomintang deserter there," she whispered. "He's got a gun."

"Is he alone?"

"Yes." She panted, biting her lips. "A big new rifle, it is."

"Have all the others gone?" The boy looked round for some support. But the sun had set behind the hills, there was only a smudge of red at the horizon, and apart from themselves the river flats were deserted.

"Can't you cope alone?" Xiumei looked up at him expectantly.

The gleam in her big eyes made him grasp his sickle more firmly and stride off towards the east. With a glance at the bright curved blade in her own hands, the girl padded after him.

"Go on," she said softly. "I'll help you."

"I don't need you."

Yuansheng came up quietly behind the deserter. The fellow looked fagged out as he bent forward to bandage his blistered feet, his rifle on the ground beside him. The boy kicked him over and ran off with the gun. Xiumei's scarf fell off as she raced after him, but she didn't stop to pick it up.

Not until they reached the village did they pause for breath.

"Now we've got a gun," gasped Xiumei. "Tomorrow you can join the guerrillas."

"It's partly yours. Let's share it."

"As if this were a clutch of eggs two of us could share! You take

着小镰跑过来,跑到原生跟前,一扯原生的袖子,就用镰刀往东一指:东面是深深一带芦苇,正叫晚风吹的摇摆。

"什么?"原生问。

秀梅低声说:

"那道边有一个逃兵,拿着一支枪。"

原生问:

"就是一个人?"

"就是一个。"秀梅喘喘气咬咬嘴唇,"崭新的一支大枪。"

"人们全回去了没有?"原生周围一看,想集合一些同伴,可是太阳已经下山,天边只有一抹红云,看来河滩里是冷冷清清的没有一个人了。

"你一个人还不行吗?"秀梅仰着头问。

原生看见了这女孩子的两只大眼睛里放射着光芒,就紧握他那镰刀,拨动芦草往东边去了。秀梅看了看自己那一把弯弯的明亮的小镰,跟在后边,低声说:

"去吧,我帮着你。"

"你不用来。"原生说。

原生从那个逃兵身后过去,那逃兵已经疲累得很,正低着头包脚上的燎泡,枪支放在一边。原生一脚把他踢趴,拿起枪支,回头就跑,秀梅也就跟着跑起来,遮在头上的小小的白布手巾也飘落下来,丢在后面。

到了村边,两个人才站下来喘喘气,秀梅说:

"我们也有一支枪了,明天你就去当游击

it and join up. What would I do with a gun?"

"I'll join up, don't worry. But you must know that song:

He's off to fight in the war,
And she to join the women's resistance corps....

Let's both go."

"I'm not going anywhere with you. It's Xiaowu you should be taking." Xiumei started cheerfully home brandishing her sickle, but turned after a few steps to call:

"I've lost my crate and scarf. You must help me find them after supper, or I'll catch it from my dad."

"All right," he said.

That was how the boy came to join up and marched off with this rifle to fight. He probably changed it later for a Japanese rifle captured from the enemy. Now he may be using an American automatic.

Xiaowu was Yuansheng's wife. She was twenty, five years older than he. Their marriage had been arranged by a go-between and his father.

At this time people did not try to prevent young men from becoming soldiers, and no objection was raised to Yuansheng's enlisting. When his father ferried him and some other lads across the river, he waved a casual, laughing goodbye to the youngsters under the willows on the dyke, among them Xiumei, her small brother in her arms.

队！"

原生说：

"也有你的一份呢，咱两个伙着吧！"

秀梅一撇嘴说：

"你当是一个雀虫蛋哩，两个人伙着！你拿着去当兵吧，我要那个有什么用？"

原生说：

"对，我就去当兵。你听见人家唱了没有：男的去当游击队，女的参加妇救会。咱们一块去吧！"

"我不和你一块去，叫你们小五和你一块去吧！"秀梅笑一笑，就舞动小镰回家去了。走了几步回头说：

"我把草筐和手巾丢了，吃了饭，你得和我拿去，要不爹要骂我哩！"

原生答应了。原生从此就成了人民解放军的战士，背着这支枪打仗，后来也许换成"三八"，现在也许换成"美国自动步"了。

小五是原生的媳妇。这是原生的爹那年在船上，夜里推牌九，一副天罡赢来的，比原生大好几岁，现在二十了。

那时候当兵，还没有拖尾巴这个丢人的名词，原生去当兵，谁也不觉得怎样，就是那登上自家的渡船，同伙伴们开走的时候，原生也不过望着那抱着小弟弟站在堤岸柳树下面的秀梅和一群男女孩子们，嘻嘻笑了一阵，就算完事。

英汉对照
English-Chinese
中国文学宝库
Gems of Chinese Literature
现代文学系列
Modern Literature

This was hardly a formal send-off. But for the fifteen-year-old it marked the beginning of night marches across the plain and battles at dawn. The soldiers trained hard on the sandy flats below Mount Dahei in Fuping, they heard the clear, urgent call of the Hutuo at Yuping, stood sentry on snowy nights in the forests of Mount Wutai, and sang at dusk in the wind north of the Great Wall.

Xiumei, part-owner of his gun, in time became one of the village cadres. So many lads from their village joined the army that she seldom remembered young Yuansheng. For her the war years passed quickly, there was so much to think about, so much to be done.

But as time went by Yuansheng's wife grew more and more restive. First she started quarrelling with her mother-in-law, then she took to going home for lengthy visits, and finally she even refused to come back and help with the harvest.

When she did come it was only to make a scene. Her mother-in-law, kindly soul, did her best to humour Xiaowu in Yuansheng's absence. When all her efforts proved wasted she protested:

"Plenty of soldiers have left wives at home, but none of them sulks the way you do."

"And haven't I good reason? The others at least come home on leave or write." She pulled a long face and looked down her nose. You couldn't have called Xiaowu fat, yet even when she was pleased there was something flabby and sulky about her features.

"I reckon he's too far away to send a letter."

"Well, you can't expect a girl to wait for ever." With this Xiaowu flounced out.

这不像是离别,又不像是欢送。从这开始,这个十五岁的青年人,就在平原上夜晚行军,黎明作战;在阜平大黑山下砂石滩上艰苦练兵,在孟平听那滹沱河清冷的急促的号叫;在五台雪夜的山林放哨;在黄昏的塞外,迎着晚风歌唱了。

他那个卡枪的伙伴秀梅,也真的在村里当了干部。村里参军的青年很多,她差不多忘记了那个小小的原生。战争,时间过的多快,每个人要想的、要做的,又是多么丰富啊!

可是原生那个媳妇渐渐不安静起来。先是常常和婆婆吵架,后来就是长期住娘家,后来竟是秋麦也不来。

来了,就找气生。婆婆是个老好子人,先是觉得儿子不在家,害怕媳妇抱屈,处处将就,哄一阵,说一阵,解劝一阵;后来看着怎么也不行,就说:

"人家在外头的多着呢,就没见过你这么背晦的!"

"背晦,人家都有个家来,有个信来。"媳妇的眼皮和脸上的肉越发搭拉下来。这个媳妇并不胖,可是,就是在她高兴的时候,她的眼皮和脸上的肉也是松松地搭拉着。

"他没有信来,是离家远的过。"婆婆说。

"叫人等着也得有个头呀!"媳妇一转脸就出去了。

英汉对照
English-Chinese
中国文学宝库
Gems of Chinese Literature
现代文学系列
Modern Literature

Her mother-in-law flared up and cried after her:

"Just what do you mean by that?"

Xiaowu soon made clear what she meant. When she came she spent little time in the house, preferring to sit in the street for hours at a stretch chatting to the other women as they worked.

"How can you bear to fritter away your time?" asked one woman, busy spinning.

"Why should I wear myself out?" retorted Xiaowu. "We can't all be busy beavers."

When her mother-in-law had milled corn and cooked a meal, Xiaowu went home and helped herself from the pan. Yet there was no end to her grumbles and complaints.

"Many of our men have joined up," the villagers told her. "Yours isn't the only one. If none of us worked, your Yuansheng would have to fight on an empty stomach."

"That would be all right by me," was her reply.

After all his years as ferryman her father-in-law set considerable store by face. As his daughter-in-law went from bad to worse he took his wife to task, till she lost her temper and started blaming her son. There was fighting not far away at the time and she often sat on her doorstep half the night, looking up at the star-sprinkled sky and listening to the gunfire, for this made her feel closer to her boy. She would sigh, "Why don't you come back? Fire a couple of shots from your big gun and teach this minx a lesson."

One day, after Xiumei had become a cadre, some young women asked for her. It was summer and a number of young wives were working in a covered entrance-way. Xiaowu, just back from her

婆婆生了气,大声喊:

"你说,你说,什么是头呀?"

从这以后,媳妇就更明目张胆起来,她来了,不大在家里呆,好到街上去坐,半天半天的,人家纺线,她站在一边闲磕牙。有些勤谨的人说她:"你坐的落意呀?"她就说:"做着活有什么心花呀?谁能像你们呀?"等婆婆推好碾子,做熟了饭,她来到家里,掀锅就盛。还常说落后话,人家问她:"村里抗日的多着呢,也不是你独一份呀,谁也不做活,看你那汉子在前方吃什么穿什么呀?"她就说:"没吃没穿才好呢。"

公公耍了半辈子落道,弄了一辈子船,是个有头有脸好面子的人,看看儿媳越来越不像话,就和老婆子闹,老婆子就气的骂自己的儿子。那几年,近处还有战争,她常常半夜半夜坐在房沿上,望着满天的星星,听那隆隆的炮响,这样一来,就好像看见儿子的面,和儿子说了话,心里也痛快一些了。并且狠狠地叨念:怎么你就不回来,带着那大炮,冲着这刁婆,狠狠地轰两下子呢?

小五的落后,在村里造成了很坏的影响,一些老太太们看见她这个样子,就不愿叫儿子去当兵,说:"儿子走了不要紧,留下这个娘娘咱搪不开。"

秀梅在村里当干部,有一天,人们找了她来。正是夏天,一群妇女在一家梢门洞里做活,

英汉对照
English-Chinese

中国文学宝库
Gems of Chinese Literature

现代文学系列
Modern Literature

mother's home and dressed in her best, was standing idle as usual, fanning herself. At the sight of Xiumei her face clouded. She turned away.

"Come in here and cool off, Xiumei," called the others happily. They offered her a straw hassock.

"Someone here's so pig-headed, we can none of us make her see reason. We want your help."

Xiumei sat down with a smile.

"Pig-headed, am I?" snapped Xiaowu. "Well, all you do is talk."

"Who does nothing but talk?" rejoined Xiumei. "Try counting the families here with a man at the front fighting Japan. There are plenty of them. But who else behaves the way you do?"

"What's wrong with the way I behave?" Xiaowu rounded on her, scowling, her dark face at variance with her gaudy clothes. "At least I've never driven someone else's husband off to be a soldier."

"Who drove your husband off to be a soldier?" said Xiumei. "To be a soldier fighting for our country, why, that's an honour."

"What good is honour?" sneered Xiaowu. "You can't eat honour, or wear it."

"Maybe not. Nor will honour keep house for you like a husband. But different people see things differently. Those who are out for an easy life think only of food and clothes. Other people think of more honourable things."

"Xiumei's dead right," chimed in another girl. "They're fighting for all of us. No decent young fellow nowadays wants to stay snug at home on his *kang*."

小五刚从娘家回来,穿一身鲜鲜亮亮的衣裳,站在一边摇着扇子,一见秀梅过来,她那眼皮和脸皮,像玩独脚戏一样,瓜搭就落下来,扭过脸去。

那些青年妇女们见秀梅来了,都笑着说:

"秀梅姐快来凉快凉快吧!"说着就递过麦垫来。有的就说:"这里有个大顽固蛋,谁也剥不开,你快把她说服了吧!"

秀梅笑着坐下,小五就说:

"我是顽固,谁也别光说漂亮话!"

秀梅说:

"谁光说漂亮话来?咱村里,你挨门数数,有多少在前方抗日的,有几个像你的呀?"

"我怎么样?"小五转过脸来,那脸叫这身鲜亮衣裳一陪衬,显得多么难看。"我没有装坏,把人家的人挑着去当兵!"

"谁挑着你家的人去当兵?当兵是为了国家的事,是光荣的!"秀梅说。

"光荣几个钱一两?"小五追着问,"我看也不能当衣穿,也不能当饭吃!"

"是!"秀梅说,"光荣不能当饭吃,当衣穿;光荣也不能当男人,一块过日子!这得看是谁说,有的人窝窝囊囊吃上顿饱饭,穿上件衣裳就混的下去,有的人还要想到比吃饭穿衣更光荣的事!"

别的妇女也说:

"秀梅说的一点也不假,打仗是为了大伙,现在的青年人,谁还愿意当炕头上的汉子呀!"

英汉对照
English-Chinese
中国文学宝库
Gems of Chinese Literature
现代文学系列
Modern Literature

Xiaowu laughed scornfully and slapped her backside with her fan.

"That's a lot of hot air. If not for you, my man wouldn't have joined the army."

"You mean Yuansheng wouldn't have gone if the two of us hadn't got hold of that rifle? I see nothing wrong with that. When Yuansheng went off with that rifle to serve our country, I felt very proud I can tell you. You should feel it an honour too."

"Keep your honour, I don't want it. You talk as if you'd done some great public service."

"Not I. Your husband, yes."

"He's not my husband," hissed Xiaowu. "You're a cadre, aren't you? All right, I want a divorce."

The others stared at Xiumei in dismay.

"You can't get a divorce," she said. "Not while your husband's fighting at the front."

"When can I, then?"

"When Japan is defeated, that's when."

"I refuse to wait. If your're so keen on waiting, why are you getting married?"

Xiumei flushed crimson at this, for her marriage was about to be settled.

"Why be such a dog in the manger?" cried one of her friends. "You've got a man to wait for, she hasn't. Why shouldn't she marry?"

Xiumei stood up and looked Xiaowu in the eye.

"All right, I won't get married. I mean it. We'll both wait."

小五冷笑着，用扇子拍着屁股说：

"说那么漂亮干什么，是'画眉张'的徒弟吗，要不叫你，俺家那个当不了兵！"

秀梅说："哈！你是说，我和原生卡了一支枪，他才当了兵？我觉着这不算错，原生拿着那支枪，真的替国家出了力，我还觉着光荣呢！你也该觉着光荣。"

"俺不要光荣！"小五说，"你光荣吧，照你这么说，你还是国家的功臣呢，真是木头眼镜。"

"我不是什么功臣，你家的人才是功臣呢！"秀梅说。

"那不是俺家的人。"小五丝声漾气地说，"你不是干部吗？我要和他离婚！"

大伙都一楞，望着秀梅。秀梅说：

"你不能离婚，你的男人在前方作战！"

"有个头没有？"小五说。

"怎么没头，打败日本就是头。"

"我等不来，"小五说，"你们能等可就别寻婆家呀！"

秀梅的脸腾地红了，她正在说婆家，就要下书定准了。别人听了都不忿，说："碍着人家了吗！你不叫人家寻婆家，你有汉子好等着，叫人家站谁呀！"

秀梅站起来，望着小五说：

"我不是和你赌气，我就不寻婆家，我们等着吧。"

英汉对照
English-Chinese
中国文学宝库
Gems of Chinese Literature
现代文学系列
Modern Literature

77

The others burst out laughing, although Xiumei was close to tears. And Xiaowu beat a retreat.

"Someone must have put her up to this," remarked one of the young women. "Trying to sabotage our work, she is."

"We'll win her over patiently," said Xiumei.

"You're too trusting, Xiumei," said another. "You think everybody else is as good as you. I'm sure Xiaowu has somebody backing her up."

"But seriously, why shouldn't you marry?" asked several others.

"Not now, I won't. I'll show those grass widows. Just think of Yuansheng. He marched off with a rifle as a boy in his teens, and he's been gone seven or eight years. I call that fine."

"Yuansheng's all right." A girl chuckled. "But you can't wait for someone else's husband."

"I'm not waiting for him," said Xiumei earnestly. "I'm waiting for victory."

Meanwhile Xiaowu had gone to a melon field outside the village. It belonged to Yin Dalian, a local grain merchant who found it a handy place for some quiet drinking and subversive talk.

He was perched up on his look-out now, fanning himself and tippling.

"Choose yourself a big melon," he called down to Xiaowu. "Have you fixed up your divorce?"

Picking her way between the vines she answered:

"They say I've got to wait till the victory."

"Hm. It's going to be a long war. A life sentence to hard labour, I call it. Besides, the ruling is: Five years without news

别的人都笑起来,秀梅气的要哭了。小五站不住走了。有的就说:"像这样的女人应该好好打击一下,一定有人挑拨着她来破坏我们的工作。"秀梅说:"我们也不随便给她扣帽子,还是教育她。"那人说:"秀梅姐!你还是佛眼佛心,把人全当成好人;小五要是没有牵线的,挖下我的眼来当泡踏!"

对于秀梅的事,大家都说:

"你真是,为什么不结婚?"

"我先不结婚。"秀梅说,"有很多人把前方的战士,当做打了外出的人,我给她们做个榜样。你们还记得那个原生不?现在想起来,十几岁的一个人,背起枪来,一出去就是七年八年,才真是个好样儿的哩!"

"原生倒是不错,"一个姑娘笑了,"可是你也不能等着人家呀!"

"我不是等着他,"秀梅庄重地说,"我是等着胜利!"

小五到村处一块瓜园里去。这瓜园是村里一个粮秣先生尹大恋开的。这人原是村里一家财主,现在村中弄了名小小的干部当着,掩藏身体,又开了个瓜园,为的是喝酒说落后话儿,好有个清净地方。

尹大恋正坐在高高的窝棚里摇着扇子喝酒,一看见小五儿来了就说:

"拣着大个儿的摘着吃吧,你那离婚的事儿谈的怎样了?"

小五儿拨着瓜秧说:

"人家叫等到打败日本,谁知道哪年哪月他们才能打败日本呀!"

英汉对照
English-Chinese
中国文学宝库
Gems of Chinese Literature
现代文学系列
Modern Literature

and you can get a divorce. Take it to court. Don't be soft."

Xiaowu went back and made such a scene with her in-laws that they consented, grudgingly, to a divorce. Then Yuansheng's mother gave way to a storm of weeping.

"Don't waste tears on her," said her husband. "I was a fool ever to fix that match. Good riddance to bad rubbish. That bitch doesn't know there's a war on, all she thinks of is herself."

After Xiaowu left, Xiumei made a point of dropping in to help about the house. She kept the water vat filled, swept the yard, unpicked and washed their padded clothes in summer with Yuansheng's mother, and helped his father with the harvesting in autumn.

When the Japanese surrendered, she ran to give the old couple the good news. They were overjoyed. But the months went by and although many demobbed soldiers came home there was no sign of Yuansheng.

"Fate's treated us shabbily," complained his mother. "Saddling us with a daughter-in-law like that."

"Forget her, Aunty," advised Xiumei. "I'm here if you need any help. You've no girl of your own, you must count me as your daughter."

"You're a good child, but aren't you going to be married some day?" Yuansheng's mother sighed. "Nearly ten years he's been gone, and not even a letter."

"Our troops have marched so far, Aunty. On the move all the time, with never a moment to spare, he just didn't get round to writing. But he'll turn up one of these days, and then how pleased

"唉！长期抗战,这不是无期徒刑吗？喂,不是有说讲吗？五年没有音讯就可以。这是他们的法令呀,他们自己还不遵守吗？和他打官司呀,你这人还是不行！"

小五儿回来就又和公婆闹,闹的公婆没法,咬咬牙叫她离婚走了,老婆婆狠狠啼哭了一场。老头说："哭她干什么！她是我一副牌赢来的,只当我一副牌又把她输了就算了！"

自从小五儿出门走了以后,秀梅就常常到原生家里,帮着做活,看看水瓮里没水,就去挑了来,看看院子该扫,就要扫干净,伏天,帮老婆拆洗衣裳,秋天帮着老头收割打场。

日本投了降,秀梅跑去告诉老人家,老人听了也欢喜,可是过了好久,有好些军人退伍回来了,还不见原生回来。

原生的娘说：

"什么命呀,叫我们修下这样一个媳妇！"

秀梅说：

"大娘,那就只当没有这么一个媳妇,有什么活我帮你做,你不是没有闺女吗,你就只当有我这么个闺女！"

"好孩子,可是你要出聘了呢？"原生的娘说,"唉,为什么原生八九年就连个信也没有？"

"大娘,军队开的远,东一天,西一天,工作很忙,他就忘记给家里写信了。总有一天,一下子回来了,你才高兴呢！"

英汉对照
English-Chinese
中国文学宝库
Gems of Chinese Literature
现代文学系列
Modern Literature

you'll be!"

"I listen for a knock every evening and wake up in the middle of the night fancying I hear him calling, 'Mum! Open up !' But it's just my imagination. So many others have come back, why doesn't Yuansheng?"

"He must be an officer by now. How can he leave his men to come home?"

"It's only right to fight for his country, I know. But that wife of his, that's what gets me down."

There was a drought that June. The first sowing of late crops had failed to sprout and the sorghum was badly parched. Rain was desperately needed. One night, at last, a storm broke and the rain poured down. At once Xiumei's room became cooler. Mosquitoes stopped biting. She said to her mother, beside her on the *kang*:

"I must help Yuansheng's family with their sowing tomorrow. The ground will be good and moist."

"Are you trying to take the place of their daughter-in-law?" protested her mother, yawning. "You've plenty to do at home, lass. If you gad about outside, your dad will have something to say."

"You don't need me at home just now. Why scold me for lending someone else a hand?"

Her mother did not answer. And Xiumei lay awake wondering whether it was raining up in the mountains too. Heavy rain there would send freshets pouring down. She might have to take the ferry the next morning. She remembered as a child playing on the boat with Yuansheng. They'd weighed anchor on the sly and with Yuan-

"我每天晚上听着门,半夜里醒了,听听有人叫娘开门哩,不过是想念的罢了。这么些人全回来了,怎么原生就不回来呀?"

"原生一定早当了干部了,他怎么能撂下军队回来呢?"

"为国家打仗,那是本分该当的,我明白。只是这个媳妇,唉!"

今年五月天旱,头一回耩的晚田没出来,大庄稼也旱坏了,人们整天盼雨。晚上,雷声忽闪的闹了半夜,才浙沥淅沥下起雨来,越下越大,房里一下凉快了,蚊子也不咬人了。秀梅和娘睡在炕上,秀梅说:

"下透了吧,我明天还得帮着原生家耩地去。"

娘在睡梦里说:

"人家的媳妇全散了,你倒成了人家的人了。你好好地把家里的活做完了,再出去乱跑去,你别觉着你爹不说你哩!"

"我什么活没做完呀!我不过是多卖些力气罢了,又轮着你这么唠哝人!"

娘没有答声。秀梅却一直睡不着,她想,山地里不知道下雨不,山地里下了大雨,河里的水就下来了。那明天下地,还要过摆渡呢!她又想,小的时候,和原生在船上玩,两个人偷偷把

83

sheng punting, Xiumei steering, had set out to cross the river. But the current in midstream was too strong for Yuansheng, and when the boat started to swivel he cried for fright. It was she who had said:

"There's nothing to be afraid of. We can't go off course if I keep a good grip on the rudder. Go ahead and punt."

She recalled that evening after they got the gun, when the two of them went back to the flats to search for her crate and scarf. The crate was easily found, but they had to wait for the moon to rise before they discovered the scarf.

She did not close her eyes until cock-crow, when the rain stopped.

When Xiumei reached Yuansheng's house she found his father out in the yard repairing the seed-hopper.

"You pull the roller, will you, lass? Your aunty can lead the ox. Other jobs can be done single-handed, I always say, even if it takes a bit longer. But hoeing and sowing, no."

"Let me sow, Uncle. I'm a dab at it. You pull the roller. I sowed those few *mu* of ours."

"That's right. I meant to ask. Have you finished your sowing?"

"We finished a couple of days ago. I left the seeds in the soil praying for rain. Timed it nicely, didn't I?"

"Young people have all the luck. When you're old your luck runs out. Well, let's get going."

Xiumei put the plough on her back and set off, barefoot and in shorts. Yuansheng's mother led their small brown ox and his father brought up the rear with the hopper. So they filed out of the vil-

锚起出来,要过河去,原生使篙,她掌舵,船到河心,水很急,原生力气小,船打起转来,吓哭了,还是她说:

"不要紧,别怕,只要我把的住这舵,就跑不了它,你只管撑吧!"

又想到在芦苇地卡枪,那天黑间,两个人回到河滩里,寻找草筐和手巾,草筐找到了,寻了半天也寻不见那块手巾,直等月亮升上来,才找到了。

想来想去,雨停了,鸡也叫了,才合了合眼。

起身就到原生家里来,原生的爹正在院里收拾"种式",一见秀梅来了,就说:

"你给我们拉砘子去吧,叫你大娘旁耧。我常说,什么活也能一个人慢慢去做,惟独锄草和耩地,一个人就是干不来。"

秀梅笑着说:

"大伯,你拉砘子吧,我拿耧,我好把式哩!我们那几亩地,都是我拿的'种式'哩!"

"可就是,我还没问你,"老头说,"你那地全耩上没有?"

秀梅说:"我前两天就耩上了,耩的'干打雷',叫它们先躺在地里去求雨,我的时气可好哩!"

老头说:

"年轻人的时运总是好的,老了都倒霉,走吧!"

秀梅背上"种式"就走。她今天穿了一条短裤,光着脚,老婆子牵着小黄牛,老头子拉着砘子胡卢在后边跟着,一字长蛇阵,走出村来。

lage.

All the roads and paths through the fields were thronged with peasants. It was a cheerful, animated scene. In spring, on those sandy flats, dust storms often blot out the sky and cast a gloom over everybody's spirits. But the day had cleared after the heavy rain, and the plain lay fresh and lovely in the sunlight.

It was nearly noon by the time they finished sowing and the three of them sat down in the field to rest. Xiumei mopped her flushed face with her head scarf and then used it as a fan. Her big eyes seemed more luminous than ever today, as if newly washed by rain.

As she picked some grass by the roadside for the ox, a horse approached from the south.

It was a large roan horse, plodding wearily forward as if it had travelled a long way and had just been galloping. It was ridden by a soldier of the Eighth Route Army, a straw hat over his shoulders, who was flicking a willow switch. He looked a quiet young fellow, deep in thought.

As the horse drew near Xiumei bent sidewise to whisper to Yuansheng's mother, "An Eighth Route armyman." The old man, puffing at his pipe, did not hear. But as his wife looked up the horse shied at the roller by the roadside and bolted.

Xiumei sprang to her feet and stared after the rider.

"I do declare it's Yuansheng, Aunty!" she cried.

The old couple looked up.

"You must be mistaken, lass."

"I'm not," insisted Xiumei.

田野里,大道小道上全是忙着去种地的人,像是一盘子好看的走马灯。这一带沙滩,每到春天,经常刮那大黄风,刮起来,天昏地暗人发愁。现在大雨过后,天晴日出,平原上清新好看极了。

耩完地,天就快晌午了,三个人坐在地头上休息。秀梅热的红脸关公似的摘下手巾来擦汗,又当扇子扇,那两只大眼睛也好像叫雨水冲洗过,分外显得光辉。

她把道边上的草拔了一把,扔给那小黄牛,叫它吃着。

从南边过来一匹马。

那是一匹高大的枣红马,马低着头一步一颠地走,像是已经走了很远的路,又像是刚刚经过一阵狂跑。马上一个八路军,大草帽背在后边,有意无意挥动着手里的柳条儿。远远看来,这是一个年轻的人,一个安静的人,他心里正在思想什么问题。

马走近了,秀梅就转过脸来低下头,小声对老婆子说:"一个八路军!"老头子正仄着身子抽烟,好像没听见,老婆子抬头一看,马一闪放在道旁上的石砘子,吃了一惊,跑过去了。

秀梅吃惊似的站了起来,望着那过去的人说:

"大娘,那好像是原生哩!"

老头老婆全抬起头来,说:

"你看差眼了吧!"

英汉对照
English-Chinese
中国文学宝库
Gems of Chinese Literature
现代文学系列
Modern Literature

Meantime the rider had reined in. He turned to ask, "Is that Yin Family Village, Uncle, in front?"

Xiumei jumped for joy.

"Look, it *is* Yuansheng. Yuansheng!"

"Xiumei." The rider dismounted.

"Yuansheng, child!" His mother scrambled to her feet.

"Mum, fancy finding you here."

She could scarcely believe that her son was really back.

It is hard to know what to say first when a long parted family is reunited. Several times it was on the tip of his mother's tongue to break the news to Yuansheng about his wife, but each time she bit the words back.

"Our unit's on its way north to storm Baoding," he said. "I asked leave to come home and see you."

"Don't tell me you're off again," protested his mother. "Why did you never write to us all these years?"

"Once we've beaten the reactionaries I'll come home for good," he promised with a smile. "When I first left home I'd no time to write. Later on, the road was cut by the Japanese. Letters wouldn't have got through. Now we've driven out the Japanese and here I am."

"Well, Aunty," interposed Xiumei. "Didn't I say he'd come back?"

"You're a good child. Whatever you say comes true."

By now peasants from all sides had gathered round them. And since it was noon, shouldering or lugging their farm tools they escorted Yuansheng back.

"不,"秀梅说。那骑马的人已经用力勒住马,回头问:"老乡,前边是尹家庄不是?"

秀梅一跳说:

"你看,那不是原生吗,原生!"

"秀梅呀!"马上的人跳下来。

"原生,我那儿呀!"老婆子往前扑着站起来。

"娘,也在这里呀!"

儿子可真的回来了。

爹娘儿女相见,那一番话真是不知从哪说起,当娘的嘴一努一努想把媳妇的事说出来,话到嘴边,好几次又咽下去了。原生说:

"队伍往北开,攻打保定,我请假家来看看。"

"咳呀!"娘说,"你还得走吗?"

原生笑着说:

"等打完老蒋就不走了。"

秀梅说:

"怎么样,大娘,看见儿子了吧!"

"好孩子,"大娘说,"你说什么,什么就来了!"

远处近处耩地的人们全围了上来,天也响午了,又围随着原生回家,背着耧的,拉着砘子的。

英汉对照
English-Chinese
中国文学宝库
Gems of Chinese Literature
现代文学系列
Modern Literature

They were met just outside the village by the chairman of the newly formed peasants' association who rushed out, his face beaded with sweat, a piece of red paper in his hand.

"Get home, quick, Uncle!" he called to Yuansheng's father. "I've great news for you."

"What is it?"

"Splendid news. Absolutely grand."

A roar of laughter went up.

"You're a bit late with your good news."

"What d'you mean? Word has just this minute come from the courty. As soon as I got it I came dashing out."

"Here's Yuansheng already home."

"Oh, is Yuansheng back?" He beamed at them. "Why then, Uncle, you've double cause for rejoicing today."

"What's that notice in your hand?" they asked.

"Don't you know? Hasn't Yuansheng told you?" The chairman flourished the red sheet of paper. "Here's official notification that our Yuansheng has distinguished himself at the front. Captured one of Chiang Kaishek's brigadiers, he did. He's been awarded a special order of merit. The whole district's to hold a meeting to celebrate."

"My, that's really something."

"Why did you keep it mum, Yuansheng?"

"Good for you, boy."

Shouting and laughing, they streamed into the village.

The rally was held the next day in the village square.

刚到村边,新农会的主席手里扬着一张红纸,满头大汗跑出村来,一看见原生的爹就说:

"大伯,快家去吧,大喜事!"

"什么事呀?"

"大喜事,大喜事!"

人们全笑了,说:

"你报喜报的晚了!"

"什么呀?"主席说,"县里刚送了通知来,我接到手里就跑了来,怎么就晚了!"

人们说:

"这不是原生已经到家!"

"哈,原生家来了?大伯,真是喜上加喜,双喜临门呀?"主席喊着笑着。

人们说:

"你手里倒是拿的什么通知呀?"

"什么通知,原生还没对你们大家说呀?"主席扬一扬那张红纸,"上面给我们下的通知:咱们原生在前方立了大功,活捉了蒋介石的旅长,队伍里选他当特等功臣,全区要开大会庆祝哩!"

"哈,这么大事!怎么,原生,你还不肯对我们说呀,你真行呀!"人们嚷着笑着到了村里。

第二天,在村中央的广场上开庆功大会。

天晴的很好,这又是个热天,全村的男女老少,都换了新衣裳,先围到台下来,台上高挂全区人民的贺匾:"特等功臣"。

各村新农会又有各色各样的贺匾祝辞,台上台下全是红绸绿缎,金字彩花。

全区的小学生,一色的白毛巾,花衣服,腰

Honour

It was another hot, cloudless day. Dressed in their best, every man, woman and child in the village crowded round the platform over which hung the congratulatory tablet from the district inscribed: "Special Order of Merit."

There were banners of every size and colour too from the peasants' associations of different villages. The platform was a mass of red silk, green brocade, golden characters and bright paper flowers.

First the district head gave an account of Yuansheng's action and urged all the young men to learn from his example, join the army and win honour for their people. Then Yuansheng spoke.

When the meeting was thrown open several women called out, "We want Xiumei!" This was greeted by approving shouts and all eyes started searching for her. Xiumei in a short-sleeved tunic with red and white stripes, a new scarf on her head, stopped gazing raptly at the platform and flushed crimson, her bright eyes darting busily this way and that.

This was the speech she made:

"Yuansheng's order of merit brings honour to our whole village. Yuansheng joined up to fight at fifteen, just a slip of a boy barely able to carry his rifle. He's twenty-five this year. That means he's fought for ten years, and he'll go on fighting till the revolution is victorious.

"Some people can't see any end to the fighting, because they don't look on it as their own business. They want a quick victory and ask other people: How soon will Chiang Kaishek be defeated? That's something we should ask ourselves, because it depends on

里系着一色的绸子,手里拿着一色的花棍,脸上搽着胭脂,老师们擦着脸上的汗,来回照顾。

区长讲完了原生立功的经过,他号召全区青壮年向原生学习,踊跃参军,为人民立功。接着就是原生讲话。他说话很慢,很安静,台下的人们说:老脾气没变呀,还是这么不紧不慢的,怎么就能活捉一个旅长呀!原生说:自己立下一点功;台下就说:好家伙,活捉一个旅长他说是一点功。原生又说:这不是自己的功劳,这是全体人民的功劳;台下又说:你看人家这个话说的。

区长说:老乡们,安静一点吧,回头还有自由讲话哩,现在先不要乱讲吧。人们说:这是大喜事呀,怎么能安静呢!

到了自由讲话的时候,台下妇女群里喊了一声,欢迎秀梅讲话,全场的人都嚷赞成,全场的人拿眼找她。秀梅今天穿一件短袖的红白条小褂,头上也包一块新毛巾,她正楞着眼望着台上,听得一喊,才转过脸东瞧瞧,西看看,两只大眼睛,转来转去好像不够使,脸飞红了。

她到台上讲了这段话:

"原生立了大功,这是咱们全村的光荣。原生十五岁就出马打仗,那么一个小人,背着那么一支大枪。他今年二十五岁了,打了十年仗,还要去打,打到革命胜利。

"有人觉着这仗打的没头没边,这是因为他没把这打仗看成是自家的事。人们光愿意早些胜利,问别人:什么时候打败蒋介石?这问自己就行了。我们要快就快,要慢就慢,我们坚决,我们给前方的战士助劲,胜利就来得快;我们不

英汉对照
English-Chinese
中国文学宝库
Gems of Chinese Literature
现代文学系列
Modern Literature

us. If we go all out to support our men at the front, we'll win more quickly. If we do nothing and leave it all to the soldiers, victory will be slower in coming. It depends on how much effort each of us makes.

"Some people say you can't eat honour. They don't understand that without honour, if nobody set any store by honour, we'd not be able to live. It's because some men put honour before their own lives that we have food to eat.

"What we set our hearts on, we get. Here we've been waiting for Yuansheng, and now he's back. What our soldiers have set their hearts on is victory. Yuansheng says very soon Chiang Kai-shek will be defeated. In a few months, a year at the most, he'll be done for.

"It's possible for all the soldiers from our village to distinguish themselves at the front. There's no reason why they shouldn't all come back wearing medals like Yuansheng. When that happens we'll hold an even bigger rally to celebrate.

"That's all I have to say."

Cheers and applause burst out below.

Next came the parade.

The four best shots in the district led the way with rifles to fire salvoes. Next came two great red silk banners inscribed: "Congratulations on Outstanding Service" and "All Honour to the Hero." Then gongs and drums flanked the tablet from the district, followed by Yuansheng on his roan horse tricked out with rosettes. His parents in new clothes for this great occasion rode behind in a handsome mule-cart, and at the back trooped the villagers and

助劲,光叫前方的战士们自己去打,那胜利就来得慢了。这只要看我们每个人尽的力量和出的心血就行了。

"战士们从村里出去,除去他的爹娘,有些人把他们忘记了,以为他们是办自己的事去了,也不管他们哪天回来。不该这样,我们要时时刻刻想念着他们,帮助他们的家,他们是为我们每个人打仗。

"有的人,说光荣不能当饭吃。不明白,要是没有光荣,谁也不要光荣,也就没有了饭吃;有的人,却把光荣看的比性命还要紧,我们这才有了饭吃。

"我们求什么,就有什么。我们这等着原生,原生就回来了。战士们要的胜利,原生说很快就能打败蒋介石,蒋介石很快就要没命了,再有一年半载就死了。

"我们全村的战士,都会在前方立大功的,他们也都像原生一样,会带着光荣的奖章回来的。那时候,我们要开一个更大更大的庆功会。

"我的话完了。"

台下面大声地鼓掌,大声地欢笑。

接着就是游行大庆祝。

最前边是四杆喜炮,那是全区有名的四个喜炮手;两面红绸大旗:一面写"为功臣贺功",一面写"向英雄致敬"。后面是大锣大鼓,中间是英雄匾,原生骑在枣红马上,马笼头马颈上挂满了花朵。原生的爹娘,全穿着新衣服坐在双套大骡车上,后面是小学生的队伍和群众的队伍。

schoolchildren.

As they gonged and drummed their way out of the village, the air above the rain-washed fields seemed to quiver with excitement.

Each village they came to resounded with gonging and drumming. Flushed, happy people crowded round to watch.

The drummers drummed like mad, the banner-bearers held themselves straight as ramrods and Yuansheng's parents took their ease in the cart, the envy of all the old people lining the roads who pointed them out and cried:

"Proud they must be to have raised such a fine son."

The women marchers kept hold of each other's tunics and looked eagerly about them as they followed close behind Yuansheng.

He, poor fellow, longed to hide himself in the crowd. But each time he tried to dismount, the photographer put a quick stop to it.

Xiumei, flushed and radiant, was leading the other marchers to shout slogans like a veteran propagandist, with the air of a peasant who has reaped a good harvest and wants others to admire the fruit of her toil. Like a sower scattering seeds, she was implanting new ideas and demands in the hearts of all around her. When she saw a girl she knew, she would dart out from the column and seize her hands.

"This is Yuansheng from our village. He joined up at fifteen and now he's twenty-five. He's distinguished himself at the front. That gold medal was awarded by Chairman Mao."

This said she would hurriedly rejoin the parade.

Each time they approached a new village Yuansheng, with a true peasant's diffidence, slipped his glittering medal into his tunic

大锣大鼓敲出村来,雨后的田野,蒸晒出腾腾的热气,好像是叫大锣大鼓的声音震动出来的。

到一村,锣鼓相接,男男女女挤的风雨不透,热汗齐流。

敲鼓手疯狂地抢着大棒,抬匾的柱脚似的挺直腰板,原生的爹娘安安稳稳坐在车上,街上的老头老婆们指指划划,一齐连声说:

"修下这样好儿子,多光荣呀!"

那些青年妇女们一个扯着一个的衣后襟,好像怕失了联络似的,紧跟着原生观看。

原生骑在马上,有些害羞,老想下来,摄影的记者赶紧把它捉住了。

秀梅满脸流汗跟在队伍里,扬着手喊口号。她眉开眼笑,好像是一个宣传员。她好像在大秋过后,叫人家看她那辛勤的收成;又好像是一个撒种子的人,把一种思想,一种要求,撒进每个人的心里去。她见到相熟的姐妹,就拉着手急急忙忙告诉说:

"这是我们村里的原生,十五上就当兵去了,今年二十五岁,在战场上立了大功,胸前挂的那金牌子是毛主席奖的哩。"

说完就又跟着队伍跑走了。这个农民的孩子原生,一进村庄,就好把那放光的奖章,轻轻

pocket. But Xiumei insisted on his displaying it.

They paraded past Xiaowu's home, where the drummers deliberately beat out a quick tattoo to tempt her out to watch. The door remained fast closed, however.

The fields and villages were stirred as never before by this rousing parade. Never had the plain witnessed such a splendid pageant. The sun blazed in the sky and flowers burst into bloom as the thrilling roll of the drums flashed a message to every heart — its theme was Honour.

Back home that evening Yuansheng told his parents, "Tomorrow I'm rejoining my unit. I didn't know when I came home to see you that I'd happen on this celebration. I shall have to fight harder to repay the people for all their goodness to me."

"Suppose you fetch back that wife of yours?" remarked his mother.

"I don't want her back. If she couldn't even wait for her husband, she'd never work with me for the revolution."

"When will you marry again, then?" asked his father. "Shouldn't be too hard now to find a wife."

"Wait till we've licked Chiang Kaishek. That won't take long. A year at most."

"Has she got to wait too?" asked his mother.

"She? Who?"

"Xiumei. She's put off marrying all this time because of you."

His mother gave him a detailed account of the scenes Xiaowu had made, Xiumei's protests, her decision to postpone her own mar-

掩进上衣口袋里去。秀梅就一定要他拉出来。

大队也经过小五家的大门。一到这里,敲大鼓的故意敲了一套花点,原想叫小五也跑出来看的,门却紧紧闭着,一直没开。

队伍在平原的田野和村庄通过,带着无比响亮的声音,无比鲜亮的色彩。太阳在天上,花在枝头,声音从有名的大鼓手那里敲打,这是一种震动人心的号召:光荣! 光荣!

晚上回来,原生对爹娘说:"明天我就回部队去了。我原是绕道家来看看,赶巧了乡亲们为我庆功,从今以后,我更应该好好打仗,才不负人民对我的一番热情。"

娘说:"要不就把你媳妇追回来吧!"

原生说:"叫她回来干什么呀!她连自己的丈夫都不能等待,要这样的女人一块革命吗?"

爹说:"那么你什么时候才办喜事呢? 以我看,咱寻个媳妇,也并不为难。"

原生说:"等打败蒋介石。这不要很长的时间。有个一年半载就行了。"

娘又说:"那还得叫人家陪着你等着吗?"

"谁呀?"原生问。

"秀梅呀! 人家为你耽误了好几年了。"娘把过去小五怎样使歪造耗,秀梅怎样解劝说服,秀梅怎样赌气不寻婆家,小五走了,秀梅怎样体

riage, and her care for the two of them after Xiaowu left.

In a flash, Yuansheng seemed to see Xiumei standing before him. A girl in a hundred she was, and how much he owed her! He remembered that evening on the flats when she had urged him to seize the deserter's gun. Sometimes after he left home with that rifle to fight, standing sentry at night while the Milky Way shimmered and twinkled overhead, or marching through the dust in the blazing sun, he had fingered his rifle and recalled that scene. But her image had passed from his mind like a shooting star, fast as a bird in flight. Now clear and vivid, it was filling his heart. He knew nothing could take its place.

Meanwhile on the look-outs in the melon fields, under the bean trellises, in the shade of willows or below cottage eaves, all the lively village youngsters were agreeing that Xiumei and Yuansheng were destined for each other. And sure as it is that rain must fall on the ground, so sure were they that this would be a perfect marriage.

1948

Translated by Gladys Yang

贴娘的心,处处帮忙尽力,原原本本说了一遍。

在原生的心里,秀梅的影子,突然站立在他的面前,是这样可爱和应该感谢。他忽然想起秀梅在河滩芦苇丛中命令他去卡枪的那个黄昏的景象。当原生背着那支枪转战南北,在那银河横空的夜晚站哨,或是赤日炎炎的风尘行军当中,他曾经把手扶在枪上,想起过这个景象。那时候,在战士的心里,这个影子就好比一个流星,一只飞鸟横过队伍,很快就消失了。现在这个影子突然在原生心里鲜明起来,扩张起来,顽强粘住,不能放下了。

在全村里,在瓜棚豆架下面,在柳阴房凉里,那些好事好谈笑的青年男女们议论着秀梅和原生这段姻缘,谁也觉的这两个人要结了婚,是那么美满,就好像雨既然从天上降下,就一定是要落在地上,那么合理应当。

1948 年 7 月 10 日饶阳东张岗

英汉对照
English-Chinese
中国文学宝库
Gems of Chinese Literature
现代文学系列
Modern Literature

Recollections of the Hill Country

A peasant delegate from Fuping came to see the Tianjin Industrial Exhibition. We were old friends meeting after nearly ten years. Going round the exhibition with him, I noticed his interest in the textiles and improved farm tools. I wanted to give him a present before he left, and decided to buy some cloth.

Why cloth specially? Because he was still wearing a light blue suit of homespun dyed with the local indigo. I don't know what to call this blue but it has countless associations for me, bringing back those three years of fighting among the barren hills and swift streams of Fuping, reminding me of many people. So to me this colour is "Fuping blue" or "hill blue."

That colour looked conspicuous in Tianjin, quite countrified. Yet in Fuping to get cloth woven and dyed was so hard that a suit like that struck you as fresh and handsome. Fuping is full of hills and they are nothing but black rock. Land is scarce and heavy rain keeps washing down soil to the Hebei plain — my home. The Fuping peasants have never seen big tracts of land but own plots the size of a *kang* or kitchen range. They take endless pains over these tiny pockets of land which may be in the odd shape of lozenges, half-moons or ladders. They shore them up with stone, surround them with mud, plant date trees round the edges and maize in the middle.

山地回忆

从阜平乡下来了一位农民代表,参观天津的工业展览会。我们是老交情,已经快有十年不见面了。我陪他去参观展览,他对于中纺的织纺,对于那些改良的新农具特别感到兴趣。临走的时候,我一定要送点东西给他,我想买几尺布。

为什么我偏偏想起买布来?因为他身上穿的还是那样一种浅蓝的土靛染的粗布裤褂。这种蓝的颜色,不知道该叫什么蓝,可是它使我想起很多事情,想起在阜平穷山恶水之间度过的三年战斗的岁月,使我记起很多人。这种颜色,我就叫它"阜平蓝"或是"山地蓝"吧。

他这身衣服的颜色,在天津是很显得突出,也觉得土气。但是在阜平,这样一身衣服织染既是不容易,穿上也就觉得鲜亮好看了。阜平土地很少,山上都是黑石头,雨水很多很暴,有些泥土就冲到冀中平原上来了——冀中是我的家乡。阜平的农民没有见过大的地块,他们所有的,只是像炕台那样大,或是像锅台那样大的一块土地。在这小小的、不规整的、有时是尖形的,有时是半圆形的,有时是梯形的小块土地上,他们费尽心思,全力经营。他们用石块垒起,用泥土包住,在边沿栽上枣树,在中间种上玉黍。

英汉对照
English-Chinese
中国文学宝库
Gems of Chinese Literature
现代文学系列
Modern Literature

It's cold up in those hills, where the sun seldom shines. No cotton grows there and when first I arrived the old women were busy twisting hemp yarn, which they use in place of cotton thread. Even the soles of socks are sewn with this.

It was all on account of socks that I got to know this family and we became friends. It was winter, the winter of 1941, and our partisan unit had fought its way to this village. Things had eased up enough for us to have a short rest there.

I went to the river every day to wash my face, squatting down on an icy rock. I made a hole in the ice, dipped my towel in the water, and by the time I'd wiped my face the towel was frozen stiff. One cold windy morning a few pale rays of sunlight were gilding the hills on the opposite bank as I squatted on my usual stone. I broke the ice and was about to wash when someone downstream shouted:

"Can't you see I'm washing greens here? Go further down if you want to wash you face!"

This sharp protest put my back up. What business was it of anybody else if I wanted to wash my face on such a cold day? I retorted angrily:

"I'm too far away to dirty your greens!"

A gust of wind carried my objection over. The other took offence in turn and shouted:

"We've to eat these greens! You wash your face and bottom up there — is that hygienic?"

"Who are you cursing?" I stood up and turned to see a girl of sixteen or seventeen. The wind had whipped a red like frosted per-

阜平的天气冷,山地不容易见到太阳。那里不种棉花,我刚到那里的时候,老大娘们手里搓着线锤。很多活计用麻代线,连袜底也是用麻纳的。

就是因为袜子,我和这家人认识了,并且成了老交情。那是个冬天,该是一九四一年的冬天,我打游击打到了这个小村庄,情况缓和了,部队决定休息两天。

我每天到河边去洗脸,河里结了冰,我在冰冻的石头上,把冰砸破,浸湿毛巾,等我擦完脸,毛巾也就冻挺了。有一天早晨,刮着冷风,只有一抹阳光,黄黄的落在河对面的山坡上。我又登在那块石头上去,砸开那个冰口,正要洗脸,听见在下水流有人喊:

"你看不见我在这里洗菜吗?洗脸到下边洗去!"

这声音是那么严厉,我听了很不高兴。这样冷天,我来砸冰洗脸,反倒妨碍了人。心里一时挂火,就也大声说:

"离着这么远,会弄脏你的菜!"

我站在上风头,狂风吹送着我的愤怒,我听见洗菜的人也恼了,那人说:

"菜是下口的东西呀!你在上流洗脸洗屁股,为什么不脏?"

"你怎么骂人?"我站立起来转过身去,才看见洗菜的是个女孩子,也不过十六七岁。风吹

105

simmon leaves into her cheeks. Her chapped hands were like frozen red radishes. She was thinly clad in shabby pants and jacket of the local blue.

There she stood in the biting wind on the cold riverbank by the village the Japanese had burned down more than once. She was holding a basket of willow leaves — probably their whole morning meal.

Something made me calm down.

"My fault," I said. "I won't wash. Come up here and rinse your greens."

She stared at me scornfully before replying:

"Wash greens where you've just been washing?"

I chuckled.

"You're not easy to please. Up here you say I'm fouling the water, though the grime from my face could never reach your greens! When I offer to change places with you, you won't. What's to be done?"

"What's to be done? I'll have to go further up."

She whirled round and walked up the shore to a jagged boulder. There she squatted down to steep her basket in the water. Tucking her hands under her tunic for warmth, she looked at me and smiled.

Not knowing whether to laugh or fume, I said:

"You're mad on hygiene."

"We believe in hygiene — you people only pretend to! You keep jeering that we hill-folk are unhygienic. Living in our homes, eating our rice, you have to rinse your mouths and wash your teeth

红了她的脸,像带霜的柿叶,水冻肿了她的手,像上冻的红萝卜。她穿的衣服很单薄,就是那种蓝色的破袄裤。

十月严冬的河滩上,敌人往返烧毁过几次的村庄的边沿,在寒风里,她抱着一篮子水沤的杨树叶,这该是早饭的食粮。

不知道为什么,我一时心平气和下来。我说:

"我错了,我不洗了,你在这块石头上来洗吧!"

她冷冷地望着我,过了一会才说:

"你刚在那石头上洗了脸,又叫我站上去洗菜!"

我笑着说:

"你看你这人,我在上水洗,你说下水脏,这么一条大河,哪里就能把我脸上的泥土冲到你的菜上去?现在叫你到上水来,我到下水去,你还说不行,那怎么办哩?"

"怎么办,我还得往上走!"

她说着,扭着身子逆着河流往上去了。登在一块尖石上,把菜篮浸进水里,把两手插在袄襟底下取暖,望着我笑了。

我哭不的,也笑不的,只好说:

"你真讲卫生呀!"

"我们是真卫生,你们是装卫生!你们尽笑话我们,说我们山沟里的人不讲卫生,住在我们家里,吃了我们的饭,还刷嘴刷牙,我们的菜饭

— are you afraid our food will dirty your mouths? Why not wash your stomachs too!" Giggling, she bent over her basket.

I was tickled. When she laughed I'd seen her teeth flash white.

"Right!" I said. "You're clean, we're dirty."

"It's true! You use the same basin for rice, greens, washing your face and feet or drinking. Call that hygienic?" Smiling, she dabbled her hands in the icy water.

"Beggars can't be choosers! Wait till we beat the Japanese invaders and take back Beiping. We'll have special pots for food and special jugs for water — the whole caboodle!"

"How long will that take?" She threw me a searching glance. "They've burnt our house down three times!"

"Maybe three years, maybe five or ten. We'll keep right on fighting no matter how long it takes. We'll never give up!" Talking to her like this cheered me up too.

"Keep on fighting barefoot?" Her eyes swept my feet before she bent over her basket again.

Puzzled, I asked:

"What do you mean?"

"What's that?" She pretended not to have heard. "Why don't you wear socks? Aren't your feet cold? Call that hygienic?"

"Hygienic?" I chuckled. "I can't help it. Since September we've been beating back this last Japanese 'mopping-up campaign,' and our Eighth Route Army doesn't issue socks till the end of October. Busy fighting, who's time to worry about socks?"

"Can't you buy a pair?" she asked softly.

"Where? In one of these pint-sized villages? We haven't passed

再不干净,难道还会弄脏了你们的嘴?为什么不连肠子肚子都刷刷干净!"说着就笑的弯下腰去。

我觉得好笑。可也看见,在她笑着的时候,她的整齐的牙齿洁白的放光。

"对,你卫生,我们不卫生。"我说。

"那是假话吗?你们一个饭缸子,也盛饭,也盛菜,也洗脸,也洗脚,也喝水,也尿泡,那是讲卫生吗?"她笑着用两手在冷水里刨抓。

"这是物质条件不好,不是我们愿意不卫生。等我们打败了日本,占了北平,我们就可以吃饭有吃饭的家伙,喝水有喝水的家伙了,我们就可以一切齐备了。"

"什么时候,才能打败鬼子?"女孩子望着我,"我们的房,叫他们烧过两三回了!"

"也许三年,也许五年,也许十年八年。可是不管三年五年,十年八年,我们总是要打下去,我们不会悲观的。"我这样对她讲,当时觉得这样讲了以后,心里很高兴了。

"光着脚打下去吗?"女孩子转脸望了我脚上一下,就又低下头去洗菜了。

我一时没弄清是怎么回事,就问:

"你说什么?"

"说什么?"女孩子也装没有听见,"我问你为什么不穿袜子,脚不冷吗?也是卫生吗?"

"咳!"我也笑了,"这是没有法子么,什么卫生!从九月里就反'扫荡',可是我们八路军,是非到十月底不发袜子的。这时候,正在打仗,哪里去找袜子穿呀?"

"不会买一双?"女孩子低声说。

英汉对照
English-Chinese
中国文学宝库
Gems of Chinese Literature
现代文学系列
Modern Literature

any towns."

"Get someone to make you a pair."

"Where's the cloth? And if there were any, who'd make them?"

"I would!" She stood up, her willow leaves washed. "We live over there." She pointed at a slope. "If you've no cloth, we've got a bit left, enough for a pair of socks."

She went off with her leaves while I finished washing my face. I looked at my feet, frozen black in their old patched shoes. I felt for a moment that I never wanted to leave these hills, this stream and this bank.

After cleaning up I went back to my unit to eat, then made my way to the girl's house. She was tending the stove and welcomed me with these words:

"Trust you to show up!"

With some idea of her temper now, I just grinned and stepped inside. The room was full of smoke. It took me a minute to see a man of forty or so and his wife seated on the *kang* by a brazier. Behind them was an old woman with white hair. Smiling, they invited me to take a seat.

"Don't wash at the river tomorrow," said the girl. "Come over here. We can easily manage one extra ladle of water."

The man said:

"Our daughter was laughing at you just now."

The white-haired granny puckered her lips in a smile.

"You mustn't mind her, comrade! That's her way."

"Suits me!" I said. "Main thing is she has a warm heart. When

"哪里去买呀,尽住小村,不过镇店。"我说。
"不会求人做一双?"
"哪里有布呀?就是有布,求谁做去呀?"
"我给你做。"女孩子洗好菜站起来,"我家就住在那个坡子上,"她用手一指,"你要没有布,我家里有点,还够做一双袜子。"

她端着菜走了,我在河边上洗了脸。我看了看我那只穿着一双"踢倒山"的鞋子,冻的发黑的脚,一时觉得我对于面前这山,这水,这沙滩,永远不能分离了。

我洗过脸,回到队上吃了饭,就到女孩子家去。她正在烧火,见了我就说:
"你这人倒实在,叫你来你就来了。"

我既然摸准了她的脾气,只是笑了笑,就走进屋里。屋里蒸气腾腾,等了一会,我才看见炕上有一个大娘和一个四十多岁的大伯,围着一盆火坐着。在大娘背后还有一位雪白头发的老大娘。一家人全笑着让我炕卜坐。女孩子说:
"明儿别到河里洗脸去了,到我们这里洗吧,多添一瓢水就够了!"
大伯说:
"我们妞儿刚才还笑话你哩!"
白发老大娘瘪着嘴笑着说:
"她不会说话,同志,不要和她一样呀!"
"她很会说话!"我说,"要紧的是她心眼儿

英汉对照
English-Chinese
中国文学宝库
Gems of Chinese Literature
现代文学系列
Modern Literature

she saw my bare feet she was sorry for the Eighth Route Army."

The girl's mother picked up a piece of coarse white cloth from one corner of the *kang*.

"She earned this by half a year's spinning. Made me a pair of padded pants, and meant to make her dad socks with what was left. She'll make you a pair first."

"No, keep it for him!" I put in hastily. "Or let me pay for it."

"There you go again!" The girl looked up from the stove. "You got any money?"

Her mother said:

"In our family, when we make a promise we keep it. She can do more spinning to get socks for her dad. We didn't know how to spin till this spring when one of your women comrades stayed with us and taught her. She's promised to teach her to weave next time she comes. Can your folks spin?"

"Sure. But where I come from we wear machine-made cloth. Once we've beaten the enemy, Aunty...."

"Once we've taken Beiping we'll have fine cloth, the whole caboodle!" put in the girl mockingly.

As it happened, things were quiet for some time after that. So we didn't have to move on. Every morning I went to the girl's house for a wash. The next day she cut out the socks, and the day after that she was sewing on the soles with fine strands of hemp.

"Do folk in your parts use hemp like this?" she asked.

"No, cotton." I fingered the soles. "Where I come from, even shoe-soles aren't so thick!"

好,她看见我光着脚,就心疼我们八路军!"

大娘从炕角里扯出一块白粗布,说:

"这是我们妞儿纺了半年线赚的,给我做了一条棉裤,下剩的说给她爹做双袜子,现在先给你做了穿上吧。"

我连忙说:

"叫大伯穿吧! 要不,我就给钱!"

"你又装假了,"女孩子烧着火抬起头来,"你有钱吗?"

大娘说:

"我们这家人,说了就不能改移。过后再叫她纺,给她爹赚袜子穿。早先,我们这里也不会纺线,是今年春天,家里住了一个女同志,教会了她。说还再过来了,还教她织布哩! 你家里的人,会纺线吗?"

"会纺!"我说,"我们那里是穿洋布哩,是机器织纺的。大娘,等我们打败日本……"

"占了北平,我们就有洋布穿,就一发齐备!"女孩子接下去,笑了。

可巧,这几天情况没有变动,我们也不转移。每天早晨,我就到女孩子家里去洗脸。第二天去,袜子已经剪裁好,第三天去她已经纳底子了,用的是细细的麻线。她说:

"你们那里是用麻用线?"

"用线。"我摸了摸袜底,"在我们那里,鞋底也没有这么厚!"

"They're stronger this way. They'll last you three years. Is that long enough to beat the Japanese?"

"Should be," I said.

In five days I was wearing my new socks.

I had found a home away from home. They were a healthy family, cheerful and lively. The girl's mother looked even sturdier than her old man. Even the ninety-year-old granny was so fit there was nothing wrong with her hearing. She seldom butted in, but listened with obvious enjoyment to our conversation.

The man was a good farmer but having nothing to do on the land just now he decided to take some dates to Quyang to sell, and asked me to lend a hand. Our army knew that the people's trading and transport work were inportant and agreed to my helping him. For several days we set out at the crack of dawn, each with a load of over a hundred catties, and took the hilly, riverside track to Quyang. The girl got up before it was light and sat up late to get our meals for us. We ate well, and one day her father said:

"I've you to thank for this, comrade!"

"What do you mean?"

"When I carried dates into town alone before, she never fed me half so well!"

I laughed. She said:

"What are you thanking him for? He's wearing our socks, he owes us something, doesn't he?"

Then she asked:

"You've been at it two weeks now. How much have you made?"

"这样坚实。"女孩子说,"保你穿三年,能打败日本不?"

"能够。"我说。

第五天,我穿上了新袜子。

和这一家人熟了,就又成了我新的家。这一家人身体都健壮,又好说笑。女孩子的母亲,看起来比女孩子的父亲还要健壮。女孩子的姥姥九十岁了,还那么结实,耳朵也不聋,我们说话的时候,她不插言,只是微微笑着,她说:她很喜欢听人们说闲话。

女孩子的父亲是个生产的好手,现在地里没活了,他正计划贩红枣到曲阳去卖,问我能不能帮他的忙。部队重视民运工作,上级允许我帮老乡去作运输,每天打早起,我同大伯背上一百多斤红枣,顺着河滩,爬山越岭,送到曲阳去。女孩子早起晚睡给我们做饭,饭食很好,一天,大伯说:

"同志,你知道我是沾你的光吗?"

"怎么沾了我的光?"

"往年,我一个人背枣,我们妞儿是不会给我吃这么好的!"

我笑了。女孩子说:

"沾他什么光,他穿了我们的袜子,就该给我们做活了!"

又说:

"你们跑了快半月,赚了多少钱?"

英汉对照
English-Chinese
中国文学宝库
Gems of Chinese Literature
现代文学系列
Modern Literature

115

"Hear that! She's checking our accounts now!" her father said. "Well, it's time we figured it out." He opened a small bundle stuffed under the quilts. "Whatever we've made or lost, it's all in here."

We counted the notes and they came to over 5,000. The girl said:

"That's enough."

"Enough for what?" he asked.

"To buy a loom! Won't you bring me back a loom from Quyang today?"

Fair enough. Neither her granny, her parents nor I had any objection. After selling our dates in Quyang that day, we went to buy a loom. Her father wanted a good one, even if it cost a bit more, and ended up by spending all he had. We took turns lugging the thing back, and arrived in a lather of sweat.

The whole family was delighted. It must have been the happiest day in the girl's life. She behaved as if she'd been given several *mu* of land, a new ox or a splendid dowry.

And it didn't take her long to learn to weave.

The day that she finished her first length of cloth, my unit set out again. After that, trudging north and south over hills and plains, I wore those socks for three years without wearing them out. In 1945, coming back from Yan'an after the defeat of Japan, I jumped into the Yellow River for a bath at Qikou and was careless enough to let the rushing water sweep away all my clothes, including this pair of socks. Then the waves of the Yellow River

"你看,她来查账了,"大伯说,"真是,我们也该计算计算了!"他打开放在被垛底下的一个包袱,"我们这叫包袱账,赚了赔了,反正都在这里面。"

我们一同数了票子,一共赚了五千多块钱,女孩子说:

"够了。"

"够干什么了?"大伯问。

"够给我买张织布机子了!这一趟,你们在曲阳给我买架织布机子回来吧!"

无论姥姥、母亲、父亲和我,都没人反对女孩子这个正义的要求。我们到了曲阳,把枣卖了,就去买了一架机子。大伯不怕多花钱,一定要买一架好的,把全部盈余都用光了。我们分着背了回来,累的浑身流汗。

这一天,这一家人最高兴,也该是女孩子最满意的一天。这像要了几亩地,买回一头牛;这像制好了结婚前的陪送。

以后,女孩子就学习纺织的全套手艺了:纺,拐,浆,落,经,镶,织。

当她卸下第一匹布的那天,我出发了。从此以后,我走遍山南塞北,那双袜子,整整穿了三年也没有破绽。一九四五年,我们战胜了日本强盗,我从延安回来,在碛口地方,跳到黄河里去洗了一个澡,一时大意,奔腾的黄水,冲走了我的全部衣物,也冲走了那双袜子。黄河的

swirled with my memories of those years in the enemy's rear, swirled with my recollections of the girl.

The day of the founding of the People's Republic of China, I took her father to the department store and we bought some cloth: two lengths of good blue cotton for him and his wife, a length of red for their daughter. He'd never seen such bright red cotton, and said:

"Let's have a few feet more of that. Some yellow too."

"What for?" I asked.

"There's new flag hanging from every door here in town — they won't have that yet back home! Give me a drawing of the red flag with five gold stars and I'll get my girl to make one. Then at meetings or at New Year, we'll hang it up!"

He told me that his daughter, though she had two children now, was just the same as before, interested in anything new and able to pick up new skills in no time.

1949

Translated by Gladys Yang

波浪激荡着我关于敌后几年生活的回忆,激荡着我对于那女孩子的纪念。

开国典礼那天,我同大伯一同到百货公司去买布,送他和大娘一人一身蓝士林布,另外,送给女孩子一身红色的。大伯没见过这样鲜艳的红布,对我说:

"多买上几尺,再买点黄色的!"

"干什么用?"我问。

"这里家家门口挂着新旗,咱那山沟里准还没有哩!你给了我一张国旗的样子,一块带回去,叫妞儿给做一个,开会过年的时候,挂起来!"

他说妞儿已经有两个孩子了,还像小时那样,就是喜欢新鲜东西,说什么也要学会。

1949年12月

英汉对照
English-Chinese
中国文学宝库
Gems of Chinese Literature
现代文学系列
Modern Literature

Little Sheng

At the end of spring 1942, a cavalry troop came to central Hebei. It was the first cavalry unit the Communist Eighth Route Army ever had in north China. Soon, the performances of the troops at commemoration meetings, military reviews and gatherings became a favourite form of entertainment of the villagers.

The horses were strong and sturdy, their colour good, their coats glossy. And the men were so young. Even their leader, a warmhearted fellow named Yang, was not more than twenty-one.

The peasants loved their own army, and they were fond of horses. Whenever the cavalry passed through a village, whether in the early morning mist or the dusk of evening, the peasants would stop their lunch or supper, pick up their buckets and help the cavalrymen water the horses. If the unit went by without stopping, the peasants would gather on the embankment to watch.

"What do they feed their horses? Every one of them is so sturdy and fat. We can never get our farm stock to look like that."

"The one on the black horse is Captain Yang, and that one in front carrying three weapons on his back is Little Jin."

"Just look at the boy! He seems glued to the horse."

Little Jin had joined the army when he was seventeen. Now at nineteen he was Captain Yang's messenger and orderly. He rode a roan horse of foreign breed captured from the Japanese.

小胜儿

1

冀中有了个骑兵团。这是华北八路军的第一支骑兵,是新鲜队伍,立时成了部队的招牌幌子,不管什么军事检阅、纪念大会,头一项人们最爱看的,就是骑兵表演。

马是那样肥壮,个子毛色又整齐,人又是那样年轻,连那个热情的杨主任,也不过二十一岁。

农民们亲近自己的军队,也爱好马匹。每当骑兵团在早晨或是黄昏的雾露里从村边开过,农民们就放下饭碗,担起水筲,帮助战士饮马。队伍不停下,他们就站在堤头上去观看:

"这马儿是怎么喂的,个个圆膘!庄稼牲口说什么也比不上。"

"骑黑马的是杨主任,在前面背三件家伙的是小金子!"

"这孩子!你看他像粘在马上一样。"

小金子十七岁上参加了军队,十九岁给杨主任当了警卫员,骑着一匹从日寇手里夺来的红洋马。

英汉对照
English-Chinese
中国文学宝库
Gems of Chinese Literature
现代文学系列
Modern Literature

The peasants from all the villages in the vicinity liked to watch the cavalry. As the last horse and rider was reluctantly allowed to depart from one village, the next village would eagerly welcome the appearance of Little Jin, who rode in front.

Today, nobody knew where the cavalry was bound. The riders looked solemn but unhurried. From the expressions on the men's faces and the pace of the horses, apparently nothing extraordinary was up.

"Are they going off to fight the Japanese, or are they just on the march?" a young peasant asked a woman beside him.

"They are going to battle, I think," answered the woman.

"How do you know? Did the captain tell you?"

"I know Little Jin. You just watch. When he pouts it means they are off on an ordinary march and he's reluctant to leave the family he's been staying with. If there's a smile on his face which he's trying to hold back, then they're going into battle. Just remember that and you'll be all right."

Little Jin, cantering in the van, was smiling broadly. He had received a delightful present before they started out. Now, he kept feeling his rucksack where the gift was hidden.

The sun had just risen above the horizon, flooding the plain with sunshine which spread like water across the wheat fields, ditches, trees and villages. The crowing of roosters echoed from hamlet to hamlet. In one village the young men of the self-defence squad had started their morning drill. Crisp commands for assembly were also heard in other villages.

远近村庄都在观看这个骑兵团。这村正恋恋不舍地送走最后一匹,前村又在欢迎小金子的头马了。

今天,队伍不知开到哪里去,走的并不慌忙,很是严肃。从战士脸上的神情和马的脚步看来,也不像有什么情况。

"是出发打仗?还是平常行军?"一个青年农民问他身边一个青年妇女。

"我看是打仗去!"妇女说。

"你怎么看的出来,杨主任告诉你了?"

"我认识小金子。你看着,小金子噘着嘴,那就是平常行军,他常常舍不得离开房东大娘。脸上挂笑,可又不笑出来,那准是出发打仗。傻孩子!你记住这个就行了。"

2

这个妇女是猜着了。过了两天,这个队伍就打起仗来,打的是那有名的英勇壮烈的一仗。敌人"五一大扫荡"突然开始,骑兵团分散作战,两个连突到路西去。一个连作后卫陷入了敌人的包围,整整打了一天。在五月麦黄的日子,冀中平原上,打的天昏地暗,打的树木脱枝落叶,道沟里鲜血滴滴。杨主任在这一仗里牺牲了,炮弹炸翻的泥土,埋葬了他的马匹。小金子受了伤,用手刨着土掩盖了主任的尸体,带着一支打完子弹的短枪,夜晚突围出来,跑了几步就大口吐了血。

这是后话。现在小金子跑在队伍的前面,轻快地行军。他今天脸上挂笑,是因为在出发

Purple pompon-like flowers brushed the belly of Little Jin's horse all along the way and dew soaked the boy's trouser-legs. He seemed in no hurry though, and let the horse saunter along freely.

"Ride a little faster, Little Jin. We must get to Shifuzhen and make camp before dark," the captain urged him.

The boy turned back and smiled. "At this speed, we'll get there long before dark."

"Do you like to stay in the sun in such hot weather? I'm thirsty."

"Beyond that grave is a melon patch. I'll buy a melon. I'm on good terms with the old keeper. The trouble is he might not want any payment. The watermelons are not quite ripe yet. I'll get you a small sweet melon."

"We can't accept gifts from the people. Give me the water-bottle."

Little Jin handed it to him and said, "I'll get you a clean, cool room free of bedbugs when we arrive at Shifuzhen."

Then he pulled something from his sack and struck his horse on the flank. The animal started galloping.

The captain charged his little black horse forward.

"What is that thing, Little Jin?" he asked.

"A quirt!" Little Jin waved it in the air. It was a short, little whip made of multi-coloured silk and cloth strips, like a child's toy.

"You imp! Where did you get it? We're cavalrymen. We don't need whips," laughed the captain.

"Who should use whips if not cavalrymen? The generals on the

的时候,收到了一件心爱的东西。一路上,他不断抽出手来摸摸兜囊,这小小的礼品就藏在那里面。

太阳刚刚升出地面。太阳一升出地面,平原就在同一个时刻,承受了它的光辉。太阳光像流水一样,从麦田、道沟、村庄和树木的身上流过。这一村的雄鸡接着那一村的雄鸡歌唱。这一村的青年自卫队在大场院里跑步,那一村也听到了清脆的口令。

一路上,大麻子刚开的紫色绒球一样的花,打着小金子的马肚皮,阵阵的露水扫湿了他的裤腿。他走的不慌不忙,信马由缰。主任催他:

"小金子同志,放快些吧,天黑的时候,我们要到石佛镇宿营哩!"

"报告主任,"小金子转过身来笑着说:"就这样走法,也用不着天黑!"

"这样热天,你愿意晒着呀?"主任说,"口渴的很哩!"

小金子说:

"过了树林,前面有个瓜园,我去买瓜!我和那个开瓜园的老头有交情,咱们要吃瓜,他不会要钱。可是,现在西瓜还不熟,只能将着摘个小酥瓜儿吃!"

主任说:

"怎么能白吃老百姓的瓜呢?把水壶给我吧!"

递过水壶去,小金子说:

"到了石佛,我给主任去号一间房,管保凉快,清净,没有臭虫!"

stage all carry whips when they go into battle."

"That's on the stage. We need both our hands to fight. We don't want this stuff. Put it away now, we're entering a village. People will laugh at you," said the captain.

Little Jin looked again at the colourful quirt, then put the beloved gift into his sack. He was a little vexed. It had been very nice of his friend to make it for him. What a pity that he couldn't show it off when he entered the village. She must have gone to a lot of trouble.

"Did you buy it, or did you ask someone to make it for you?" the captain asked.

"It was sent from home."

"Why should they send you a thing like that?"

"They must have thought that since I've become a cavalryman I'd need a quirt and would be glad to have one."

"Why is it so colourful and fancy?"

"It was made by a young girl. They like them colourful."

"Who is she?"

"A neighbour. We grew up together."

Captain Yang asked no more questions. After a while he said:

"Don't forget to thank her the next time you go home on leave or when we pass through your village."

Two days later, the cavalry clashed with the Japanese. It was a heroic battle, a counter-attack to the enemy's "mopping-up campaign." The fight raged until the sun dimmed and the sky darkened over the central Hebei plain. It was May. The wheat had just turned golden. Captain Yang died in battle. Little Jin was wound-

他从兜囊扯出了那件东西,一扬手在马屁股上抽了一下,马就奔跑起来。

主任的小黑马追上去,主任说:

"小金子!那是件什么东西?"

"小马鞭儿!"小金子又在空中一场。那是一杆短短的,用各色绸布结成的小马鞭,像是儿童的玩具。

"你总是顽皮,哪里弄来的?我们是骑兵,还用马鞭子?"主任笑着。

"骑兵不用马鞭,谁用马鞭?戏台上的大将,还拿着马鞭打仗哩!"小金子说。

"那是唱戏,我们要腾开手来打仗,用不着这个。进村了,快收起来,人家要笑话哩!"主任说。

小金子又看了几看,才把心爱的物件插到兜囊里去,心里有些不高兴。他想人家好心好意给做了,不能在进村的时候施展展,多么对不住人家?人家不知道费了多大工夫哩!

主任又问了:

"买的,还是求人做的?"

"是家里捎来的。"

"怎么单捎了这个来?"

"他们准是觉得我当了骑兵,缺少的就是马鞭子,心爱的也是这个。"

"怎么那样花花绿绿?"

"是个女孩子做的,她们喜欢这个颜色!"

"是你的什么人呀?"

"一家邻舍,从小儿一块长大的。"

主任没有往下问,在年岁上,他不过比小金子大两岁。在情感这个天地里,人们会是相同

英汉对照
English-Chinese
中国文学宝库
Gems of Chinese Literature
现代文学系列
Modern Literature

ed. With his bare hands, he dug a pit and buried the captain. His gun empty, he broke through the encirclement that night and returned home. But he could not eat or sleep. The captain, the horses running in all directions, the comrades fighting and dying in the ditches... all these appeared before his eyes and would not let him rest. Day and night, he seemed to hear bugle calls, the captain's commands, and the galloping of horses. At other times he heard nothing. He was ill and getting worse.

Little Jin's father was already fifty-nine. The boy was his only son. He decided to dig a tunnel with its entrance behind an old and shabby cabinet in their little house, and its exit in the house of their neighbour Little Sheng, the girl who had sent Little Jin the whip.

Little Sheng's father was a small pedlar in Shanxi Province. He had been away for more than ten years. After Little Jin's mother had died and there was no one to sew and mend in the family, Little Jin's father went to Little Sheng's mother with a length of cloth and a favour to ask.

"Don't call it a favour," said the kind neighbour. "Although we're not related we live so near we are just like members of one family. Whatever you want made, just bring it over. I know how difficult it is to have no one do necessary things. Leave the cloth here, I'll cut it and sew it for you."

Since then the two households had been on very good terms.

Little Sheng's mother hugged Little Jin in her arms when he came back from the battlefield. Patting his ragged uniform, she said: "How you must have crawled and rolled in the battle, my

的。过了一刻,他说:

"回家或是路过,谢谢人家吧!"

3

五月里打过仗,小金子受伤回到家里,他饭也吃不下,觉也睡不着。主任和那些马匹,马匹的东奔西散,同志们趴在道沟里战斗牺牲……老在他眼前转,使他坐立不安。黑间白日,他尖着耳朵听着,好像那里又有集合的号音,练兵的口令,主任的命令,马蹄的奔腾;过了一会又什么也听不见。他的病一天一天重了。

小金子的爹,今年五十九岁了,只有这一个儿子。给他挖了一个洞,洞口就在小屋里破旧的迎门橱后面。出口在前邻小胜儿家。小胜儿,就是给小金子捎马鞭子的那个姑娘。

小胜儿的爹在山西挑货郎担儿,十几年不回家了。那年小金子的娘死了,没人做活,小金子的爹,心里准备下了一堆好话,把布拿到前邻小胜儿的娘那里。小胜儿的娘一听就说:

"她大伯,你别说这个。咱们虽说不是一姓一家,住的这么近,就像一家似的,你有什么活,尽管拿过来。我过着穷日子,就知道没人的难处,说句浅话,求告你的时候正在后头哩。把布放下吧,我给你裁铰裁铰做上。"

从这以后,两家人就过的很亲密。

小金子从战场回来,小胜儿的娘把他抱在怀里,摸着那扯破的军装说:

"孩子,你们是怎么着,爬着滚着的打来呀,

boy! Why, you've got your brand-new tunic torn to shreds. Little Sheng, find something for your brother to change into at once."

"Aw, don't bother," said Little Jin.

"You'll have to lie down and rest anyway, you silly child," said Little Sheng's mother. "Look at the colour of your face. Take off your tunic and let Little Sheng mend it for you. Look at the bloodstains. Did you shed all that blood?..."

"Some is mine. Some is the blood of my comrades," said Little Jin.

That night, mother and daughter helped Little Jin's father dig the tunnel and persuaded the boy to hide in there so that he could rest and heal his wound.

The enemy started a dragnet search through the fields. The village became their base and they searched and checked each household. Little Sheng and her mother were very worried about Little Jin. They could not eat properly and they would not allow him to come out. Every morning Little Sheng took food to him in the tunnel.

One day, the small oil lamp in the tunnel suddenly went out. Little Sheng, her hair covered by a kerchief, crawled in with the food.

"It's me," she whispered and put the food down. She fished a box of matches out of her pocket and struck several before she got the lamp lit. The tunnel was smoky. Little Jin reclined mutely on the damp earth, his face as white as a sheet of paper.

"How do you feel?" she asked.

新布就撕成这个样子!小胜儿,快去给你哥哥找衣裳来换!"

小金子说:

"不用换。"

"傻孩子,"小胜儿的娘说,"不换衣裳,也得养养病呀!看你的脸成了什么颜色!快脱下来,叫小胜儿给你缝缝。你看这血,这是你流的……"

"有我流的,也有同志们流的!"小金子说。

母女两个连夜帮着小金子的爹挖洞,劝说着小金子进去养病养伤。

4

敌人在田野拉网"清剿",村里成了据点,正在清查户口。母女两个整天为小金子担心,焦愁得饭也吃不下去。她们不让小金子出来,每天早晨,小胜儿把饭食送进洞里去,又把便尿端出来。

那天,她用一块手巾把头发包好,两只手抱着饭罐,从洞口慢慢往里爬。爬到洞中间,洞里的小油灯忽的灭了,她小声说:"是我。"把饭罐轻轻放好,从身上掏出洋火,擦了好几根,才把灯点着。洞里一片烟雾,她看见小金子靠在潮湿的泥土上,脸色苍白的怕人,一言不发。她问:

"你怎么了?"

英汉对照
English-Chinese
中国文学宝库
Gems of Chinese Literature
现代文学系列
Modern Literature

"I'm going to die if I have to go on like this."

"What else can we do?" She sat down on his quilt. It was virtually soaked with damp. "The Japanese soldiers seem to be settling down in this place. They're not going to leave if we don't fight." Then she inquired. "Was Captain Yang killed?"

"Yes. He's always in my mind. I was with him for two years. We were about the same age. I always feel that he is still alive. One minute I keep thinking that I should bring him his meal and the next that it's time to get his horse ready for him. Of course I'm only dreaming. I'll never be able to see him again."

"I still remember his face," said Little Sheng. "I saw him when he came to our house with you that day. Was he from the southern provinces?"

"From Guizhou Province, nine thousand *li* away. But he learned to speak perfect northern dialect. Don't you think so?"

"Does his family know about his death? How bad they'll feel when the news reaches them. Of course, he was a soldier in wartime...."

"At first he and I were covering the retreat of the others. Then I was wounded. An enemy soldier rushed towards me and Captain Yang jumped out from behind the shelter and came to grips with him. No one could match his courage in battle but he was always telling us to be careful. He was very strict with himself but very considerate of others. One day when we were marching and he was thirsty I offered to get him a melon but he wouldn't let me."

"Why? Was there anything wrong with the melon?" asked Little Sheng.

"这样下去,我就死了。"小金子说。

"这有什么办法呀?"小胜儿坐在那像在水里泡过的褥子上,"鬼子像在这里住了老家,不打,他们自己会走?"她又说,"我问问你,杨主任牺牲了?"

"牺牲了。我老是想他。"小金子说,"跟了他两三年,年纪又差不多,老是觉着他还活着,一时想该给他打饭,一时想又该给他备马了。可是哪里去找他呀,想想罢了!"

"他的面目我记的很清楚。"小胜儿说,"那天,他跟着你到咱们家来,我觉着比什么都光荣。说话他就牺牲了,他是个南方人吧?"

"离我们有九千多里地,贵州地面哩。你看他学咱这里的话学的多像!"小金子说。

小胜儿说:

"不知道家里知道他的死讯不?知道了,一家人要多难过!自然当兵打仗,说不上那些。"

小金子说:

"先是他同我顶着打,叫同志们转移,后来我受了伤,敌人冲到我面前,他跳出了掩体和敌人拚了死命。打仗的时候,他自己勇敢的没对儿,总叫别人小心。平时体贴别人,自己很艰苦。那天行军,他渴了,我说给他摘个瓜吃,他也不允许。"

"为什么,吃个瓜也不允许?"小胜儿问。

英汉对照
English-Chinese
中国文学宝库
Gems of Chinese Literature
现代文学系列
Modern Literature

"No. He didn't like to take anything from the people. You see, he wasn't the only one who was thirsty. He always knew when I had something on my mind! That same day he criticized me for playing with that quirt you sent me."

"That was just for fun. Why should he criticize you?"

"He said it was too fancy for a soldier. I put it away immediately. But later he told me to thank you for it."

"Don't thank me for getting you criticized!" laughed Little Sheng. "We must avenge him. You have to get well quickly."

When Little Sheng came out of the tunnel she said to her mother, "Let's buy some eggs and noodles for Little Jin."

"We haven't reaped any wheat nor sown anything to be harvested in the autumn this year because of the invaders. We can't even afford to eat sorghum and millet, and it's difficult to borrow money at such times."

"Let's weave a length of cloth and sell it, Ma."

"We are running and hiding all the time. How can you talk about weaving? If you set up the loom how do you know the Japanese devils won't rush in on you?"

"Perhaps we can sell something. His health is more important."

"He's not an outsider, child. I look upon him as your brother. But what can a poor household sell? There's nothing of value here."

Little Sheng raised her head, meditated for some time, then said, "Suppose we sell that coat of mine."

"Your coat! That flowered silk coat?" asked the mother. "Are

"因为不只他一个人呀。我心里有什么事,他立时就能看出来。也是那天,我玩弄你捎给我的小马鞭儿,他批评了我。"

"那是闹着玩儿的,"小胜儿说,"他为什么批评你哩?"

"他说是花花绿绿,不像个战士样子,我就把马鞭子装起来了。可是,过了一会,他又叫我谢谢你。"

"有什么谢头,叫你受了批评还谢哩!"小胜儿笑了一下,"我们别忘了给他报仇就是了!你快着养壮实了吧!"

5

小胜儿从洞里出来,就和她娘说:

"我们该给小金子买些鸡蛋,称点挂面。"

娘说:

"叫鬼子闹的,今年麦季没收,秋田没种,高粱小米都吃不起,这年头摘摘借借也困难。"

小胜儿说:

"娘,我们赶着织个布卖了去吧!"

娘说:

"整天价逃难,提不上鞋,哪里还能织布?你安上机子,知道那兔崽子们什么时候闯进来呀?"

"要不我们就变卖点东西?人家的病要紧哩!"小胜儿说。

"你这孩子!"娘说,"什么人家的病,这不像亲兄弟一样吗?可是,咱一个穷人家,有什么可变卖的哩,有什么值钱的物件哩?"

英汉对照
English-Chinese
中国文学宝库
Gems of Chinese Literature
现代文学系列
Modern Literature

you selling your wedding outfit before you are married?"

"We are in hiding all the time, I won't be wearing it for the time being anyway. It will either rot in the earth where we buried it for safekeeping or the enemy soldiers will take it away. We had better sell it."

"I've been thinking of marrying you off," said the mother with a smile, "if we can make a suitable match. Times are bad. I am worried about you. You shouldn't sell the coat. I've set my heart on your wearing it at your wedding."

"But he had nothing fit to eat this evening. Do you mean we should give him coarse sorghum meal?" said Little Sheng. "It's market day. Go and sell the coat."

In the end the daughter persuded the mother to take the coat to market. But the market looked quite different from ordinary days. There were no young people nor proper buyers and sellers to be seen. The booths selling thread and coloured cotton cloth were not there anymore. Holding the coat, Little Sheng's mother stood at the crossroads a whole morning without finding a buyer. It was only in the afternoon that a man who worked for the Japanese appeared with a tart. He wanted to buy her a coat. Little Sheng's mother sold the coat without daring to haggle over the price. Her heart ached as if she had sold her daughter's flesh. With the money she had received, she bought a catty of noodles and ten eggs. These she gave Little Sheng as soon as she reached home. She could not hold back a sob when she thought of the coat, and that evening she was so upset she went to bed before it was dark.

Little Sheng said nothing but set to cooking supper for Little Jin.

小胜儿也仰着脖子想,她说:
"要不,把我那件袄卖了吧!"
"哪件袄?你那件花丝葛袄吗?"娘问着,"哪有还没过事,就变卖陪送的哩?"
小胜儿说:
"整天藏藏躲躲的,反正一时也穿不着,不是埋坏了,就是叫他们抢走了,我看还是拿出去卖了它吧!"
"依我的心思呀,"娘笑着说,"这么兵荒马乱,有个对事的人家,我还想早些打发你出去,省的担惊受怕哩!那件衣裳不能卖,那是我心上的一件衣裳!"
"可是,晚上,他就没得吃,叫他吃红饼子?"小胜儿说,"今儿个是集日,快拿出去卖了吧!"
到底是女儿说服了娘,包起那件衣服,拿到集上去。集市变了,看不见年轻人和正经买卖人,没有了线子市,也没有了花布市。胜儿的娘抱着棉袄,在十字路口靠着墙站了半天,也没个买主。晌午过了,才过来个汉奸,领着一个浪荡女人,要给她买件衣裳。小胜儿的娘不敢争价,就把那件衣裳卖了。她心痛了一阵,好像卖了女儿身上的肉一样。称了一斤挂面,买了十个鸡蛋,拿回家来,交给小胜儿,就啼哭起来,天还不黑就盖上被子睡觉去了。

小胜儿没有说话,下炕给小金子做饭。现

英汉对照
English-Chinese
中国文学宝库
Gems of Chinese Literature
现代文学系列
Modern Literature

It was getting dark. She broke dry willow branches into small pieces, staring at the firelight flickering on her face and arms. She seemed to see Captain Yang's blood and Little Jin's pale face, but quickly the boy's thin face grew plump and rosy again. She turned her mind to her cooking. When everything was ready she barred the gate and pulled the string attached to the bell in the tunnel. There was a muffled tinking. Then Little Jin crawled out.

Little Jin ate a very good meal that evening. He finished the two bowls of noodles and four eggs at one sitting and seemed to have appetite for more. After he had eaten, he wiped his mouth and said: "You should just give me whatever you have. Why do you spend extra money to feed me?"

Little Sheng's mother said from the *kang*, "We haven't any money. Your sister sold the coat which was meant for her wedding to buy you proper nourishing food. If only it was sold to a nice person. It pains me to think of the coat falling into the hands of that tart. Don't forget your sister for this."

"This is merely treating the Eighth Route Army. There's no need for thanks or repayment," smiled Little Sheng as she cleared away the chopsticks and bowls.

Little Jin lay down on the *kang*. Little Sheng covered the window snugly with a quilt and barred the door. Then she lit the oil lamp, put it in a niche in the wall and began to sew while listening attentively for any strange sounds outside. She knew that countless women and children of the central Hebei plain were spending the night in the fields, full of fear and anxiety as they listened to the sound of guns.

在天快黑了,她手里劈着干柳树枝,眼望着火,火在她脸上身上闪照,光亮发红。她好像看见杨主任的血,看见小金子苍白的脸,看见他的脸慢慢变的又胖又红润了。她小心地把饭做熟,早早地把大门上好,就爬到洞口去拉暗铃。一种微小的柔软的声音,在地下响了。不久,小金子就钻了出来。

这一顿饭,小金子吃的很多,两碗挂面四个鸡蛋全吃了,还有点不足心的样子。吃完了饭,一抹嘴说:

"有什么吃什么就行了,干什么又花钱?"

"哪里来的钱呀,孩子,是你妹子把陪送袄卖了,给你养病哩!卖了,是叫个好人穿呀!叫那么个烂货糟蹋去了,我真心疼!你可别忘了你妹子!"小胜儿的娘在被窝里说。

"我们这是优待八路军,用不着谢,也用不着报答!"小胜儿低着头笑了笑,收拾了碗筷。

小金子躺在炕上。小胜儿用棉被把窗子堵了个严又严,把屋门也上了。她点起一个小油灯,放在墙壁上凿好的一个小洞里,面对着墙做起针线来,不住尖着耳朵听外面的风声。

在冀中平原,有多少妇女孩子在担惊,在田野里听着枪声过夜!她回过头来说:

英汉对照
English-Chinese
中国文学宝库
Gems of Chinese Literature
现代文学系列
Modern Literature

"We are luckier than others," Little Sheng turned and said. "We can still sit on our own *kang*. Are you asleep?"

"Your Ma is asleep but I'm not," answered Little Jin. "I've eaten a lot today and I feel better. Besides, I slept during the day in the tunnel. I'm not sleepy now. What are you doing?"

"I'm making a pair of shoes. Shoes wear out quicker with so much running in and out of shelters."

"I can do without shoes since I stay in the tunnel all day," said Little Jin. His woeful tone made a lump rise in Little Sheng's throat.

"You're wounded and ill. Don't think of anything now but just take good care of yourself. When you recover, you can go across the railway to look for the army. When I finish these shoes of mine, I'll make a pair for you."

Little Sheng's eyes glistened in the dark. On a night like this, the enemy was at work, setting fire to nearby villages, and searching, plundering and killing in fields, villages, forests, and haystacks the innocent people of central Hebei.

1950
Translated by Yu Fanqin

"我们这还算享福哩,坐在自己家里的炕上——怎么你们睡着了!"

"大娘睡着了,我没睡着。"小金子说,"今天吃的多些,精神也好些,白天在洞里又睡了一会,现在怎么也睡不着了。你做什么哩?"

"做我的鞋,"小胜儿低着头说,"整天东逃西跑,鞋也要多费几双。今年军队上的活,做的倒少了。"

"像我整天钻洞,不穿鞋也可以!"小金子说,听着他的声音,小胜儿的鼻子也酸了,她说:

"你受了伤,又有病,这说不上。好好养些日子,等腿上有了力气,能走长路了,就过铁道找队伍去。做上了我的,就该给你铰底子做鞋了!"

小胜儿放下活计,转过身来,她的眼睛在黑影里放光。在这样的夜晚,敌人正在附近村庄放火,在田野、村庄、树林、草垛里搜捕杀害冀中的人民……

1950年1月19日

英汉对照
English-Chinese
中国文学宝库
Gems of Chinese Literature
现代文学系列
Modern Literature

The Blacksmith and the Carpenter

1

What things in childhood leave the deepest impressions? If you grew up in a village in the old days, you know how impoverished material life was and how few cultural activities there were. You saw an opera only once every several years. Once a year you might hear the drums and cymbals of some variety troupe that had arrived. Except for the fields and cemeteries and abandoned kilns and willow groves in the outskirts, there were few places in the village that were any fun for the children.

And so, the ringing of a hammer in anyone's courtyard drew them immediately. They would run flocking in whenever a household hired a carpenter to build a cart or put up a door. A long carpenter's bench with a wedge on one end of it would be placed in the courtyard. On this would be laid a board that was to be planed. Then the carpenter astride the bench would lean forward and shavings like strips of satin would come curling out of the plane he was pushing and fall to the ground. The children would rush forward but, just as they got their hands on them, the owner of the house, watching the work, would bark:

"Get out of here, you kids. Go outside and play."

铁木前传

1

在人们的童年里,什么事物,留下的印象最深刻?如果是在农村里长大的,那时候,农村里的物质生活是穷苦的,文化生活是贫乏的,几年的时间,才能看到一次大戏,一年中间,也许听不到一次到村里来卖艺的锣鼓声音。于是,除去村外的田野、坟堆、破窑和柳杆子地,孩子们就没有多少可以留恋的地方了。

在谁家院里,叮叮当当的斧凿声音,吸引了他们。他们成群结队跑了进去,那一家正在请一位木匠打造新车,或是安装门户,在院子里放着一条长长的板凳,板凳的一头,突出一截木楔,木匠把要刨平的木材,放在上面,然后弯着腰,那像绸条一样的木花,就在他那不断推进的刨子上面飞卷出来,落到板凳下面。孩子们跑了过去,刚捡到手,就被监工的主人吆喝跑了:

"小孩子们,滚出去玩。"

英汉对照
English-Chinese
中国文学宝库
Gems of Chinese Literature
现代文学系列
Modern Literature

The Blacksmith and the Carpenter

Yet that slithering sound was so fascinating! And how charming the art of carpentry was! And in the corner of the compound wall, the crackling fire — for heating fishbone glue and straightening warped boards — that too was hard to leave. Particularly since most of the carpentry work was done in winter, when a good fire was doubly appealing.

Sooner or later, however, the children, unhappily, would have to go. Let the lovely ring of hammers sound far beyond the compound walls. May those gleaming flames dance forever before their eyes. The children often had a ridiculous thought: Why can't we invite a carpenter to work at our house? When they got home, they would express this wish to their father during the evening meal. He would get angry and say:

"We hire a carpenter? We haven't been able to afford one in generations. Maybe we'll start with yours, little wretch, if you're fated to be rich! Or I could send you to Old Li to be his apprentice. You can fool all day with hammers and awls."

Old Li was the village's only carpenter. Tall, he had a brown beard and a pock-marked face. There seemed little likelihood of anyone becoming Old Li's apprentice. The children knew he wasn't taking on any. He had six boys of his own, and not one of them was a carpenter. They spent all day with wicker baskets on their backs, picking dried bean stalks for fuel, just like the other kids.

But hope springs eternal, and there were always chances for enjoyment. If it were late spring or early summer, the village street would resound with clanging and the roar of a fiery furnace. The clanging seemed especially heroic, the flames especially fierce.

然而那呦呦的声音,多么引诱人!木匠的手艺,多么可爱啊!还有生在墙角的那一堆木柴火,是用来熬鳔胶和烤直木材的,那噼剥噼剥的声音,也实在使人难以割舍。而木匠的工作又多是在冬天开始,这堆好火,就更可爱了。

在这个场合里,是终于不得不难过地走开的。让那可爱的斧凿声音,响到墙外来吧;让那熊熊的火光,永远在眼前闪烁吧。在童年的时候,常常就有这样一个可笑的想法:我们家什么时候也能叫一个木匠来做活呢?当孩子们回到家里,在吃晚饭的时候,把这个愿望向父亲提出来,父亲生气了:

"你们家叫木匠?咱家几辈子叫不起木匠,假如你这小子有福分,就从你这儿开办吧。要不,我把你送到黎老东那里学徒,你就可以整天和斧子凿子打交道了。"

黎老东是这个村庄里的唯一的木匠,他高个子,黄胡须,脸上有些麻子。看来,很少有给黎老东当徒弟的可能。因为孩子们知道,黎老东并不招收徒弟。他自己就有六个儿子,六个儿子都不是木匠。他们和别的孩子一样,也是整天背着柴筐下地捡豆楂。

但是,希望是永远存在的,快乐的机会,也总是很多的。如果是在春末和夏初的日子,村里的街上,就又会有叮叮当当的声音,和一炉熊熊的火了。这叮叮当当的声音,听来更是雄壮,

英汉对照
English-Chinese
中国文学宝库
Gems of Chinese Literature
现代文学系列
Modern Literature

The Blacksmith and the Carpenter

You could hear and see them from ever so far! They meant that Old Fu's travelling blacksmith forge had come once more to the village.

He came every year, as punctually as the swallows returning to the eaves at nesting time. Just before the wheat harvest and the busy autumn season, sickles and hoes and all sorts of tools had to be mended and other implements forged. As soon as he appeared, people brought out their worn and broken farm tools, and the scrap metal they had been saving for the repairs.

In the course of fifty years, Old Fu's lean face had assumed the colour of the pincers he held in his left hand and the hammer he wielded with his right and the anvil resting on the big wooden block. Even the short beard that fringed his face was rusty in hue. He worked stripped to the waist. The oilcloth apron covering his legs was so pitted with holes, large and small, burned through by flying sparks of many years, that it resembled a hornet's nest. On his feet Fu wore a pair of very tattered stockings, also intended as a protection against the sparks that flew each time his hammer struck the glowing metal.

He had two apprentices. The older one swung the sledge hammer and sharpened tools, the younger worked the bellows and cooked their food. His grimy face streaked with sweat, the younger boy would stand proudly, his head high, his feet firmly planted one before the other, pulling and pushing the piston of the big wheezing bellows, while the village children who had gathered round gazed at him with the utmost admiration. "Watch out!" he would cry softly as Old Fu drew a cherry-red piece of iron from the

那一炉火看来更是旺盛,真是多远也听得见,多远也看得见啊!这是傅老刚的铁匠炉,又来到村里了。

他们每年总是要来一次的。像在屋梁上结窠的燕子一样,他们总在一定的时间来。麦收和秋忙就要开始了,镰刀和锄头要加钢,小镐也要加钢,他们还要给农民们打造一些其他的日用家具。他们一来,人们就把那些要修理的东西和自备的破铁碎钢拿来了。

傅老刚被人们叫做"掌作的",他有五十岁年纪了。他的瘦干的脸就像他那左手握着的火钳,右手抡着的铁锤,还有那安放在大木墩子上的铁砧的颜色一样。他那短短的连鬓的胡须,就像是铁锈。他上身不穿衣服,腰下系一条油布围裙,这围裙,长年被火星冲击,上面的大大小小的漏洞,就像蜂窠。在他那脚面上,绑着两张破袜片,也是为了防御那在锤打热铁的时候迸射出来的火花。

傅老刚是有徒弟的。他有两个徒弟,大徒弟抡大锤,沾水磨刃,小徒弟拉大风箱和做饭。小徒弟的脸上,左一道右一道都是污黑的汗水,然而他高仰着头,一只脚稳重地向前伸站,一下一下地拉送那忽忽响动的大风箱。孩子们围在旁边对他这种傲岸的劳动的姿态,由衷地表示了深深的仰慕之情。

"喂!"当师傅从炉灶里撤出烧炼得通红的铁器,他就轻轻地关照孩子们。孩子们一哄就

英汉对照
English-Chinese
中国文学宝库
Gems of Chinese Literature
现代文学系列
Modern Literature

The Blacksmith and the Carpenter

forge. The kids would hurriedly scatter, and the ringing big hammer would send sparks flying after them in all directions. If their mothers or fathers didn't call them home, the kids would remain indefinitely. They had no idea what was being made. Was it a ring for a door-knocker, or a chain of iron circlets? Ah, children! While you silently watch, what really is going on in your minds?

The blacksmith's team spent over a month in this village every year, rising early and going to bed late. At daybreak, when everyone else was wrapped in their quilts, the sound of the team's hammers resounded down the village street. The fire in their forge still glowed long after dark. They slept beside the forge at night, in the open, for they had neither shed nor tent. Only in the rainy season did they dismantle their portable furnace and wheel it into a villager's home.

Usually they stayed with Old Li, the carpenter. Old Li was very poor. His wife had died, leaving him with six children. A few years before, steeling his heart, he had sent the oldest boy to Tianjin to learn commercial trading; the others he boarded among relatives and friends. Then, shouldering his carpenter's kit, he had set out for the northeast provinces. In those distant parts, he endured many hardships and saw much that was new. But in the end, he returned home empty-handed. He and a few of his kids set up house in an unused compound. He was having an increasingly difficult time making ends meet.

Old Li was a friendly fellow. He knew the hardships a man faced when working away from home. He and the blacksmith were good friends. He addressed Old Fu affectionately as "relative."

散开了,随着叮当的锤打声,那四溅的铁花,在他们的身后飞舞着。

如果不是父亲母亲来叫,孩子们是会一直在这里观赏的,他们也不知道,到底要看出些什么道理来。是看到把一只门吊儿打好吗?是看到把一个套环儿接上吗?童年啊!在默默的注视里,你们想念的,究竟是一种什么境界?

铁匠们每年要在这个村庄里工作一个多月。他们是早起晚睡的,早晨,人们还躺在被窝里的时候,就听到街上的大小铁锤的声音了;天黑很久,他们炉灶里的火还在燃烧着。夜晚,他们睡在炉灶的边旁,没有席棚,也没有帐幕。只有连绵阴雨的天气,他们才收拾起小车炉灶,到一个人家去。

他们经常的下处,是木匠黎老东家。黎老东家里很穷,老婆死了,留下六个孩子。前些年,他曾经下个狠心,把大孩子送到天津去学生意,把其余的几个,分别托靠给亲朋,自己背上手艺箱了,下了关东。在那遥远的异乡,他只是开了开眼界,受了很多苦楚,结果还是空着手儿回来了。回来以后,他拉扯着几个孩子住在人家的一个闲院里,日子过得越发艰难了。

黎老东是好交朋友的,又出过外,知道出门的难处。他和傅老刚的交情是深厚的,他不称呼傅老刚"掌作的",也不像一些老年人直接叫他"老刚",他总称呼"亲家"。

英汉对照
English-Chinese
中国文学宝库
Gems of Chinese Literature
现代文学系列
Modern Literature

When the rains came, the blacksmith's team set up shop in the carpenter's old mill shed. As a token of thanks to his "relative," in his spare time Old Fu would repair and sharpen the carpenter's tools. And Old Li in turn, when he wasn't busy, would replace the handles of the blacksmith's hammers and mend his bellows, without charge.

No one was sure what was behind this appellation "relative" which the two men used so freely. Did Old Li want one of his sons to accept Old Fu as his foster father? Or had they arranged a match with Old Fu's daughter?

"What sort of 'relatives' are you, anyhow?" people would ask inquisitively. "Foster relatives, or relatives by marriage?"

"Foster relatives?" Old Li was a talkative fellow who liked to laugh. "I have six boys. If you want a foster son, take your pick."

"Relatives by marriage? Why not?" Old Fu, who seldom joked, this time also laughed. "I've a growing daughter at home, you know."

But whenever Old Fu mentioned his daughter, his ruddy face grew sombre, like a glowing red iron billet after being plunged into the water bucket. His wife had died, and Nine, their only child, was left at home alone.

"Bring the girl with you next year." The two old friends were seated opposite each other, smoking their pipes in the old mill shed one evening. Old Fu wasn't saying a word, and Li made this proposal because he knew it would open his friend's tightly locked mouth and release some of the bitterness pent up in his heart.

"That would mean another mouth to feed." Old Fu spoke with

下雨天,铁匠炉就搬到他的院里来。铁匠们在一大间破碾棚里工作着。为了答谢"亲家"的好意,傅老刚每年总是抽时间给黎老东打整打整他那木作工具。该加钢的加钢,该磨刃的磨刃。这种帮助也是有酬答的,黎老东闲暇的日子,也就无代价地替铁匠们换换锤把,修修风箱。

"亲家"是叫得很熟了,但是,谁也不知道这"亲家"的准确的含义。究竟是黎老东的哪一个儿子认傅老刚为干爹了呢,还是两个人定成了儿女亲家?

"亲家,亲家,你们到底是干亲家,还是湿亲家?"人们有时候这样探问着。

"干的吧?"黎老东是个好说好笑的人,"我有六个儿子,亲家,你要哪一个叫你干爹都行。"

"湿的也行哩!"轻易不说笑的傅老刚也笑起来,"我家里是有个妞儿的。"

但是,每当他说到妞儿的时候,他那脸色就像刚刚烧红的铁,在冷水桶里猛丁一沾,立刻就变得阴沉了。他的老婆死了,留下年幼的女儿一人在家。

"明年把孩子带来吧。"晚上,黎老东和傅老刚在碾棚里对坐着抽烟,傅老刚一直不说话,黎老东找了这样一个话题。他知道,在这个时候,只有这样一把钥匙,才能通开老朋友的紧紧封闭着的嘴,使他那深藏在内心的痛苦流泄出来。

"那就又多一个人吃饭,"傅老刚低着头说,

英汉对照
English-Chinese
中国文学宝库
Gems of Chinese Literature
现代文学系列
Modern Literature

downcast eyes. "Girls are a nuisance to have around."

"Look at me," said Old Li trying to hold back the tears in his eyes. "I've got six kids."

They were revealing their innermost thoughts, but it was difficult for them to go on. For although each longed to help the other, both knew they were powerless. Even words of comfort seemed to be in vain.

At that moment, Six, Li's youngest son, came in to tell his father that it was time to go to bed. Fu raised his head and looked at the boy.

"It seems to me that Six is the most intelligent, the most quick-witted, of your six children."

"I wish you'd take him on as your apprentice," said Li, hugging the boy to his chest. "Is Nine as old as he?"

"How old is Six?"

"Nine," the boy answered for himself.

"My girl is nine years old too. But she's a head shorter than you. She'll have to call you Big Brother."

2

The following year when the wheat was ripe Fu did indeed bring his daughter from their old home. He fixed a small perch for her on one side of his wheelbarrow. She sat cross-legged on a bit of old padding, leaning inward and holding on with her right hand. They travelled for five or six days, eating plenty of dust, and stopping at little inns. But the child was very happy. To be with her father,

"女孩子家,又累手累脚。"

"你看我,"黎老东忍住眼里的泪说,"六个。"

这种谈话很是知心,可是很难继续。因为,虽然谁都有为朋友解决困难的热心,但是谁也知道,实际上真是无能为力。就连互相安慰,都也感到是徒然的了。

这时候,黎老东最小的儿子,名字叫六儿的,来叫父亲睡觉。傅老刚抬起头来,望着他说:

"我看,你这几个孩子,就算六儿长得最精神,心眼儿也最灵。"

"我希望你将来收他做个徒弟哩。"黎老东把六儿拉到怀里说,"我那小侄女儿,也有他这么大?"

"六儿今年几岁了?"傅老刚问。

"九岁。"六儿自己回答。

"我那女儿也是九岁。"傅老刚说,"她比你要矮一头哩,她要向你叫哥哥哩。"

2

第二年头麦熟,傅老刚真的从老家把女儿带来了。他在小车的一边,给女儿安置了一个座位。这座位当然很小,小孩子用右手紧把住小车的上装,把脚盘起来,侧着身子坐在垫好的一小块破褥上。他们在路上走了五六天,住了几次小店,吃了很多尘土。然而女孩子是很高

her only dear one, to be together for a long time — nothing could make her happier.

Arriving in the village, they went directly to Old Li's house. The carpenter was delighted. He summoned all the little girls in the neighbourhood to play with the small guest.

"What's your name?" they asked her.

"'I'm called Nine."

"You mean you're the ninth child?"

"No, I'm the only one."

"Then why are you called Nine?" The girls were puzzled. "Here, you get your nickname according to the order you're born in. Like Six, for instance. He was the sixth child in the family."

"That was the name my ma gave me before she died," the little newcomer said sadly. "I was born on the ninth day of the ninth month."

"Oh." The girls understood. "And where you come from, they still wear braids?"

"Yes," the guest said shyly. The woollen thread binding the end of her single thick braid was a dazzling shade of red!

She got to know the local girls well after playing with them for a few days, and Six too. She and Six formed a close affection, just like their fathers. Old Fu was too busy working to look after his daughter. One night, he made her and Six an axe head each. Old Li fitted the handles. During the day, they sent the two children out into the hills to cut brushwood. A big rattan basket on his back, axe in hand, Six proudly led the way. Nine followed, carrying a somewhat smaller basket. They went far into the hills.

兴的,她可以跟父亲,这唯一的亲人,长住在一起,对她说来是最幸福的了。

到了村里,先投奔了黎老东家。黎老东很是高兴,招呼左邻右舍的女孩子们来和小客人玩。

"你叫什么名儿呀?"那些女孩子们问她。

"我叫九儿。"小客人回答。

"你姐妹九个?"女孩子们问。

"就我一个哩。"小客人说。

"那你为什么叫九儿?"女孩子们奇怪了,"在我们这里,谁是老几就叫几儿,比如六儿,他就是老六。"

"这是我娘活着的时候,给我起的名儿。"小客人难过地说,"我是九月初九的生日哩。"

"啊。"女孩子们明白了,"那么,你们那里还兴留小辫儿吗?"

"唔。"小客人有些害羞了,缠在她那独根大辫上的绳儿,红得多么耀眼呀!

和女孩子们玩了几天,和六儿也就熟了。九儿看出,六儿和她很亲近,就像两个人的父亲在一起时表现得那样。傅老刚活儿忙,女孩子跟在身边不方便,他打夜作,给六儿和九儿每人打了一把拾柴的小镐儿,黎老东给他们拾掇上镐柄,白天就打发他们到野外去。六儿背着红荆条大筐,提着小镐儿,扬长走在前头,九儿背一个较小的筐子,紧跟在后面,走到很远很远的野地里去。

英汉对照
English-Chinese
中国文学宝库
Gems of Chinese Literature
现代文学系列
Modern Literature

Six didn't like to cut brushwood near the village. He preferred uninhabited places, new places which he felt he was discovering. But he didn't do much work, wasting most of his time along the road. He would suddenly flush a bird brooding eggs and chase it in its short bursts of flight. Brooders always fly close to the ground, and never very far. The bird seemed to be teasing him, taking off each time he nearly caught up.

Or he would pursue a half-grown rabbit. Sure he could nab it, he was still always disappointed.

"Let's cut some brush," Nine would urge.

"What's the hurry?" Six would retort. "As long as we bring back a full basket each before dark it'll be all right."

"Is there any rule that says we can't gather two baskets apiece?"

"Even if we each collect three, we'll never become rich!" Six would rebuke her.

One day, he was walking slowly through the grass, watching the ground. Marking a certain spot, he stopped and examined the surroundings. Then, throwing his basket aside, he called Nine.

"Stay here and guard this burrow entrance. Don't let him escape."

He returned to the marked place, leaned over and began to dig, his small axe flying.

That evening, the children returned home happily with a short-tailed little mole. They put it in a wooden box. Carpenters' homes are full of wooden boxes.

The next morning, the wind was very strong, and the children remained at home. After his father left for work, Six brought out

六儿不喜欢在村边村沿拾柴,他总是愿意到人们不常到、好像是他一个人发现的新地方去。可是,走出这样远,他并不好好的工作,他总是把时间浪费在路上。他忽然轰起一个寠卵儿鸟,那种鸟儿贴着地皮飞,飞不远又落下,好像引逗人似的,六儿赶了一程又一程。有时候,他又追赶一只半大不小的野兔儿,他总以为这是可以追上的,结果每次都失败了。

"我们赶紧拾柴吧。"九儿劝告地说。

"忙什么?"六儿说,"天黑拾满一筐回去就行。"

"我们不许一人拾两筐吗?"九儿说。

"就是一天拾三筐,也过不成财主!"六儿严肃地驳斥着。

他慢慢地走在草地里,注视着脚下。在一处作个记号,又察看着。后来,他把柴筐扔在一旁,招呼着九儿:

"你守住这个洞口,不要叫它从这里跑了。"

他回到作记号的那里,弯下腰,用小镐儿飞快地掘起来。

这天,他们高兴地捉住了一只短尾巴的小田鼠,晚上带回家里来,装在一只小木匣里。木匠家总是有很多木匣子的。

第二天,风很大。他两个没有到地里去,在六儿家里玩。父亲出去作活了,六儿拿出小田

英汉对照
English-Chinese
中国文学宝库
Gems of Chinese Literature
现代文学系列
Modern Literature

the mole. He said to Nine:

"He's been in that box all night. He must be stifling. We ought to let him run around a bit."

"Suppose we can't catch him again?"

"Just guard that water drain and nothing will happen." Six put the little mole down on the floor. At first, it crouched motionless at the boy's feet. But then Six "whish"-ed at it, and stamped his feet. The little animal scampered along the base of the wall, then popped into a hole.

Six was frantic. "Is there any water in the vat?" he asked Nine.

The vat was empty. Six grabbed a ladle, scooped some brine juice from the pickling jug and poured it into the rat hole. But it did no good. He started for the pickling jug again.

"Your father will scold you," Nine warned. "Salt is expensive."

The boy angrily flung the ladle to the ground with such force that it split.

Playing together that day was a failure. Six was unhappy over the loss of his mole. Nine felt badly about the wasted brine juice. A poor family's child, she had learned to cherish every needle and thread.

The wind blew harder and the children took refuge in the old mill shed. A seldom-used stone mill stood in the middle. Nine sat on the dusty stone roller base. Six crawled into the big winnowing machine, curling up like a shrimp, face to the ceiling.

"Come on in," he said to Nine. "There's still room."

"I won't," said Nine.

She was thinking, facing reality. Outside, the wind was howl-

鼠来,对九儿说:

"它在匣里住了一夜,一定很闷,我们叫它在地下跑跑吧。"

"捉不住了,怎么办?"九儿说。

"不要紧,你把水道守住就行了。"六儿把小田鼠放在地下。起初小田鼠伏在他的脚下,一动也不动。六儿"嘘"它,跺脚轰它,它跑开了,绕着房根儿转,突然钻进了一个洞。

六儿发急了,他命令九儿:

"你看瓮里有水没有?"

瓮里干着。六儿抓起瓢来,跑到咸菜缸那里,掏来一瓢盐水,灌进了鼠洞。看看不顶事,又要去掏。

"大叔回来要骂了,"九儿说,"盐是很贵的。"

六儿用力把瓢扔在地下,瓢摔裂了。

这一回,两个人玩得很不好。六儿失去了小田鼠,心里很难过。九儿心疼那一瓢盐水,她也是个穷人家的孩子,她在家里,是一针一线也不敢糟蹋的。

风越刮越大,他俩躲到破碾棚里去。那座不常有人使用的大石碾,停在中间。碾台上蒙着一层尘土,九儿坐在上面。六儿爬到那架大空扇车里面,蜷起身子像只虾米一样,仰天睡下了。他招呼九儿:

"你也进来吧,盛得下。"

"我不进去。"九儿说。

她在思想,面对着现实。外面的风,刮得天

英汉对照
English-Chinese
中国文学宝库
Gems of Chinese Literature
现代文学系列
Modern Literature

ing. Spiderwebs danced wildly in the eaves. A big spider was blown down by a fierce gust of wind. It hastily scurried back up its thread. I've no mother, Nine was thinking. My father is out working in that gale and my new friend is lying asleep in the winnowing machine....

Childhood memories of every kind remain long in people's hearts. When you're living in a highrise, will the recollection of that afternoon in the low-roofed mill shed surge up often among your deepest thoughts?

3

That was the year the War of Resistance against Japan began. It was the first of the great storms that swept across the plain and shook the foundations of the old way of life. From that year on, people were tested in battle. They learned the meaning of class struggle. The vast majority of the people, who had known nothing but hardship all their lives, as well as the children they formerly considered burdens and never could afford to educate, started to break the traditional fetters, tangible and intangible, that had bound them for so long. Both of Old Li's elder sons joined the army.

What with all the troop movements and general chaos, Old Fu was unable to return to his home village. His daughter was with him, and he didn't want to risk the dangers of the long journey. During those years, carpenters and blacksmiths not only helped the needs of agriculture, they also aided the war effort. Old Fu's two

黑地暗,屋顶上的蜘蛛网抖动着,一只庞大的蜘蛛,被风吹得掉下来,又急遽地团回去了。她没有母亲,她的父亲,现时在外面的大风里工作着。她新结交的小伙伴,躺在扇车里睡着了。童年的种种回忆,将长久占据人们的心,就当你一旦居住在摩天大楼里,在这低矮的碾房里的一个下午的景象,还是会时常涌现在你沉思的眼前吧?

3

就在这一年,开始了抗日战争。这是在平原上急骤兴起的,动摇旧的生活基础的第一次大风暴。从这一年起,人们在战争的考验里,接受了阶级斗争的新道理,广大的劳苦半生的人们,包括他们那从前以为累赘、无法养教的儿女们,开始打破有形无形、传统久远的束缚和枷锁。黎老东在家的两个较大的儿子,都参军去了。

在兵荒马乱里,傅老刚没有能够按时回到老家去,好在女儿也在身边,他不想去冒那长远路途上的危险了。在这些年月里,木匠、铁匠除去为农业生产服务,还都要为战争服务。傅老

apprentices went to work in an arsenal belonging to the Eighth Route Army. All that winter, Old Fu and his daughter shod horses for the cavalry that came and went in increasing numbers. To Nine the work was very exciting.

Once, she grew careless and looked up to watch some passing troops. The jittery horse she was shoeing kicked her, leaving her with a small permanent scar on her temple. But when the army first-aid man was bandaging her head, Nine didn't shed a tear.

Amid wind and rain and the roar of guns, suffering through hunger and cold, rejoicing in victory, the youngsters finished their childhood, those precious years. Because he got along well with people, Old Fu was known and liked by everyone in the surrounding villages. When he and Nine were refugees away from home, local women always volunteered to look after the girl. As soon as they heard she was the blacksmith's daughter they would offer to feed her and give her a place to live.

In the last two years of the war, because she was more grown up and had acquired some experience in guerrilla tactics, Nine usually travelled with Six. The boy was bold and clever, and he took very good care of her. She was just reaching the age of understanding, and when they were together she felt fortunate to have a companion. But it was more than that — there seemed to be a mutual reliance between them. They never ran into danger when they were together. At times she really believed Six's boastful claims.

"Just stick with me," he would say. "The Japanese devils are scared to come near me."

"All you can do is brag," Nine, walking behind, would scold

刚的两个徒弟,不久也参加了八路军附设的兵工厂。在这一年冬天,傅老刚和女儿,给来往不断和越聚越多的骑兵打钉马掌。九儿兴奋地工作着,有一次她只顾观望那过往的部队,被一匹性劣的马踢了一脚,从此在额角上留下一块小小的伤痕。当时,部队上的卫生员替她包扎好,她连一声也没哭。以后,大家公认,这块小伤痕,不但没有损害九儿的颜面,反而给她增加了几分美丽。

孩子们在风雨里、炮火里、饥饿和寒冷的煎熬里,战斗和胜利的兴奋里,完成了他们的童年,可珍贵的童年的历程。傅老刚在村里人缘很好,附近村庄的人们也都认识他。在逃难的时候,那些妇女们看到九儿,都自动地愿意带着她,跑到哪个村庄,人们一听说是铁匠的女孩子,也愿意收留吃饭和安排住宿。在战争的最后二年,因为年岁大些了,游击经验也丰富些了,九儿总是好和六儿一同走。六儿胆子很大,很机警,照顾九儿也很周到。当他们在一块儿的时候,在九儿那刚刚懂事的心里,除去有人作伴仗胆,感到幸福,还产生了一种相依相靠的感情。当她和六儿在一块的时候,也真的没有遇到什么大的危险。因此,她有时也真的相信六儿自我吹嘘的话了。

六儿常常对她说:

"你谁也不要跟着,就跟着我吧,日本鬼子不敢着我的边。"

"你净瞎说。"九儿跟在他身后边说。

him.

"Stick with me, and you'll never starve or go thirsty," Six would state cockily. "I can find food for you anywhere, like an old mother bird."

In Nine's eyes, Six was quite efficient. When it rained, he could always find shelter for her, even in the wilds. When she was hungry, he would go off on long treks, and always come back with something to eat. Many people were taking refuge out in the open then; they generally were willing to help children. But more important, when she was with Six, Nine felt a kind of gratitude and joy that could overcome both hunger and cold.

After the Japanese surrendered, Old Fu was eager to go back to his native village with his daughter. They hadn't been home in several years.

The evening before they departed, Old Li heated a pot of wine and gave Old Fu a farewell dinner. Ordinarily, the old blacksmith wasn't very talkative, even when he drank. On the other hand, words would gush from Old Li's mouth like water pouring through a break in a Yellow River dyke as soon as wine touched his lips. But this night the two old friends sat with a vegetable oil lamp and the pot of wine between them, drinking in silence. Not until it was nearly time to say goodbye did Old Li manage to force out a few commonplace phrases. Then he again lapsed into silence, his head down.

This was an unusual state for the carpenter. Old Fu asked him: "Is something troubling you, relative?"

"Yes, there is." Old Li suddenly grew animated. He had been

"你跟着我,饥不着也渴不着,"六儿自信地说,"我会像一只大老家(雀),给你打食儿吃。"

在九儿的眼里,六儿的办法就是多一些。下雨时候,他总是能很好地把九儿安置起来,就是在野地里,也淋不湿。在九儿觉饿的时候,他能跑出多远,找些吃的东西回来。那时候,在野外躲藏的人很多,人们是愿意帮助孩子们的。而更重要的是,九儿从心里发生的那一种感激和喜欢的心情,也确实能战胜一时的饥饿和寒冷。

日本投降以后,因为多年不回老家,老铁匠急于要带女儿回去看望一下。

临走的那天晚上,黎老东打了一壶酒,给傅老刚送行。平日,傅老刚即使在喝酒的时候,话也是很少的;黎老东酒一沾唇,那话就像黄河开了口子一样,滔滔不绝。可是今天晚上,俩个老朋友中间放上一盏菜油灯,一把酒壶,在快要分别的时候,黎老东只是勉强地说了几句普通话。以后,就也把头低下来,一直沉默着。

这是很稀奇的现象。傅老刚问:

"亲家,你心里有什么事?"

"有点事儿。"黎老东突然兴奋起来,他是单

英汉对照
English-Chinese
中国文学宝库
Gems of Chinese Literature
现代文学系列
Modern Literature

just waiting for his friend's question. "I want to request a favour of you, relative. You know I have six sons. We're so poor — there isn't anything I hope for myself. But my boy Six, believe me, he may amount to something."

"You've spoiled him a bit, relative," Old Fu interjected. "You can't be too soft with boys."

"It's this way." The carpenter refused to be diverted. "Let's not beat about the bush. Without being prejudiced, it seems to me that Nine and Six like each other pretty well. Of course, a pauper like me has no right to have a daughter-in-law, but, well, I can't help dreaming...."

He gulped down the remaining wine and again dropped his head.

"I know what you mean," said Old Fu. "You're poor, but am I any richer?"

"A man with a daughter naturally wants to find her a husband who's well off," Old Li mumbled.

"The kids are still young. Why not wait until Nine and I come again before we decide. What do you say?" With these cool words, Old Fu concluded a meeting that should have warmed both parties' hearts. Old Li's enthusiasm at once diminished by half.

That evening Nine went around saying goodbye to the local women and girls. All hated to see her go; they trooped along with her as she went from house to house. Six tailed her every step.

"What are you following her for, you silly boy?" the women scolded. "You're not hiding out in the hills anymore!"

"He's also come to say goodbye to Nine," explained some of the

等着老朋友这句问话的。"亲家,我想向你请求一件事。你看,我有六个儿子,穷得这样,我这一辈子也不打算什么了。不过六儿这孩子,我看还许有些出息。"

"亲家,"傅老刚插断他的话,"你就是娇惯了他一些。孩子们是要管得严紧些的。"

"是这样。"黎老东急于要把话说完,"咱也别绕圈子,据我冷眼观看,九儿和六儿,两个人的感情还合得来。按说,像我这个穷光蛋,还想支使儿媳妇?不过,咳!"

他一口把壶里的酒喝干了,就又低下头去。

"我明白你的意思了。"傅老刚说,"你穷,我就富吗?"

"不过,不过,养女儿总是要攀个高枝儿的。"黎老东低着头说。

"孩子们年纪还小。等我们从老家回来再定规,你说好不好?"傅老刚这样冷漠地结束了这场本来应该激动人心的交谈,使得老朋友的心冷了半截。

这一晚上,九儿在附近的姊子大娘家里辞行。姐妹们留恋她,在这家停一会儿,又一群一伙地到另一家去。六儿也一直跟在后面,就有姐妹们说他:

"你老是跟着干什么?一个小子家。这又不是打游击的时候了。"

"人家也是来送九儿哩。"有的姑娘说。

girls.

"Hurry home, Six, and go to bed," one of the older women scolded.

"I won't go to bed! I will follow her! What are you going to do about it?" Six muttered to himself.

Nine continued to chat and laugh with the others.

Early the next morning, Six and his father helped Nine and the blacksmith load the wheelbarrow. In shadows, Nine said to Six softly:

"We'll be coming back."

4

After Old Fu and Nine left, there was no news of them. It was said that the region where their village was situated was occupied by Kuomintang troops.

During the past two years, the War of Liberation had swept the plains. In its wake had come momentous changes. Old Li, as a poor peasant and the father of two boys in the people's army, received a good allotment of land in the land reform. Later, his second son was killed in battle, and the carpenter was given a death benefit. When Tianjin was liberated, his eldest son, who was in business there, sent home some of his earnings. The family's standard of living rose precipitously.

Li was quite miserable when he learned that his second son had been killed. The boy had endured nothing but hardships from the day he was born; he and his brother Four had begged on the streets

"快家去睡觉吧,六儿。"有的大娘斥责他。

"我就是跟着!"六儿有些气愤地在心里说,"我就是不去睡觉! 你们管得着吗?"

九儿一直和别人说笑着。

第二天,打早起,六儿跟着父亲,帮九儿家收拾小车。在黑影儿里,九儿小声对他说:

"我们还要回来的呀。"

4

傅老刚和九儿走了以后,就一直没有音讯。听说在他们家乡那一带,是蒋匪军盘踞着。这二年,平原上进行着解放战争,人们又经历了许多重大的事件。土地改革以后,黎老东因为是贫农,又是军属,分得了较多较好的地。后来,二儿子在解放战争里牺牲了,领到一笔抚恤粮。天津解放了,在那里做生意的大儿子又捎来一些现款,家里的生活,突然提高了很多。黎老东听到二儿子牺牲的消息以后,悲痛了一个时期。他想起这个老二从小没有得过一点儿好,母亲死了以后,还曾带着四兄弟讨要过一个时期的饭。

英汉对照
English-Chinese
中国文学宝库
Gems of Chinese Literature
现代文学系列
Modern Literature

for a time after their mother died.

Now the carpenter was nearing sixty. Only Six and Four were at his side. For some reason Li didn't like Four much, and lavished his affection on Six. Now that life was better, he wanted Six to have some of the pleasures which he and his other sons had lacked.

And so Six grew increasingly spoiled. Although quite big already, he was unwilling to work in the fields like Four. And he wouldn't even consider carrying manure or cleaning the pig pens. At the same time, he couldn't very well remain idle. So he took up a small trade. After autumn, he roasted shelled peanuts and sold them. In the winter evenings, he hawked hot beancurd on the street corner, banging a bamboo segment to attract attention. What he couldn't sell, he ate himself. Every night, when his father was already in bed, Six would come home with a large bowl of hot beancurd spiced profusely with garlic and ginger, and place it down beside the old man's head, saying:

"Eat, Pa, it's nice and hot."

Old Li would sit up and eat the beancurd. "How understanding the boy is," he would think to himself. "What a filial son!"

Sometimes, Six would bring a bowl to his brother Four who was giving the animals their nightly feed. Four had learned frugality as a child. He never would accept.

"Sell it," he would say. "It will be that much more money earned. I'm going to bed now anyway. What's the point of eating?"

And Six would think: "This fellow doesn't appreciate good treat-

现在,黎老东是将近六十岁的人了,身边只有四儿和六儿。但是,不知道为了什么,黎老东不大喜爱四儿,只喜爱六儿。老人的心里想:自己受了一辈子苦,没有过出头之日,几个大孩子,小的时候也没有赶上好年月,现在既然生活好了,应该叫六儿多享些福。

这样,六儿就越发娇惯起来了。他已经长大成人,他不愿意像四哥一样到地里去做活,起猪圈送粪这些事,他连边也不愿沾。可是,也不好净闲着,他就学做些小买卖。秋后,搓大花生仁儿,炒了到街上卖;冬天煮老豆腐,晚上在大街十字路口敲着梆子。卖不完的,就自己吃。每天夜里,父亲已经钻被窝了,他盛上一大碗老豆腐,多加蒜、姜,送到老人脑袋头起说:

"爹,吃了吧,热的。"

老人爬起来,喝完老豆腐,心里想,这孩子多懂事儿,多孝顺呀!

有时,六儿也盛上一碗送给在夜里喂着牲口的四哥,老四是从小知道省细的,总是不愿意吃。他对六儿说:

"多卖一碗,就多赚一碗,我这就要睡觉了,喝一碗这个有什么用?"

这使得六儿有时想:这个人真不知好歹哩。

ment."

But whether he peddled peanuts or beancurd, Six was never able to earn any money. He had many friends. This one would grab a handful, that one would help himself to a bowl. Even when he kept a record, Six couldn't make himself go around and demand payment. At the end of the year, Four had to collect the bills for him.

The girls were the worst. Whenever they saw Six on the street, they would gather around and ask: "Are your peanuts crisp? Are they tasty?"

"Just try them!" Six would say with a laugh, quickly opening his cloth bag.

There was no charge for "trying," and the girls were many. Not only did each take a handful; Six generously helped them stuff their pockets, which were deep although their openings were small.

Of medium build, with very fair skin and an affable disposition, Six was a great favourite among the girls. He was not unaware of this, and he took pains to consolidate and strengthen the good impression he was making. After the war, he was the first man in the village to comb his hair long, with a part. Scorning the regular itinerant head shaver, on county fair days he would hurry to the county seat and have his hair done in a "modern" barber's shop. He was also the only one in the village to use a flashlight at night. He played its beam all over the street. Laughing, the girls would surround him and say:

"Six, are you trying to blind me!"

但是,不管卖花生仁儿,还是卖老豆腐,六儿总是赚不下钱。在街面上,他的朋友多,这个抓一把,那个喝一碗,就是记上账,六儿也拉不下脸皮儿去要,到年底,还是得老四去讨账。特别是那些姑娘们,看见六儿提着花生仁儿来了,就说:

"你这花生仁儿脆不脆?香不香?"

"你们尝尝呀!"六儿赶忙张开布袋口儿笑着说。

"尝"是不要钱的,可是姑娘们很多,又都下得手,一个人一大把不算,六儿还自己抓着送到她们手里,替她们装进那口儿虽小底儿却深的衣裳口袋里去。

六儿长得个儿适中,脸皮儿很白,脾气儿又好,他在街上成了姑娘们十分喜欢的对象。六儿已经能够自觉到这一点,他就更加注意去巩固和扩大这个良好的影响。战争结束以后,在这个村里,他第一个留起大分头,还不叫担挑的剃头匠理发,总是在集日跑到城南关的理发店去。夜晚,村里只有他有一筒手电,在街上一晃一晃的,姑娘们嘻笑着围着他:

"看你,六儿,照坏了我的眼!"

英汉对照
English-Chinese
中国文学宝库
Gems of Chinese Literature
现代文学系列
Modern Literature

"Six, let me have it a while!"

For rainy weather, he had a pair of shiny rubber halfboots. He would put these on and go calling, being especially courteous to those families possessing pretty daughters and flooded courtyards. When, peering through the window, a fair maiden would see him entering the yard she would hurry to the door to greet him.

"Six, you've come exactly at the right time. Take them off and lend them to me. I want to go out to the latrine!"

"They're just your size," Six would say, pulling off the boots and handing them to her. "You ought to buy a pair."

"Where would I get enough money?" the girl would laugh. "The next time you go into town, buy me a pair of stockings, will you?"

"What colour?"

"You decide. You're always buying things. You've got good taste." Thus expressing her confidence in him, the girl would reach into her pocket. "Here's some money."

"Not now. Wait until I've bought them."

But when he would later appear with the stockings, although the girl would praise the quality, and approve the size, the subject of money somehow wouldn't come up again.

5

Old Li was too involved in his new business to be concerned about his son's shortcomings. He had recently traded his old grey donkey for a roan horse. Although the horse was also a bit on the elderly side, its legs and colour were good. The animal was much

"来,六儿,给我拿拿!"

在雨天,他有一双双钱牌胶鞋,故意穿上去串门儿,谁家的姑娘好看,谁家庭院里积的雨水深,他就特别到谁家去。那家的姑娘在窗户眼儿里看见他进来,就赶紧爬下炕来说:

"六儿,你来得正好,脱下来给我穿穿,我正要到茅房里去!"

"你穿着正合适。"六儿说,一边脱下胶鞋来递给她,"你也该买一双。"

"我哪里有这些钱呀?"姑娘笑着说,"六儿,你什么时候再进城,给我捎一双袜子来吧!"

"什么色儿的?"六儿问。

"你看着吧,你常买东西,又懂眼。"姑娘信任地说,在腰里掏摸着,"你带着钱吧!"

"不用。"六儿说,"买回来,再说吧。"

等到买回来,姑娘们只称赞他买得货色好,尺寸合适,就再也不提钱的事了。

5

黎老东目前也顾不上管教他,老人正在为新兴的家业操心。新近他把那匹老灰驴换成了一匹红马。这匹马虽然口齿老一些,但蹄腿毛

too handsome, in fact, for the dilapidated cart which had been allotted to Li during the land reform. After shopping around, Li brought home some logs of elm and locust. He had decided to build himself a big new cart.

The carpenter's skill at cart-making was famed near and far. He had built innumerable carts for others, in his time. Now he was old. He would build a fine one to leave to his sons. The idea made Old Li very happy. In his search for proper lumber, he had come across a sandalwood sapling. Carpenters love this kind of tree best of all. He planted it outside his bedroom window and tended it carefully. It would be the symbol of the new life he was starting. He also raised a flock of chickens in the yard and bought two new piglets for the pig pen.

He told Four to help him saw the logs into boards. In the courtyard, the first log was propped up at one end so that it pointed into the sky like an anti-aircraft gun. The old man stood on the raised end, while Four sat on the ground, and both worked a two-man saw back and forth along a black line. Old Li kept complaining that Four was "stupid." He wasn't holding the saw to the line, he wasn't pushing it correctly.... Four proposed that Six take his place. The old man wouldn't agree. Four said he was playing favourites. Father and son wrangled loudly. The carpenter picked up an axe and chased Four all around the yard.

What Four hated worst was for anyone to say he was stupid. Ever since the War of Resistance against Japan he had been studying hard, reading books and newspapers every day, going to school every night and taking an active part in the village youth work. He

色都很好,架上那辆分来的破车,实在显得不调和。老人四处去观看,买回几棵榆树槐树,想自己打一辆大车。黎老东打的大车是远近知名的,一辈子给人家打了无数的车,现在年老了,也给孩子们打一辆吧,他的心情是十分愉快的。在转游着买树的时候,他还得到一棵小檀木树的秧子,做木匠的最喜爱这种树,他把它栽到自己的窗台下,小心养护着,作为自己新的生活开始的标志。院里养了一群鸡,猪圈里新买来两个猪崽儿。

他叫老四和他解树,在院子里,被解的树木斜竖起来,像一架高射炮。老人登在上面,俯身向下,老四坐在地下,仰身向上,按着墨线拉那大锯,一推一送。老人总是埋怨老四笨,不是说他走了线,就是说他不会送锯。老四建议叫六儿来拉锯,老人又不肯。老四说他有偏心,父子两个争吵起来,老人甚至举起锛斧,绕院子追赶。

老四最不喜欢人家说他笨。他从抗日战争以来,学习很努力,每天看书看报上夜校,积极参加村里的青年工作,他觉得在家庭里,他比父

英汉对照
English-Chinese
中国文学宝库
Gems of Chinese Literature
现代文学系列
Modern Literature

felt that he was more progressive than his father or Six, that he understood things much better.

Feeling lonely in the silence that followed the quarrel, the old man began to reminisce.

"When I was your age," he said to Four, "I was already a full-fledged craftsman, and not only in our county. Even in the northeast, in Harbin no one could match me.

"Those partitions in the main hall of the big moneylending shop in the south part of town — I made them. In the old days the big medicinal herbs merchants from Yunnan and Guangxi always came to the county merchandise fairs we held every tenth lunar month. They all admired the carvings I made on those partitions," Old Li recalled happily. "The Pu family ran the moneylending shop. The old gentleman and I got along fine."

"Wasn't that the family exposed by the Poor Peasants' Association as tyrant landlords? You'd better not talk that way about them outside our home. People will say you were in league with them."

"I also built a fine carriage for the Cui family. The old madame never allowed anyone except herself to ride in it."

"Another big landlord family. That carriage was given over to the poor peasants long ago. They carry manure to the fields in it, now."

The old man pushed the saw so hard he nearly knocked Four down on his back.

When the carpentry work on the big cart was nearing completion, Old Li thought frequently of his friend Old Fu. Iron fittings had to be forged before the cart could be assembled. Of course

亲和六儿都进步得多,懂事得多。

吵过架,老人又不甘寂寞,说:

"我像你这个年纪,早就出师了。我的手艺,不用说在这一县,就是在关外,在哈尔滨,那里有日本木匠,也有俄国木匠,我也没叫人比下去过。'哈拉索',有钱的苏联人总是这样对我说。"

"那时他们不是苏联人,那时他们是白俄。"老四说。

"县城南关福聚东银号的大客厅的隔扇,是我做的。那些年,每逢十月庙会,远从云南广西来的大药商,也特别称赞那花儿刻得好。"老人越说越高兴,"这字号是卜家的买卖,老东家和我很合适。"

"卜家不是叫贫农团斗倒了吗?"老四说,"你这话只能在家里说,在外边说,人家会说你和地主有拉拢。"

"南关西后街崔家的轿车,也是我打的。"老人说,"那车只有老太太出门才肯用。"

"那也是大地主。"老四说,"那辆车早分给贫农,装大粪用了。"

老人把锯用力往下一送,差一点没把老四顶个后仰。

大车的木工程序越是接近完成的时候,黎老东越是怀念他那老朋友傅老刚,因为还要有段铁工程序,大车才能制造成功。附近当然也

英汉对照
English-Chinese
中国文学宝库
Gems of Chinese Literature
现代文学系列
Modern Literature

there were other blacksmiths in the vicinity, but none of them suited Old Li. He had often built carts together with Old Fu in the past, and when one of these vehicles rolled smoothly down the road, people easily recognized the fine craftsmanship of Li the carpenter and Fu the blacksmith. Li wished very much that his old friend could help him construct this cart. It would be a representative work of their years of co-operation, a symbol of their everlasting friendship. Today, the Li family no longer had to worry about food. Old Li wanted to send a letter to the blacksmith, inviting him and his daughter. The children had reached marriageable age. In his present economic status, Li could propose their marriage with complete confidence.

But people said they were still fighting down in Fu's part of the country. It was difficult to deliver mail.

The question of marriage naturally led Li to think of the housing problem. The run-down old compound in which he now lived had been confirmed as his property by the village authorities. But if his sons should marry, there would not be enough space for them. At a time like this, he wouldn't feel right as a father unless he could prepare a place for them to live. The summer and autumn harvests had both been good that year. With his surplus grain, he could buy another compound. Originally he had been considering buying more land, but people had advised him against it. Land wasn't dependable any more, they said, but houses would remain your personal property no matter how society changed. So Old Li decided to buy a compound.

Four suggested that they discuss the matter with the brother in

有其他的铁匠,但是这些人的手艺,都不中黎老东的意。过去,他是常常和傅老刚合打一辆大车的。而他们合打的大车,据说一上道,格登格登一响,人们离很远,就能判断出这是黎老东砍的轴,挑的键,傅老刚挂的车瓦。他很希望老朋友能来帮他把这一辆车成全好,成为他们多年合作中的代表作品,象征他们终身不变的深厚友谊。现在家里又有吃有喝,他想给傅老刚捎上个信儿,叫他带女儿来。孩子们的年岁也到了,凭眼下这日子光景,再求婚也就理直气壮了。

可是,听说那边还在打仗,信儿也不好捎。

想起儿女的婚姻,黎老东就想起住宅的问题,现在住的这个破院,虽说村里已经固定给他,要是儿子们结婚,还是很不够住的。当父亲的赶上这个年月,还不能替孩子们安排下几间住处,也感觉于心有愧似的。今年一个麦季,一个秋季,收成都很好。他想把粮食合起来,换处宅院。原先,他是想多买几亩田地的,听人说,这年头田地总不牢靠,宅院到什么社会,终归是自己的,他就下了决心买宅子。

关于买宅子,老四提议要和军队上的哥哥

英汉对照
English-Chinese
中国文学宝库
Gems of Chinese Literature
现代文学系列
Modern Literature

the army, but the carpenter disagreed. "It's no use," the old man said. "He's a revolutionary cadre. He wouldn't approve of the family acquiring too much private property."

Li directed a local middleman to find him a house. The man soon returned with a report that a widow had a place for sale. The compound contained a three-room building, facing south, with walls of earthen brick and plastered on the outside. Its wooden frame, doors and windows were all quite sturdy. The courtyard was very large; Old Li could add an east and west wing. Now the only other structure was a large entrance way. It was cheap too — only ten piculs of wheat. What's more, it was quite near Old Li's present home. He could easily go from one place to the other.

Old Li wanted the place very much, but when he went to close the deal he discovered that the widow had a condition: She would sell now, but the new owner couldn't move in until she died. The carpenter hesitated. Who knew how many more years she would last? She looked quite healthy.

But not long after, the middleman came with a report that the widow's nephew wanted the compound and was willing to give twelve piculs. Old Li got worried; he rushed over and paid the widow a deposit. The nephew raised a terrific row, but the village authorities stepped in and mediated. They allowed Old Li to buy the property.

With the purchase of the compound his troubles increased. Every few days he went over to inspect the place. Neighbours' chickens had got in; he shooed them out. Children had knocked down the compound wall; he set it up again. Plaster had peeled off the

商量一下,黎老东说:"不用。他是革命干部,不同意我们置家业过活。"

他托了村里的说合人,替他物色宅院。很快,说合人就来告诉他,后街二寡妇那宅子要卖。这所宅子包括三间土坯抹灰北房,木架门窗都还很坚固,院子很大,以后可以盖三合房,现在就有一个大梢门洞儿。价钱不贵,十石麦子。另外,这所宅院距离黎老东现在住的地方很近,以后来往也方便。

黎老东想了想,很中意这宅子,就要下定钱。但是老寡妇有一个附带条件,要卖"养老腾宅",就是说要等她死了,新主人才能搬进来。对于这一点,黎老东有些犹豫,谁知道老寡妇哪年死哩,看来她还很健康。不久,说合人又来说,老寡妇有个侄儿要争这宅院,出十二石麦。黎老东一听着了急,下了定钱,还和老寡妇那个侄儿闹了一场纠纷,经过村里调解,黎老东是军烈属,才得买到了手。

买了宅子,黎老东操心的事情叫就多了。他隔几天就要到那宅子里转转,看见院子里跑着一群别人家的鸡,他就轰出去,看见墙头又叫孩子们登倒了,他就垒起来,看见房墙上的泥皮

side of the house; he repaired that too. He had to watch every inch of the compound. The old widow lay wheezing on the brick bed all day, not bothering about a thing.

That winter, the carpenter wanted to move Four into one of the empty rooms and keep the horse and trough in an outer shed. He asked the widow's permission, but she absolutely refused. She said the horse would drop its manure into her rice pot. The widow and Li had a violent quarrel. In a fit of rage, the widow packed her things, moved out and went to live with her daughter. Rumour had it that Li had forced her to go, and this made a nasty impression in the village. Somehow the son in the army got word of it. He wrote a letter criticizing the old man.

Old Li felt badly about the matter for several days. He thought he had bought himself a packet of trouble. But since the place was his, why not move in? He chose an auspicious day and, together with his two sons, took occupancy of their new home. The neighbours insisted that he serve drinks by way of celebration; he had no choice but to comply.

That night, Six returned very late. The old man was still awake, waiting for him.

"Why did I buy this cursed place, if not for you?" Li grumbled.

"It's awfully cold here," Six said in a muffled voice, his head beneath the quilts.

"You ought to behave better," Li admonished him, "instead of running around all day." But Six was already asleep. His gentle rhythmic snores warmed Li's heart. For what could make an old man happier than to have his young son sleeping sweetly by his

掉了,就和泥抹上。他关心宅院的每一个细小部分,而老寡妇好像什么也不管,在东间屋里炕上喘嗽着。

　　冬天,黎老东想叫老四到这北屋西间来住,捎带喂牲口,马槽就安在外间。他和老寡妇商量,老寡妇不同意,说马会把粪拉到她做饭的锅里。因为这个争吵起来,老寡妇一生气,收拾东西,到女儿家住去了,声言是黎老东把她逼走,在村里影响很不好。在军队里的儿子,不知怎么也知道了,来信批评了父亲。

　　黎老东为这件事也懊悔了好几天,觉得是找了麻烦。但是既然买了,就搬来住吧,选择了一个日子,他和六儿四儿搬进了这一所新居。人们还要他请酒,他也只好应酬了一下。

　　夜里,六儿很晚才回来,黎老东一直没睡着,在等着他。

　　"我为什么买这个冤孽?"黎老东说,"不就是为了你?"

　　"嗯。"六儿把头蒙在被窝里,"新房子怎么这样冷呀?"

　　"你要学点好。"黎老东又规诫着,"不要整天瞎跑。"

　　而六儿已经呼呼入睡了,鼾声是那样匀称和舒心,老人是喜爱听这种声音的,年老的人,身边有个小儿子甜蜜地睡着,是会感到幸福的。

英汉对照
English-Chinese
中国文学宝库
Gems of Chinese Literature
现代文学系列
Modern Literature

side?

6

That winter Six and a family of ne'er-do-wells formed a partnership to sell beef dumplings. Every evening, carrying a small wooden container on his back, Six hawked dumplings on the main street.

"Beef dumplings! Hot beef dumplings!"

Until late at night.

The dumplings were made at the west end of the village in the home of Stupid Li. Stupid's wife came from a family whose house had always been a popular hangout for fancy ladies and gamblers. Ugly, with a right foot that twisted inward, she had a darkly spotted face. On the lid of her left eye, which had been blind since her childhood, a large wart sprouted. In spite of several years of the new society she still retained her spoiled self-indulgent habits. A greedy eater, she could think up the most amazing devices to satisfy her rapacious appetite.

Stupid always had to make sure she approved before he ventured to do anything. After the war of resistance ended, the couple received shares of property confiscated from local tyrants during various campaigns, but they squandered it all. They sold the land and the coarse grain that had been given them and bought wheat. This they converted into noodles which they peddled on the street. But before long, they ate their way through both capital and profits.

In the dumpling venture with Six, Stupid's wife was unwilling to

6

这一年冬天,六儿和村里的一家懒人,合伙卖牛肉包子,每天晚上,他背着一个小木柜子,在大街上来回游逛。

"牛肉包儿呀!好热的牛肉包儿呀!"

一直到深夜。

包子房设在村西头黎大傻家。黎大傻的老婆,原是县城东关一户包娼窝赌不务正业的人家的长女。这女人长得既丑且怪,右脚往里勾着,黑麻脸,左眼从小瞎了,有一大块萝卜花向外冒突着。她的性情很是刁泼,在新社会里,也长期改造不好,又非常好吃,为了满足她那馋嘴,她会想出一些奇奇怪怪别人绝想不到的办法。

黎大傻行什么事,也是要看着女人的眼色,听着女人的鼻息的。抗日战争以后,经过几次社会运动,他们每次都把分得的一些东西泼撒了。过程是:把分得的土地和一些粗粮变卖了,换回麦子卖面条儿,结果,一家人把本儿利儿全吃进肚里去。

今年和六儿卖包子,就是和面擀皮儿这些

英汉对照
English-Chinese
中国文学宝库
Gems of Chinese Literature
现代文学系列
Modern Literature

perform even the trifling task of making and rolling the dough. She brought her younger sister from her old home, ostensibly to help her. But what her real purpose was, anybody could guess.

The girl bore no resemblance to her whatsoever. People said she had been adopted from another family, that they weren't born of the same mother.

Nineteen, the girl's name was Man'er, and she was already married. Her husband worked away from home for long periods. Man'er grew better-looking year by year. When she walked she was like a flower on display. Everyone in the neighbourhood knew her. She was the cynosure of all eyes.

When she first arrived at her sister's home, Man'er seemed very quiet. She rarely left the house. Every day, when her sister went gadding about, Man'er sat cross-legged on the heated brick platform, preparing the dumplings, seldom even raising her head. Stupid Li moved busily back and forth, picking up the dumplings, putting them into the steam hampers, while tending as well to the stove and the steamer. Six had nothing to do. He sat on a stool beside the brick platform, smoking and staring at Man'er.

At dusk one day when Stupid's wife returned, the girl asked what she should make for dinner. As usual, the older woman replied decisively:

"Why should you make anything? We've got meat dumplings! Just heat up a little gruel."

"Is Six going home to eat, or will he dine with us?"

"What a question!" Stupid's wife laughed. "He's our employer. We've got to treat him right!"

极为轻微的工作,黎大傻的老婆也是不愿意担负的,她不久就从娘家接了一个妹妹来,名义上是帮忙做活,她的实际目的在哪里,谁也猜得着。

这位妹妹,外表和姐姐长得非常不同,人们传说,这孩子原是那些年,从别人家领来的,和她的姐姐,并非一母所生。

她今年十九岁了,小名叫满儿。已经结了婚,丈夫长年在外面。小满儿一年比一年出脱得好看,走动起来,真像招展的花枝,满城关没有一个人不认识她,大家公认她是这一带地方的人尖儿。

刚到姐姐家来,小满儿表现得很安静。她不常出门儿,每天,姐姐出去串门儿,她就盘腿卧脚地坐在炕上剁馅儿,包包子,连头也不轻易抬起。黎大傻在地下来往,装着笼屉,兼在灶上烧火。六儿没事做,放一条板凳在炕沿儿下面,呆呆地望着她抽香烟。等到天黑,姐姐回来,小满儿问做什么吃,姐姐照例是说得很干脆的:"还做什么吃?熬点米汤儿,就包子吃!"

"六儿不用回家,就在一块儿吃吧?"小满儿问。

"那还用你说吗?"姐姐笑着,"人家是咱们的大东家哩,要好好照应!"

英汉对照
English-Chinese
中国文学宝库
Gems of Chinese Literature
现代文学系列
Modern Literature

Six hung around Stupid's house day and night.

Gradually, Man'er grew restless. She began standing at the door. It's hard to say how word got around, but after Man'er moved in with her sister, pedlars of cosmetics and fragrant soaps started flocking to the village, and they all hawked their wares directly in front of her compound gate. If Man'er didn't appear immediately, they twirled their little rattle drums, luring her out with noisy provocative rhythms.

Then, on the pretext of using the village grist mill, Man'er took to walking down the main street.

The little village was thrown into a turmoil whenever she did so. Long before it was her turn to use the mill — she had only to put her small broom down to indicate her place in line and then go home — young men would start gathering in the vicinity. The crowd would keep growing larger and larger, much to the puzzlement of whoever happened to be grinding meal.

Then, when the roller was unoccupied, some young fellow would notify Man'er. After a few minutes, she would round the corner of her lane, the eyes of every young man present swinging with her. There was a variety of expressions in those eyes. Some were bolder, some were more timid, but all flickered ardently, like dancing tongues of flame.

Holding a large flat basket on her head with one hand, Man'er would approach, innocently oblivious of the stares. Her new fashionably cut tunic of flowered cloth, when blown open by the breeze, revealed a lining of fresh rose. The bell-like cuffs of her heavy padded trousers slid against each other in cadence with her

现在,六儿就黑夜白日地在这一家鬼混。

渐渐,小满儿就不能安静地坐在炕上了。她每天要抽空儿到门口儿站一站。自从她搬到姐姐家,不知道是谁传播的消息,那些卖胭脂粉儿香胰子的小贩,也都跟踪到这村里来了。他们像上市一样,常常把三副几副的担子放在她姐姐家的门口,如果小满儿还没有出来,他们就用力摇动那小货郎鼓儿,用繁乱的、挑逗的节奏把她招引出来。

以后,小满儿又借口占碾子借磨,到大街上去。

每逢小满儿到街上来推碾,就会在这小小的村庄里引起一场动乱。当她还没有得到推碾的机会,只是放下一把笤帚在碾子旁边占着,自己一径回家去了,就有一些青年人趁到碾子附近来了,青年人越聚越多,常常使得那正在推碾的人家,感到非常的奇怪。

后来,碾子空下了,就有青年自动去给她报信。过了一会儿,小满儿从她姐姐家的胡同里转出来,青年们的眼睛就一齐转向她那里。青年们的眼神是多种多样的,有的勇迈些,有的怯弱些,然而都被内心的热情和狂想激动着,就像无数的接连爆发的一片火焰。

小满儿头上顶着一个大笸箩,一只手伸上去扶住边缘,旁若无人地向这里走来。她的新做的时兴的花袄,被风吹折起前襟,露出鲜红的里儿;她的肥大的像两口大钟似的棉裤角,有节

英汉对照
English-Chinese
中国文学宝库
Gems of Chinese Literature
现代文学系列
Modern Literature

191

walk. Her embroidered cloth shoes trod the ground in neat even steps, so lightly that they seemed incapable of leaving any print.

Man'er's unoccupied hand, swinging back and forth like a dancer's, was smooth and tender. Her face was slightly flushed, and she kept her glistening red lips closed so as not to reveal any exertion in breathing. The top button of her tunic was opened at the neck.

Coming down the long street, she was like a victorious general reviewing his troops. Some of the young men would fall back a few paces. Others would mount the incline at the base of a compound wall to get a better look at her beauty.

One day when she arrived at the grist mill, Man'er put her large basket on the floor and smoothed the glossy black hair which hung down to her shoulders. Then she swept a look over her audience.

Man'er had come to grind rice. She spread the grain on the flat stone base and waited for her sister. But evidently something had delayed her. After waiting for some time, Man'er began to push the heavy roller alone.

She was sure that someone would help her. But today, although the young men watching grimaced and nudged each other, no one had the courage to step forward.

Trudging around the circular mill stone, each time she came to the street side of the shed Man'er looked towards the west end of the village, hoping to see Six. He was more understanding than these louts. He certainly would hasten to give her a hand.

But Six apparently had forgotten their appointment. There was no sign of him. Man'er was exhausted, but she didn't want to show

奏地相互摩擦着。她的绣花鞋,平整地在地下迈动,像留不下脚印似的那样轻松。

她那空着的一只手,扮演舞蹈似地前后摆动着,柔嫩得像粉面儿捏成。她的脸微微红涨,为了不显出气喘,她把两片红润的嘴唇紧闭着,把脖子里的纽扣儿也预先解开了。

她通过这条长长的大街,就像一位凯旋的将军,正在通过需要他检阅的部队。青年们,有的后退了几步,有的上到墙根高坡上,去瞻仰她的丰姿。

小满儿来到石碾旁边,一转身,把大笸箩放在了地下。然后,她掠了掠齐肩的油黑的头发,向青年们扫射了一眼。

她是来碾米。她把谷子铺在碾盘上,等候着她的姐姐。她姐姐叫什么事耽搁住了,一直没有来,她就一个人推动了石碾。

她心里明白,不会没有人来帮她的忙。但是今天,青年们都在观望着,做着各种丑态,甚至互相推挤,却谁也没有勇气上前。

每当小满儿推着碾子转到街道旁边,她就转身向村西头望望,看看六儿来了没有。她很希望六儿在这个时候来,他比这些屠头们懂事,会跑着过来帮她的忙。

可是,六儿也好像忘记了和她约好的这回事儿似的,一直没影儿。她实在推不动了,又不

英汉对照
English-Chinese
中国文学宝库
Gems of Chinese Literature
现代文学系列
Modern Literature

weakness in front of these young people. Pretending that she had finished, she halted and swept the grain together, then picked up her winnowing basket.

"I'm afraid that's still too coarse," the young man standing in the front ranks said. His name was Big Fellow.

In spite of his size, Big Fellow was extremely timid. But he could bear the silence no longer. He felt so sorry for Man'er that he screwed up his courage and took over for her at the roller. This remarkable action so astonished his mates, they even forgot to tease him, as was their custom. Suddenly, from the end of the street there came a cry, one of those terrifying screeches which women alone at home utter when they are awakened from their dreams in the middle of a winter's night by a weasel getting at their hens.

It was Big Fellow's wife. He had been only a child when they married; she was eight years older than he, and she had suffered through a long period. From the time he reached the age of understanding, she had loved him, and the more she loved him, the more strictly she treated him. Big Fellow was afraid of her, the way he feared his elder sister, or his mother. For many years not only had she looked after his wants, she had even taught him how to speak and behave. But he had never thought her finding him in a chance encounter with another woman would evoke such a storm of rage. He stood holding the handle of the roller, gazing at his wife in stupefaction.

She charged up to him. "You shameless creature! It's almost time for me to cook supper and you still haven't fetched me any

愿意在这些青年人面前示弱,她装做碾得了头合,突地停下来往回折扫着,转身抓起了簸箕。

"怕还不行吧!"这时站在最前边的一个青年叫大壮的,开了口。

这个名叫大壮而实际上非常胆小的青年,是耐不过这种沉寂的场面,又实在心疼对方,才鼓足勇气去抓起了那根闲着的推碾棍。他这种异乎寻常的举动,使得全体青年吃了一惊,连平日向他开玩笑的习惯都忘记了。但是,忽然从街东头传来一声喊叫,这一声喊叫,就像在冬天的夜晚,有黄鼬来拉鸡,孤处的女主人从梦中惊醒,喊叫出来的那种声音一样凌厉吓人。

这是大壮的媳妇。大壮早婚,她比丈夫足足大八岁。她熬过很长的一段岁月,自从大壮渐渐懂得事理,她就越发爱他,并且越发管教得严格了。大壮平日很怕她,他怕她就像怕自己的姐姐,甚至像怕自己的母亲一样。因为,在多年的印象里,她不只照顾了他的饮食起居,而且也教导着他的言语行动。但是大壮从来也没想到,在他偶尔同别的女人在一起的时候,会引起自己的女人这样大的愤怒。他扶着碾棍,呆呆地望着自己的女人。

"你这个不要脸的东西!"大壮的女人急急走过来说,"快做晚饭了,你不去担水,跑到这里

英汉对照
English-Chinese
中国文学宝库
Gems of Chinese Literature
现代文学系列
Modern Literature

water. What are you doing here?"

"What?" Confronted by his wife's full fury he didn't know what to say in the presence of so many onlookers.

"Are you dumb, or only deaf?" Her voice grew sharper. "I asked what you're doing here. You're almost eighteen. It's time you learned how to behave!"

"Excuse him this time, he's still only a child!" the young men hooted.

"A child is he?" Big Fellow's wife hated nothing more than for people to refer to her husband's youth. "Then what do you call a man? And are you children too? No pants-wetting kid would ever act in such a disgusting manner! You're a pack of dogs! A little bitch trots down the street with her tail between her legs and you all swarm after her! You've been staring at her till you're glassy-eyed and stiff in the neck. I've been watching you for a long time — I've seen your wanton airs! Do you know what you look like? Get some water from the well and take a good look at your reflection!"

This indiscriminate attack aroused great dissatisfaction among the young men, but none of them wanted to clash with her. With their eyes, with coughs, they encouraged Big Fellow, hoping he would pull the large wooden handle out of the stone roller. But Big Fellow showed not the faintest sign of resistance. He even retreated a few paces, and seemed about to go home.

The young men watched Man'er as she winnowed the rice, her face scarlet. She was known for not being easily put upon, even by men. But today, under these circumstances, she hung her head in

来干什么?"

"唔?"在众人面前,在女人的盛怒之下,大壮不知道怎样回答才好。

"你是哑巴,是聋子?"大壮女人的声音更严厉了,"我问你跑到这里来干什么?你年下就十八岁了,不学正经!"

"他还小哩,原谅他这一次吧!"青年们在一边打哈哈。

"他还小?"大壮的女人最不喜欢别人说她的丈夫年纪小,"什么才叫大人?你们小吗?吃屎的孩子,也干不出这样没出息的事儿来!你们是一群狗,有一只小母狗儿,在街上夹着尾巴一遛跶,就把你们都引出来了!就把你们的脖子勾引得硬了,就把你们的眼睛勾引得直了!我在那边瞧了老半天,看看你们那下流样子!你们自己不觉?快到井台上,弄点儿水来照照吧!"

她这种不分敌友、一律混杂的教训,引起了青年们的极度不满,但是没有人愿意在这个时候和她冲突。他们用眼睛、用咳嗽鼓励大壮,很希望大壮就手抽出那根大推碾棍来。但是大壮连丝毫反抗的意思也没有,他甚至移动脚步,要想回家去了。

青年们注视着小满儿,小满儿簸着米糠,脸涨的像块红布。这女孩子,过去在多少男人面前,也是号称难惹的,但是今天遇到这样的场面,她低着头,连一句话也没讲。

silence.

Battles don't remain at a standstill for long. Man'er's sister had already appeared at the west end of the street. She tore forward as if rushing to put out a fire. Because she was fat and had a twisted leg, and particularly because her vision was faulty, she ran like a soccer player jockeying a ball down the field — now bending forward at the waist, now flopping arms akimbo, now right and left foot mincing one over the other, now tripping and staggering across the ground. "Who are you calling a little bitch?" she bellowed challengingly at Big Fellow's wife, while still ten paces away.

"Whoever the shoe fits, let her wear it!" the other woman retorted, straightening up.

"My sister is pure," cried Stupid's wife. "Her backside is cleaner than your face! You just tend to your little husband. Nobody can insult my sister and get away with it!" She dashed over to the roller to pull out the wooden handle, but Man'er prevented her.

"When did you turn into such a softy?" she berated Man'er. "Do you want me to lose face completely?"

Dragging out the handle, she ran full tilt at Big Fellow's wife. The latter calmly grasped the end of the handle and jerked it sharply towards herself.

Stupid's wife fell flat on her face.

7

It was at this moment that Old Fu and his daughter, who had

斗争总是要展开的,她的姐姐已经在西街口那里出现。她之奔赴这里来,就像抢救水火一样迫切。因为肥胖,因为她的一只脚有点毛病,特别因为她的视力不能集中,她那奔跑的姿式,就像足球场上,带着球奋勇突击的前锋一样:一时曲偻着上身,一时弯架着胳膊,一时左右脚交攀着,一时在地下滚动着。

"你说谁是小母狗?"她离大壮的女人还有十码远,就发出了战斗的檄文。

"谁自认,我就说的是谁!"大壮的女人挺着身子说。

"我的妹妹是黄花少女!"黎大傻的女人说,"她的屁股也比你的脸干净!你管教你的小女婿行,欺侮我的亲戚就办不到!"

她跑到石碾那里抽出一根棍,但是叫小满儿给拦住了。"你怎么变得这样老好子?"她吆喝着妹妹,"叫你把我的人都丢净了!"

她举着大棍,奔向大壮媳妇,大壮媳妇以逸待劳,接住棍头,往怀里一带,黎大傻的老婆就来了个嘴啃地。

7

就在这个时候,久别的傅老刚父女,回到了

The Blacksmith and the Carpenter

been away so long, returned to the village.

As usual Old Fu was pushing his barrow with its portable blacksmith's furnace. Up front, pulling, was his daughter Nine.

The blacksmith looked older and thinner. The barrow was quite dilapidated now; its creaks had lost their previous smartness. Nine was taller, but her clothes were very tattered. Her face was quite drawn, dust coated her hair, her shoes were open at the toe. Only the joy shining in her eyes revealed how happy she was to return.

At the street corner, Old Fu set the barrow down and greeted everyone. Nine pulled the towel from around her neck and mopped her perspiring face.

"We're here again," said the blacksmith. "But why are you quarrelling?"

"No particular reason," the young men replied. "These two woman comrades have eaten their fill and have nothing better to do. So they're practising acrobatics."

"You mustn't do that," Old Fu said seriously. "This village has always been in a liberated area. You're living in paradise. You should have seen our place. Life was terrible under the Kuomintang occupation. When Nine and I went back, we fell into the net. Luckily, we lived through it."

"How is production down there now?" the young men asked.

"Just getting back to normal. But we had drought again this year," said Old Fu. "Life is good here. If you don't get along with each other, you'll be letting down the Communist Party and Chairman Mao. These last few years I've thought of you folks all the time. I knew you must be making fast progress in this old liberated

这个村庄。傅老刚还是推着他那铁匠炉,前面拉车的,是九儿。

傅老刚越显得年老和削瘦,小车已经破烂不堪,吱扭的声音,也没有了当年的气派。九儿长高了,但穿的衣服也很破旧。她的脸蛋儿很是干瘦,头发上挂满尘土,鞋面儿已经飞裂,只有那一对大眼睛里射出的纯洁亲热的光芒,使人看出她对于回到这里来,是感到多么迫切和愉快。

把小车推到十字街口,傅老刚放下绊带,和人们问好。九儿拉下脖里围着的旧毛巾,擦着脸上的汗水。

"我们又回来了,"傅老刚说,"可是,你们为什么吵架呀!"

"不为什么,"青年们说,"两位女同志,吃饱了没事儿,在这里练把式。"

"不要这样。"傅老刚郑重地说,"你们一直生活在咱们的根据地,真是生活在天堂里了。你们看我们那里,在国民党占据着的时候,人们的生活困难到了什么地步!我同九儿回去,正好陷在网儿里。还好,总算是逃了个活命儿出来。"

"你们那里生产怎么样?"青年们问。

"正在恢复,今年又遇到荒年。"傅老刚说,"你们有好日子,不好生过,就对不起共产党和毛主席。这些年,我一直想念你们,我想这里是老解放区,工作一定进步得多。六儿哩,怎么不见六儿?"

英汉对照
English-Chinese
中国文学宝库
Gems of Chinese Literature
现代文学系列
Modern Literature

area. Where's Six? Why isn't he here?"

While searching among the crowd, the blacksmith glanced at his daughter. Evidently she had also looked in vain, and now she was gazing at the beautiful girl with the lively eyes who was standing by the grist mill. Nine didn't know her. She assumed she must be someone's new bride from another village.

"I saw Six in the northern outskirts a while ago, flying his pigeons. Maybe he's gone home by now," a young man said. "You ought to go and see your old 'relative.' Old Li has come up in the world these past two years!"

Old Fu said goodbye and lifted the handles of his barrow. Nine took her place up front. As they walked off, she kept turning her head to gaze at Man'er.

Old Li was overjoyed to see his old friend again. He led him to the new compound and showed him the cart he was building.

"We've been waiting for you, relative," the carpenter said excitedly. "Tomorrow, we'll set your forge up in this courtyard. See how big and light it is. Won't it be a pleasure to work here?"

"It's really fine," said Old Fu. "You could even build a carpentry shop here. There's plenty of room."

"When I finish this cart, I'm going to retire," Old Li said with satisfaction. "You know, there's a lot of money in transport these days. Every time the cart wheel turns, the cash comes rolling in. Tianjin has been liberated, and my eldest boy has been doing very well in business there. Winter's only just begun, and he bought me this. But how can I do any work wearing this thing?"

Looking at the fine black cloth robe whose flaps the carpenter

傅老刚在人群里巡视着,转身望了望他的女儿。女儿好像已经寻觅过了,她现在只是站在那里,注视着正在推碾的那个长得极端俊俏,眉眼十分飞动的女孩子,她不认识这个女的,以为是谁家新娶的小媳妇。

"刚才,我看见六儿在村北边趁鸽子,这会儿,也许回家去了。"一个青年说,"你也该去看望看望你的老亲家了,黎老东这二年的生活,可提高大发了!"

傅老刚和人们告别,架起小车。九儿拉着牵绳,还不断地回头看小满儿。

见到老朋友,黎老东高兴极了。他带着亲家到他那新宅子里去看他打制的大车。

"亲家你看,就等你来了。"黎老东兴奋地说,"明天,咱们就在这院里支起炉灶来。你看,这院子多么豁亮,做起活儿来多醒脾?"

"真是好哩,"傅老刚说,"就是在这里开个木货厂,也满宽绰呢。"

"打上这辆车,我也就该休息了。"黎老东十分得意地说,"你知道,现在运销很赚钱,车轱辘儿一动,就是大把的票子。天津解放了,老大挣钱也多了,你看,刚一进冬天,就给我买来了这个。可是穿上这个,我还能做活吗?"

傅老刚打量着亲家高高翻起的新黑细布面的大羊羔皮袍,忽然觉得身上有些寒冷似的。

英汉对照
English-Chinese
中国文学宝库
Gems of Chinese Literature
现代文学系列
Modern Literature

raised high to show the thick fleece lining, Old Fu suddenly felt cold. It never occurred to Old Li that his guest, who had come so far, might want to rest. He told in detail his plan for building more rooms in the compound, then brought his "relative" to see his pig pens. Only after he had exhibited his horse as well did he finally lead his guest into the house and invite him to be seated.

Nine was about to follow when she happened to look up and see Six on the roof. He was waving to her and indicating that she should mount the ladder. Nine lightly clambered up. Screened behind a row of dry branches, Six was playing with a flock of tame pigeons. When the birds saw a stranger approaching, they took flight. The sun was sinking in the west, and scarlet clouds reflected pinkly on the flat white-plastered roof. Red and white pigeons wheeled over head, chasing, soaring.

"I saw you long ago," said Six. "But I didn't dare call you because my father was here."

"What are you raising these pigeons for?"

"They're fun. A couple of days ago, my friend Yang Mao brought back a pair of pure white ones from Beijing, a foreign breed. They're real beauties. I'd like to buy them, but he won't sell at any price."

"Didn't the Youth League criticize you?"

"I'm not a member." Six waved his arms at the pigeons to make them fly higher and then lower. "Are you?"

"I just joined," said Nine. She fell silent.

"When you learn how to play with these birds, they are great sport." Six stood up and shouted to the sky: "Here pigeon-pi-

黎老东还没有让远来的客人进屋休息的意思,他详细地说明了建设这所宅院的计划,又带着亲家去看猪圈。最后,推开北房门,叫亲家看马,这才顺便把客人让到里间坐下来。

当两个老人进了屋,九儿刚要跟进去的时候,她抬头看见,六儿站在房顶上向她招手儿,并且指给她上房的梯子所在。九儿轻轻上到房上,看见六儿躲在一排干树枝后面,引逗着一群鸽子玩儿。鸽子看到生人上来,都拍翅飞向天空,现在太阳西沉,西天的红霞映照到白灰抹平的房顶上,红色的白色的鸽子在他们头顶上奋飞着,追逐着,翻腾着。

"我早就看见你来了。"六儿说,"有我父亲,我不敢大声叫你。"

"你喂这些鸽子干什么?"九儿问。

"好玩呗。"六儿说,"新近,杨卯儿从北京弄来一对纯白的外国种,实在好,我还想买来哩,人家就是贵贱不卖。"

"青年团不批评你吗?"九儿问。

"我不是青年团。"六儿扬手引逗着天空的鸽子,使它们飞下来又飞上去,"你加入了吗?"

"我也是刚加入。"九儿说着沉默了。

"这东西玩熟了,最有意思。"六儿说着站立起来,向天空呼叫着,"鸽儿,鸽儿。"

geon!"

Obediently, one by one, the birds returned to the roof.

"Six, who's that girl?" Nine suddenly noticed on a roof several courtyards away the beauty she had seen at the grist mill. The girl was gazing in their direction, smiling challengingly, with an expression difficult to fathom.

"That's Stupid Li's young sister-in-law, Man'er. The dumplings must be ready. I've got to load my hamper. Let's go down."

At supper time, Six still hadn't come back. Four was delighted when he learned that Nine was also a Youth Leaguer.

"Did you bring your credentials?" he asked. "You can join our study group tonight."

"I carry them wherever I go," Nine laughed. "I'd like very much to be in your study group. What's your job in the League branch, Brother Four?"

"I'm responsible for public education. There's a lot of sand in this region and the winds are strong. In spring, we never have enough rain. Our superiors are urging us to dig wells and plant trees, and bring irrigation to our parched fields so that we can grow rice. It's a fine plan, but many people in the village don't understand how important it is."

"But you do, of course," Old Li growled caustically. "You've got to stop being such a blasted busybody. You're bringing down curses on my head."

"Why hasn't Six joined the League?" Nine asked.

"Who knows?" replied Four. "He says there's something wrong with his brain. The minute a meeting starts, his head aches. Does

鸽子们先后驯顺地落在房檐儿上。

"六儿,那个姑娘是谁?"九儿忽然看见,在西边隔几户人家的一间房上,站着刚才推碾的那个姑娘。那姑娘直直地望着这里,脸上带着那么一种逼人而又难以理解的笑容。

"那是黎大傻的小姨子小满儿。"六儿说,"包子蒸熟了,我该去装柜子了,我们下去吧。"

吃晚饭的时候,六儿也没有回家来。当四儿知道九儿也是个青年团员的时候,非常高兴地说:

"你的关系带来了吗? 今天晚上,你先参加我们的学习会吧。"

"我一路上,把关系转了来。"九儿笑着说,"我很愿意参加你们的学习会,四哥在团支部负责吗?"

"我是宣传委员。"四儿说,"咱这一带地方风沙大,每年春天缺雨,上级号召人们打井栽树,变旱田为水田,这是好事儿。可是村里还有很多人认识不清楚。"

"就是他妈的你认识清楚,"黎老东说,"你少在外头给我挣骂吧。"

"六儿为什么不参加青年团?"九儿问。

"谁知道他为什么?"四儿说,"他说脑筋不好,一开会就头痛。你看他像脑筋不好的人吗?"

英汉对照
English-Chinese
中国文学宝库
Gems of Chinese Literature
现代文学系列
Modern Literature

he look like a boy with a weak brain to you?"

"You ought to help him. His interest seems to be in other things."

"Maybe if you talk to him it'll be better," Four sighed. "He has no respect for me at all. In our family, my prestige is very low."

"Stuff and nonsense," snorted Old Li. "Outside, your prestige is high, and where does it get you?"

"It's good for young people to be progressive," Old Fu said soothingly. "If it weren't for this new society, relative, would you be getting along so well?"

"True," Old Li conceded. "The times keep improving. But in our private lives, the old ways are still the best."

8

Because Nine was very concerned, Four agreed that they should talk to Six together. After he had fed the stock, Four gathered his study material and took a small oil lamp. He left the house with Nine, asking the two old men to open the compound gate for them when they came back.

"Why are you taking that lamp?" asked Nine.

"It's our group's study lamp. I can't leave it in the classroom. People might waste the oil."

On hearing the word "oil," Old Li shouted after him:

"Four! Are you using our oil again? That Youth League of yours is a league of paupers! You work for them and give them free oil, to boot! Son of a bitch! Your prestige is high because you swipe

"你要帮助他。"九儿说,"我看他把心都用到旁处去了。"

"你劝劝他也许好些。"四儿叹气说,"他一点儿也瞧不起我。我在我们家里,威信太低。"

"胡说八道。"黎老东又斥责他,"你在外边威信高,高了什么来?"

"年轻人进步是好事。"傅老刚劝说着,"亲家,要不是这个世道,你的生活能过得这样好吗?"

"你说的这话对。"黎老东说,"时代是不断前进的,可是,我们过日子,还得按照老理儿才行。"

8

由于九儿表示十分关怀,四儿提议一同找六儿谈一谈。四儿把牲口喂上,叫两个老人在家看门,装好学习文件,又带上一个小油灯,同九儿出来。

"你带个油灯干什么?"九儿问。

"这是我们团里的学习灯。不敢放在讲堂上,怕浪费油。"

黎老东在屋里听到"油"字,就冲着窗台喊:

"四儿!你又添上了咱家的油?你们青年团真成了穷人团,哪里有赔着灯油做工作的?他妈的,你的威信高,还不是高在这点灯油上!"

英汉对照
English-Chinese
中国文学宝库
Gems of Chinese Literature
现代文学系列
Modern Literature

our damned lamp oil!"

The boy did not reply. When he and Nine reached the street, he halted and said: "Six sells meat dumplings at night. I don't know whether he's started yet or not."

But that night Six was not hawking dumplings. In place of his clear young shout was the raucous bellow of Stupid Li:

"Beef dumplings! Steaming hot meat dumplings!"

Four asked him where Six was.

"How do I know?" Stupid retorted surlily. "I'm not his boss."

As Four and Nine walked to the west end of the village, they heard Six's voice coming from a large courtyard. Through the partly open gate they could see several trees and some piles of brushwood. A tall poplar reared up beside the compound wall. Beneath this tree, Six and a girl were standing very close together.

Nine halted at the gate. Four impetuously pushed it open, entered and shouted:

"Six!"

The girl leaped aside as if she had been hit.

"What are you yelling about?" Six demanded in a low angry tone.

"What?" Four hadn't moderated his voice. "What's the secret?"

"Quit that noise!" Six whispered frantically.

Four said no more, but he struck a match and lit the small oil lamp. Holding it high, he looked around.

"Old Lord of the Heavens!" Six dashed over to him and with one puff blew it out. "Do you have to shine that wretched lamp all over the place!"

四儿没答言,领着九儿出来,他在街上停了停,说:

"六儿晚上卖包子,不知道出来没有。"

今天晚上,六儿没有出来做买卖,代替他那清脆的声音,是黎大傻那大劈拉嗓子:

"牛肉包子咧!好热的牛肉包子咧!"

四儿问他六儿到哪里去了,他有些不屑于管理地说:

"谁知道。我又不是他的掌柜的。"

当四儿和九儿转到西街口上,在村边一处大场院里,传来六儿说话的声音。场院的门虚掩着,隐约地看出:院里栽着很多树木,堆着几个柴垛,靠墙边,有一棵大杨树高高矗立着。在杨树下面,六儿和一个女人贴身站立着。

九儿在门口站住了。四儿性急,一推门进去,并且大声喊叫了一声:

"六儿!"

那女的好像从什么东西上撞了回来一样,很快地往旁边一闪。

"你喊叫什么!"六儿压低声音,愤怒地说。

"怎么啦?"四儿并没有调整自己的嗓门儿,"有什么秘密?"

"不许你嚷!"六儿更发急了。

四儿停止了说话。但是,忽然擦的一声,他划着了一根火柴,把手里的小油灯点了起来,高高举起,向四下里照耀。

"天爷!"六儿跑上去,一口把他的油灯吹灭,说,"到处点你这穷灯干什么!"

"真的有什么见不得光明的勾当,在这里进

"Is some dirty business going on here that can't be exposed to the light?" said Four. With large strides he made a circuit of the poplar, unexpectedly bumping into Man'er who was hiding on the other side of the tree. The two began to wrangle loudly.

"Ruined!" Six stamped his foot. There was a fluttering sound on the branches above. "The pigeons have flown!"

"Only one of them is gone." Man'er stopped shouting at Four to look up. "Everybody keep quiet!"

They didn't know what sex it was, but the bird that had flown off couldn't bear to leave its mate. It circled once in the dark sky, then returned to the branch. It was only then that Six told his brother softly that Yang Mao's foreign-breed pigeons had escaped; he was just in the process of catching them.

In the black night the tall poplar seemed to reach up to caress the stars, and its bark was as smooth and shiny as a girl's skin. But Six had already removed his shoes and socks. Spitting on his hands, he started up the tree.

"Are you trying to kill yourself, in the darkness!" said Four. "I'll go home and tell Pa!"

"Stop playing the big brother," said Man'er. "Those birds cost thirty yuan each. You're a good student. Figure out what two of them will bring."

Nine could restrain herself no longer. "Six," she called, "they're not worth risking your neck for!"

"Tsk-tsk," said Man'er mockingly. "Words from someone who really cares about you!"

"Who are you?" Nine demanded. "We've never met; why

行着吗?"四儿一边说着,一边大步地绕着杨树行进,冷不防撞在躲在杨树后面的小满儿的身上,两个人吵了起来。

"完了!"六儿一跺脚,大杨树上扑楞楞一响,"鸽子跑了!"

"只是跑了一只。"小满儿停止吵闹,向上观看着,"谁也别说话了!"

飞起的那只鸽子,不知是属于什么性别,它是留恋眷属的,在黑暗的天空里绕了一遭,又落到了杨树上。这时六儿才低声告诉他的四哥,杨卯儿那外国种鸽子跑出来了,他正想法上去抓住它。

在黑夜里看来,这杨树一直高到抚摩着群星,而它那树皮,又像女人的肌肤一样光滑。六儿已经脱下鞋袜,在手里唾着口沫,要攀登上去了。

"这样黑天,你要玩命?"四儿说,"我回家叫父亲去!"

"少在这里拿大哥架子吧!"小满儿说,"抓住一只三十万,抓住两只,你学习好,给算算是多少钱?"

"六儿,"九儿忍不住,说,"你不要冒这样的危险吧!"

"好。"小满儿喷着嘴儿说,"心疼你的人儿发言了。"

"你是什么人,"九儿说,"我们从来又不认识,和我犯嘴?"

英汉对照
English-Chinese
中国文学宝库
Gems of Chinese Literature
现代文学系列
Modern Literature

should you want to pick a quarrel?"

"Who am I?" Man'er laughed coldly. "I'm exactly the same kind as you!"

"Don't fight," Six pleaded. "You'll scare the birds off again. Here pigeon-pigeon!"

He quickly scrambled up to the crotch of the big branch.

"Let's go," Four said to Nine. "There's nothing we can do. If he falls and kills himself, it'll be his own fault."

Extremely angry and uneasy, Nine left with Four.

"A fine pair!" Man'er drawled.

"What?" cried Six, up in the tree.

"I'm talking about the pigeons! They're on that south branch."

Four and Nine could hear her keeping up a flow of derisive comment, while directing Six's dangerous operations.

9

In a compound that been confiscated from a landlord during the land reform, Nine met the members of the village Youth League. Many were old friends, and they greeted her warmly. Four lit the lamp and led them to a large room in the west wing which was used in common by the Youth League and the local theatrical company.

The room was frigid, for all the windows were broken. Ripped and hanging in patches, the flowered paper ceiling was covered with dust and cobwebs. One of the double doors was missing. A small blackboard hung on one wall; before it stood an old oil-stained table for six. Low platforms of bricks laid with mud fillers

"我是什么人?"小满儿冷笑着说,"我是和你一模一样的那种人。"

"别吵了。"六儿哀告着,"别再吓跑了我的鸽子,鸽儿,鸽儿。"

他很快地就上到了树的老权那里。

"我们走吧!"四儿对九儿说,"没有办法,摔死了,怨他命里活该。"

九儿的心里非常气愤和极度不安,但她还是同四儿走出来了。

"也好像是一对儿哩!"小满儿放长声音说。

"你说什么?"六儿在树上问。

"我说的是鸽子啊!它们在靠南边的那一枝儿上。"

他们听见小满儿站在树下,不停地说着淡话,并指引着六儿的冒险行动。

9

在土地改革时没收的一家地主的宅子里,九儿和这村的青年团员们会面了。很多人原先是认识的,他们热情地问候九儿。四儿点着油灯,把人们招呼进西屋里,西屋原是三间,现在已经打通,青年团和本村的剧团都利用这个地方进行活动。屋里十分寒冷,窗子都破碎了,顶棚上的花纸一块块带着灰尘蛛网垂下来,门子也缺了一扇。北墙上挂着一块小黑板,黑板前面放着一张破旧油垢的六人桌,地下用土坯和泥,垒成一堵堵的矮墙,也不知道是要人当作桌案还是当作座位。坐在上面,感到十分冰冷,

英汉对照
English-Chinese
中国文学宝库
Gems of Chinese Literature
现代文学系列
Modern Literature

could serve as either benches or desks. The girls, in their thin clothes, found the bricks icy cold, but they remained seated quietly.

Four and a young fellow called Kitchen Stove were the teachers. Crowding close to the little lamp, they told the Youth Leaguers how to explain to the peasants the advantages of digging wells and planting trees. Then everyone talked it over.

As the night deepened, the room became colder than the air outside. But the young people went on talking earnestly.

"Comrades, we must change our village into a place of prosperity and plenty," said Four. "Then, our Youth League won't have to meet in a cold room like this. We'll build ourselves a fine clubhouse."

"You're getting too far off the subject," Kitchen Stove warned him. "The question at hand is how to overcome the obstacles in the way of our educating the public."

"It seems to me there are two things blocking our path," said Four. "The first is Li the Seventh's big rubber-tired cart. It's earning a lot of money on transport jobs and is making people see only what's right in front of their noses; it's encouraging selfish capitalist-type thinking. The second is Stupid Li's dumpling house. All the carrying-on there is enticing young people away from their proper work. If we want to succeed in our propaganda, we've got to limit Li the Seventh's transport hauls and put an end to Stupid Li's dumpling business. Otherwise we'll just be making a lot of empty talk. As long as they've got something concrete to offer, our efforts will be in vain."

那些女孩子们,穿的衣服很单薄,但是,她们还是安详地坐在上面了。

四儿和一个叫锅灶的青年是教员,他们守着油灯,给团员们讲解怎样向广大农民进行打井造林的宣传,讲完了一节就进行讨论。

夜深了,这屋子里实在比屋子外面还要冷一些。他们还是认真地讨论着。

"同志们,我们一定要把我们的村庄,建设成一个富裕繁荣的村庄。"四儿说,"到那个时候,我们青年团就不会再在这样冷的屋子里开会,我们要盖起一座很好的礼堂来。"

"离题太远了。"锅灶警告他说,"目前是研究怎样克服宣传上遇到的阻碍。"

"依我看,在我们村里,横在我们前进道路上的,有两大障碍。"四儿转回来说,"一是黎七儿的胶皮大车,运输很发财,助长着人们只看眼前,只顾个人的资本主义思想;一是黎大傻家的包子房,男女混杂,减低着人们的生产热情。如果要想宣传得好,就得限制黎七儿出车和取消黎大傻的包子买卖。不然,我们只是空口宣传,他们那里却有实际利益,我们是白费劲儿。"

"我同意你的看法。"锅灶说,"可是,第一,

"I agree with you," said Kitchen Stove. "But, in the first place, Six is your brother. It's up to you to get him out of that bad environment. Second, your father is building a large cart too; he wants to take the road to private wealth. These two big obstacles are right in your own family. What are you going to do about them?"

"The problem is this," Four said frankly. "My father doesn't listen to me. I asked him: 'Are you against the call of the Party?' He said: 'I support it one hundred per cent.' I said: 'Then let's dig a well here this winter.' He said: 'There's no hurry about it.' That's my difficulty. But I'm certainly not going to give up."

"I can help," said Nine. "I look at this differently than the rest of you. Old men can be won over too. When we were living at home, my father liked to hear me talk about the new thinking. As to Six, we ought to help him progress also."

"Right!" cried the girls sitting behind her. None of them had spoken for some time, and now they all burst out in chorus.

Kitchen Stove laughed. "Helping Six progress isn't going to be easy. That Man'er has a much greater attraction for him than our Youth League."

The girls disagreed.

"If you don't believe me, just try and pull him away from her," Kitchen Stove said gloomily, coming down from the teacher's platform.

After the meeting ended, they returned, singing, to their homes. The girls insisted that Nine sleep with them. Kitchen Stove had a large family and little space; every winter, he lived with

六儿是你兄弟,你应该首先叫他脱离那个坏环境。第二,你家大伯正在打大车,也想要走个人发财的路。这两大障碍,不在别处,就在你们家里,你把克服它们的办法说一说吧。"

"困难就在这里。"四儿真诚地说,"我的父亲根本不听我的话。我问他:你反对党的号召吗?他说:我完全拥护。我说:我们今年冬天打一眼井吧?他说:现在还不忙。这就是我遇到的困难。但是,我绝不在困难面前低头。"

"我可以帮助你。"九儿说,"我的看法和你们不大一样,老人也是可以说服的。在老家,我的父亲就很喜欢我把新道理讲给他听。至于六儿,我们也应该帮助他进步。"

"是啊!"坐在她后面的那些姑娘们,半天没人言语,现在像有人指挥着的合唱队一样,一齐喊叫出来。

"帮助六儿进步,这又是一个难题。"锅灶笑着说,"那个叫小满儿的,对他的吸引力,要比团强烈得多。"

姑娘们反对他这种看法。

"不信,你们就去试试,看能不能把六儿从她那边拉过来。"锅灶无可奈何地从台上走下来说。

散会以后,他们歌唱着各自回到自己的家里去,九儿被姐妹们拉去一块儿睡觉。锅灶家里人口多,房屋少,每年冬天是和四儿做伴的,这样便于共同学习,和互相辩论。他们一同回

英汉对照
English-Chinese
中国文学宝库
Gems of Chinese Literature
现代文学系列
Modern Literature

Four. It was more convenient that way for studying and arguing together.

Kitchen Stove went to Four's house. Four fed the stock, then shared with Kitchen Stove a couple of leftover, cold sweet potatoes. As the two boys got into bed, Kitchen Stove grinned.

"These quilts are cold! With neither wood to heat the platform bed nor wives to warm us, we're in a bad way!"

"Don't surrender!" cried Four, taking a breath of icy air. "If you want to remain a bachelor, you must have the courage to stick it out!"

"Are you sure we have to remain bachelors? Better not jump to conclusions!"

In the next room, the roan horse was munching hay. Although his teeth were old, they made a noise like grating iron. But the two boys soon fell asleep. Shimmering moonbeams shone in through the window.

10

At this time, Six and Man'er were still in the empty courtyard. Six had long since caught the pigeons. When he slid down from the tree, Man'er pulled him to a large stack of wheat stalks, and the two buried themselves in the soft warm pile. Tying the pigeons' wings with a red woollen threads. Man'er played with the birds merrily, now making them kiss, now placing one on top of the other in a mating position.

"I'll sell them and buy you a padded tunic," Six said to her.

来,四儿喂好牲口,在灶台上捡了几块早饭剩下的凉山芋,和锅灶分吃了,两个人就去钻被窝。

"被窝好凉啊!"锅灶笑着说,"既没有柴烧炕,又没有小媳妇给暖暖,我们太困难了!"

"战胜它吧!"四儿一边吸着冷气,一边说,"要想打光棍儿,就得有这样一种克服困难的精神!"

"你认为我们一定打光棍儿吗?"锅灶说,"据我看,那可不能过早的下结论哩!"

红马在外间屋里吃草,它虽然口齿老了,但那嚼草的声音,还像斩钉截铁一样铿锵。两个青年很快就睡着了,月亮把清水一样的光亮,洒到他们的窗子上来。

10

这时,六儿和小满儿,还没有离开那所空场院。鸽子,六儿早已抓到。他从树上滑下来,小满儿把他拉到一个大麦秸垛后边,两个人埋在绵软温暖的麦秸里。小满儿掏出红绒绳儿,把两只外国种鸽子的翅膀别起来,欢乐地抚弄着它们。一会叫它们亲嘴儿,一会又叫它们配对儿。

"卖了它,给你买一件棉袄。"六儿对她说,"见面分一半,何况你帮了我不少的忙。"

"I'll gladly share everything with you; besides you've helped me a lot."

"Our friendship isn't based on material things," said Man'er seriously. "Give the robe to that Nine. Buy her one."

"Why?"

"Because her face is black," said Man'er, repressing a giggle. "A true blacksmith's daughter!"

"She's a very good worker. And she's in the Youth League."

"What if she is? At home, I was in the Youth League too. They criticized me. I left them flat and came straight to my sister's. As for working in the fields, you call that woman's special talent?"

"What is woman's special talent, then?"

Man'er smilingly raised her head. Six stared at her lovely face, even more alluring in the mornlight. He soon learned the answer to his question.

As dawn approached, a heavy mist spread, and frost coated the branches and grass and the eaves of the houses. Only then did Six and Man'er rise and brush the wheat stalks from their hair and clothing. They discovered that one of the precious foreign-breed pigeons had been crushed to death under Man'er's body. Holding the dead bird, a crested male, in his hands, Six was very distraught. He would have given anything to bring it back to life. But its heart had ceased to beat; beneath its wings it was already cool.

At Stupid Li's house, they found the compound gate and the house door closed but not locked. Their late return evoked no surprise from Man'er's sister. Stupid didn't even hear them come in. He continued snoring beneath his quilts.

"你和我的交情并不在吃穿上面。"小满儿认真地说,"给那位九儿,买一件吧。"

"为什么?"六儿问。

"就为她那脸蛋儿长得很黑呀,"小满儿忍着笑说,"真不枉是铁匠的女儿。"

"人家生产很好哩,"六儿说,"又是青年团员。"

"青年团员又怎样?"小满儿说,"我在娘家,也是青年团员。他们批评我,我就干脆到我姐姐家来住。至于生产好,那是女人的什么法宝?"

"什么才是女人的法宝?"六儿问。

小满儿笑着把头仰起来。六儿望着她那在月光下显得更加明丽媚人的脸,很快就把答案找了出来。

当黎明以前,天空弥漫着浓雾,树枝、草尖和柴垛的檐顶上结满霜雪的时候,六儿和小满儿才决定回家。他们站起身来,各自掸扫着头发和衣服上的草末儿,发见那珍贵的外国种鸽子,有一只压死在小满儿的身下了。那是一只大蓬头的雄鸽,六儿把它托在手里,表示了非常的沉痛。在这一时刻,他愿以任何代价换回这只鸽子的逝去的生命,但是,它的心脏确实停止跳动了,翅膀下面的部分也发了凉。

回到黎大傻的家,大门和房门都是虚掩着。小满儿和六儿在这样晚的时候同时进来,也没有引起她姐姐的任何惊怪,而黎大傻好像根本就没有听见似的,在自己的被窝里呼呼地鼾睡着。

小满儿告诉姐姐,今天夜里,她同六儿捉鸽

Man'er told her sister how she had helped Six catch the pigeons, and how badly Six felt because one of the birds had been crushed!

"What difference does it make?" Stupid's wife laughed. "Scald it, pluck out its feathers, and we'll save four ounces of beef for our dumplings! A cold night like this, I thought you were out on regular business, not playing around chasing pigeons. Hah! Come up on the platform bed, quick. Get under my covers and warm up."

Opening her bedding, she crawled out naked, and crept into the quilts with Stupid.

Six left at daybreak. He met the pigeons' owner, Yang Mao, at the compound gate.

Not very tall, smartly dressed, Yang had a small pointed head topped by a little felt skullcap. But even this looked too big. His head kept nodding erratically, and his tiny round eyes moved with startling rapidity.

"You're up early, Brother," he hailed Six.

"You too," said Six deiectedly. "What's on your mind?"

"Been looking for you." Yang Mao shoved his hands into the pockets of his tunic. "We've always been good friends. Give me back my pigeons. The female will be laying eggs this year. I'll give the first brood to you. I'm a man of my word."

Six did not reply.

"Or else — " Yang Mao came a step nearer. " — I trained a good rabbit hawk not long ago. The hunting season's just starting. I can give him to you."

Six remained silent.

"If it's money you want — naturally that could never come be-

子去了,并且说六儿正为一只鸽子被压死难过哩!

"那有什么难过的?"姐姐在被窝里笑着说,"烫一烫,拔了毛剁剁,又省下四两牛肉!这样冷的天,我以为你两个抽空儿去干点正经事儿哩,倒去捉鸟儿玩了?唉,你们快到炕上来,钻进我这被窝里暖和暖和吧。"

她说着,把自己的热被窝让了出来,光着身子爬进黎大傻的被窝里去了。

等到天明,六儿从这一家出来,在门口遇到了鸽子的主人杨卯儿。

杨卯儿个子不高,打扮得很利落,他的脑袋很小很尖,戴一顶毡帽头儿,还显得分量过重。他那脑袋不停地上下颤动着,两只又圆又小的眼睛,非常灵活地转动着:

"六兄弟,起来得早啊!"

"你也早。"六儿垂头丧气地说,"有什么事情吗?"

"来找你。"杨卯儿把两只手插进短袄上的褡包里,"咱弟兄平日交情不错,你把鸽子还给我吧。今年它们卜了蛋,孵出第一窠,我就送给你,我这人说话算话。"

六儿没有答言。

"不然,"杨卯儿上前一步,"我近来玩好了一只抓兔子的鹰,现在正是行围射猎的时候,我可以把它送给你。"

六儿还是没有话。

"如果你要钱——其实咱兄弟们不过这个,"杨卯儿的嘴唇抖颤着,脑袋扭向一边,"也

tween us — " Yang Mao's lips trembled. He cocked his head to one side. " — You can have that too. First give me my pigeons. I'll gradually raise some money."

"Let's talk about it some other time." Six began to walk away. "I'm going home to eat."

"What!" Yang's eyes glittered blue with agitation. "You're usually good to your friends. How can you treat me so badly? Give those pigeons back! Otherwise, you're a usurper!"

Six halted and turned. "What do you mean — usurper?"

"You've usurped my birds, and you usurped a girl who's somebody else's wife!"

"Did you see me do it?"

"Others have — with their own eyes! If they won't speak up, *I'll* expose you!"

"Go ahead and expose." The gate of Stupid Li's compound creaked and Man'er appeared. She evidently had just combed her hair and made up her face; her rouge was spread somewhat unevenly. Hands behind her back, she leaned against the gate post and faced Yang Mao.

"I'd like to see what you can expose. What proof have you got? Have you caught the man, or the woman? Let's hear it! Who told you to come here so early in the morning and spit turds all over the place? Now get out before I slap your face!"

11

Yang Mao formerly was a needle and thread pedlar. Every win-

可以。你先把鸽子给我,我慢慢去筹划。"

"回头再说吧,"六儿拔腿就要走,"我吃饭去。"

"怎么!"杨卯儿的两眼急得发出蓝光,"你素日为朋好友,对我这样不讲交情?你趁早把鸽子还给我,不然,你就是霸占!"

"什么叫霸占?"六儿站住,回过头来问。

"霸占我的鸽子,还霸占有主的青年妇女。"

"你看见了?"六儿问。

"有人亲眼看见,不然,我们就抖露出来!"杨卯儿喊叫着说。

"你抖露出来,又怎样?"黎大傻家的门子一响,小满儿站了出来。她显然是刚刚梳装打扮好,脸上的粉脂还没有擦匀,她倒背着手在门框上一靠,面对着杨卯儿。"我倒要看看你能抖露出什么来?你有什么证据吗,你抓住了男的,还是抓住了女的?你说呀!别他妈的大清早起在这里满嘴喷粪了,小心我过去拿大耳光子拍你!"

11

杨卯儿原先也是一个卖针头线脑儿的货郎小贩。过去,每年腊月,他到保定府贩些女人年

ter, he used to go to Baoding, buy up various items that women needed in the mountain villages on the other side of the railway. There were some strange stories about his wanderings through the mountains, all of them of a romantic nature. Though he worked at the trade for many years, Yang Mao was never able to earn much money. Now, the only thing he had left of that period was a small earthenware teapot with a blue glaze.

A few days before, a man had arrived from the provincial government, from all appearances, a high-ranking official. According to custom, such a person would be put up in the home of a cadre, or with one of the village activists. But he asked to be quartered with an ordinary family, saying he would also like to meet some of their backward elements. The village cadres wanted to give the matter more thought. Could he be on some sort of special mission? But the vice-chairman of the village, who was always getting queer ideas, simply breezed right along. He led the comrade to the house of Yang Mao.

Yang Mao was a bachelor. He welcomed the guest and gave him a place on the platform bed — although on the least warmly heated section. The visitor's health was poor, so the village authorities also set up a small coal stove for him.

"Comrade Yang," said the provincial official, "there's nothing on the fire. I wonder if you could borrow an iron kettle for me to boil some water in?"

"No need to borrow. I've a kettle here." Yang reached down to a shelf under the table, brought out his blue teapot, filled it with water, and placed it on the stove.

节用的物品,过铁路到山地里去卖。关于他在西山做买卖,很有一些奇异的传说。这些传说,都带有很大的浪漫性质。但是,多年来他并没有发财,现在,在他身边遗留下的,只有那时用过的一把沙胎蓝釉小水壶。

前几天,县里介绍了一位从省里来的干部到村里来。这位干部,从各方面看,都像一个高级干部。在解决住房问题的时候,却使得村干部们觉得他有些古怪和不近人情。按习惯,像这样的干部,应该住在村干部或是积极分子的家里,那样在相互接近和负责保卫上,都会便利一些。但是,这位干部提出要住在一个普通的人家,并且说除去先进的方面,他还要看看村里落后的部分,这就使得村里的负责同志有些踌躇,以为他负有什么特殊的使命,前来私访。而那位惯出古董主意的副村长,竟顺水推舟,把他领到杨卯儿的家里来了。

杨卯儿是个光棍儿,最初,对来客很表示欢迎,在炕上腾出一段地方,虽然那一段地方是属于炕的寒带。这位干部身体弱,在屋里又生起了一个小煤火炉。

"杨同志,火闲着也是闲着,能不能借把铁壶来,弄点开水喝呀?"干部说。

"不用去借,咱家里就有。"杨卯儿说着就从桌子底下的横板上,取出他那把水壶,到瓮里注上水,坐在炉口上。

"这是把磁壶呀,能坐水吗?"干部问。

英汉对照
English-Chinese
中国文学宝库
Gems of Chinese Literature
现代文学系列
Modern Literature

"Can you boil water in that crockery pot?"

"That's the beauty of this pot. It has an earthenware base and a porcelain glaze. It comes to a boil quickly and never leaks."

But the stove lid immediately became moist and began to hiss. At first the comrade from the province thought the outside of the teapot had got wet when it was being filled. He raised the teapot and looked. The bottom had several cracks which had widened with the heat. Not only wouldn't he have any water to drink — there was a danger that the fire would be extinguished.

"The pot's no use, Comrade Yang," he said. "It leaks."

"It does not!" cried Yang, his little eyes glaring. "If I say it doesn't leak, it doesn't leak!"

"But it's obviously leaking."

"Living here with me isn't suitable. Move to someone else's house," Yang Mao said brusquely.

His guest was bewildered. He showed Yang: the water was leaking from the cracked base. Big drops were going hiss, hiss, hiss as they hit the hot stove. Yang Mao wouldn't even turn his head.

The comrade had no choice but to roll up his bedding and seek the vice-chairman. He told him what had happened. The vice-chairman laughed.

"You wanted to see something of the backward side of this village, comrade. Perhaps we can consider Yang Mao a typical example. I can tell you quite a bit about his background, if you're interested. When I was young, he and I formed a small trading partnership. As you can imagine, it was very hard to get along with him: He was quarrelsome and stubborn. He'd never admit an er-

"这壶好就好在这里。"杨卯儿说,"磁面沙胎,在火上坐水,就像沙吊儿一样,又快又不漏。"

但是炉口马上被水阴湿,一个劲儿嘶嘶地响。最初干部以为刚从瓮里提出,是带来的水。后来提起一看,壶底裂了好几道缝,这缝被火一烤,裂得更宽了,不但水喝不成,而且有火灭的危险。干部说:

"不行啊,杨同志,壶实在漏了,不能用。"

"不漏!"杨卯儿睁大一双小圆眼睛说,"我说不漏就不漏。"

"那不是明明在漏吗?"干部说。

"在我这屋里,你住着不合适。你搬到别人家去吧。"杨卯儿二话不说,就宣布了逐客令,这真使得干部大惑不解了。

干部指给杨卯儿看:一大滴一大滴的水,从壶底漏下来,漏到火里,嘶,嘶,嘶嘶!

杨卯儿连头也不转过来。

干部只好卷起铺盖,找带他来的副村长去,把事情发生经过讲了一遍,副村长笑着说:

"同志,你要看村里的落后部分,我不知道杨卯儿,能不能算是一个典型?关于他的出身历史,我还可以向你介绍一些比较详细的材料。我年轻的时候,和杨卯儿搭伴儿做小买卖。像你看到的,和这样一个人作伙计,是最困难不过的了。他抬硬杠,一根筋,死赖账,翻脸不认

英汉对照
English-Chinese
中国文学宝库
Gems of Chinese Literature
现代文学系列
Modern Literature

ror. The least little thing and he'd ignore you as if you didn't exist. But he knew every path in the Western Hills. So I controlled my temper and played along with him.

"He'd stay up in the hills until he went broke. Then he'd come home. It happened every year. He'd go broke not because he was lazy, or dissolute. It was always due to his peculiar emotional make-up. As soon as he entered the hills, he'd immediately start hunting for beautiful women. As to who was beautiful and who was ugly — that was entirely a question of his personal taste. That fellow, anything that belonged to him was good, nobody could criticize it. If he liked it, even a scrawny chick was a gorgeous phoenix.

"Every year, he was sure to meet one beauty. As soon as he discovered her, he'd head straight for her village and hawk his wares outside her door, regardless of wind or rain, and never go any place else. But in one little hamlet, after all how much could you sell? You'd soon eat up your capital.

"One winter he found another beautiful woman. She lived way up in the hills. I got a look at her from behind once, and it's true she wasn't bad-looking. Dressed in clean blue homespun, nicely combed glossy black hair with a bun in the back — Yang Mao was enchanted. By the end of the lunar year, I was ready to go home, but he kept going to her village and sitting outside her door all day. When he got hungry he'd eat dry rations and take a sip of cold water from his teapot. Though he twirled his little hawker's drum till the skin on both sides was broken, the woman wouldn't come out anymore.

人。但是他对西山的地理很熟,哪一条道儿也摸得清,我就忍着气和他做伴。每年,他都是吃净赔光才肯回来的。他赔光,不是好吃懒做,也不是为非作歹,只是为了那么一股感情上的劲儿。他进了山,就像打猎的进了林一样,专门要找好看的女人。至于什么女人叫丑叫俊,那全看对不对他的眼光。这个人,凡是他的东西,都是好的,别人不能批评的。他喜欢的,死小鸡子也是凤凰。每年他总会遇到一个美人儿。一旦发见了这个美人儿,他就哪里也不再去,只到这个庄儿上来。不管刮风下雨,只坐在这家门口儿上去卖货。你想,一个小庄儿上,能销多少货物?坐吃山空,他就这样赔光了老本儿。一年冬天,他又发见了美人儿。这家人住在一个高山坡上,那女人我也见到一次背影儿,倒是长得不错,穿一身干净蓝衣服,头发梳得光光的,在后面盘成一朵圆花。杨卯儿被她迷住了,一直到腊月二十几,我要回家了,他还是每天到那庄儿上去,在人家门口,一坐就是一整天,饥了就吃些干粮,提起他那把小壶,喝些冷水。他一个劲儿的摇动他那小鼓,小鼓两边的皮都打穿了,人家那女的再也不出来。有一天,他实在忍不

"He couldn't stand it. One day he walked into her courtyard — and ran into her husband, who had just come home from the mountains. The man chased him out with a carrying pole and kicked his merchandise box and teapot down the slope. Yang Mao came rolling down next, his head split and bleeding. He was so dizzy, he passed out. I rushed over to him and brought him round and put his things in order. There wasn't much damage to the merchandise, but the small teapot was cracked. I said: 'Yang Mao, your teapot's broken.' He was very annoyed. 'It's not broken,' he said. 'At most, it's got a tiny crack in it.' I said: 'That's right, a tiny crack — like that gash you've got in your skull!'

"That's the sort of fellow Yang Mao is, comrade. He still thinks of that woman to this very day. He says she loves him; it's only her husband who's standing in the way!... Don't be offended. I'll find you another place to stay. We've got another backward family in this village...."

Never in his life had Yang Mao seen such a beautiful girl. He was simply overwhelmed by Man'er's pink and white splendour. He hopped forward like a sparrow in te winter snow, his trunk rigid, his small pointed cranium aimed straight ahead. His eyes devoured Man'er, every inch of her, and he docilely accepted her upbraiding like a repentant sinner accepting a reprimand from Heaven.

But then the sound that was music to his ears suddenly terminated. Man'er had gone in and slammed the gate.

12

The blacksmith work on Old Li's cart formally commenced. The

铁匠炉安设在新买来的宅院里。早晨,天晴得很好,六儿的鸽群在天空飞翔着。

黎老东最后修整着车的上装,在他心里,只等铁匠完工,就可以开始油漆了。傅老刚把铁匠炉点着,一股浓烟翻转着升向天空,然后折下来在庭院里散开。九儿拉着风箱,四儿被派练习抡大锤。

黎老东把几年来积累的烂铁和新买来的铁料,搬到炉下来。

九儿今天穿的很单薄,上身只穿了一件蓝色夹袄,她把擦脸的毛巾绺起来,齐着脑门把头发捆住,就像绣像上孙悟空戴的戒箍一样。她的脸色是更显得明朗了,充满了工作之前的热情和虔诚,轻捷而又稳重地推动着风箱。

傅老刚炼好第一块铁,用大铁钳夹着放在铁砧上,四儿赶过去抡起大锤。傅老刚用小锤敲点着砧子边教导着他,他还是不能用最适当的力量打在最适当的地方,有时把锤空落在砧子上,有时竟打在傅老刚的小锤上。九儿放下风箱把,来打给他看,在她的热心的示范和帮助下,四儿抡锤的技术,开始进步了。

黎老东在一边做着木匠活,注意力主要放在这边来了。他不断地斥责着四儿,说他笨,没有出息,唠叨不休。傅老刚在休息的时候,走到黎老东的身边说:

"You've become bad-tempered, relative," he said. "You can't treat children like that. It doesn't help them work better; it only makes them do worse. When you keep picking on him, he doesn't know what to do with his hands and feet."

"How can you talk that way? Didn't you say I'm not strict enough with my boys? My whole heart is in that cart. The sooner it's finished, the sooner it'll start earning money. Relative, let's use our very best skill on this job!"

Building a friendship is as hard as raising a flowering shrub. A careless slip can make a shrub wither. As the two old men worked together on the cart, they gradually realized that it wasn't the same as in the old days. In the past when they were working together on a job, there was a close brotherly tie between them. Now, Fu felt that Old Li wasn't co-operating — he was supervising. Li was driving him hard. The carpenter showed dissatisfaction even when Old Fu stopped for a smoke. What depressed Old Fu most was that although he had returned at last after a long journey, Old Li didn't once mention the matter of Nine and Six. It was as if the carpenter had never proposed the match.

During the final few days of the metal work on the cart, Old Li gave no help at all. He paraded around in his new fleece-lined robe, issuing orders. Six was also dressed up like a guest. Sometimes he came to the courtyard and looked around, then he vanished.

Old Fu wasn't feeling too well. Although the weather was quite cold, he wore only a tattered shirt, and he was working very hard. Every day, people came to watch. They were all old friends and

"亲家,我看你的脾气变坏了,对孩子们不能这样。这样不能使他工作得好,反会使他工作得更坏。他工作着,你一个劲儿斥责他,他的脚手就不知道往哪里放了。"

"你怎么说这样的话,你不是说管孩子应该严格些吗?"黎老东说,"打制这辆车是我心上的大事,早打成一天,好早一天用它去赚钱。亲家,让我们老兄弟把最好的手艺都施展出来吧!"

建立友情,像培植花树一样艰难。花树可以因为偶然的疏忽而枯萎。在黎老东和傅老刚这一次合作里,两个人心里都渐渐觉得和过去有些不一样。过去,两个人共同给人家做工,那是兄弟般的、手足般的关系。这一次,傅老刚越来越觉得黎老东不是同自己合作,而是在监督着。赶工赶得过紧,简直连抽袋烟,黎老东都在一旁表示着不满意。最使他闷气的是,自己远道赶来,黎老东却再也不说九儿和六儿的事,好像他从前没提过似的。

最后几天,黎老东只是穿着大皮袄,在院里察看着,指点着;八儿也打扮的像个客人似的,有时来在院里转游一下,就不见了。傅老刚身体有些不舒服,在这样冷的天气里,他穿着一件破旧的小衫,还是辛勤地工作着。天天,有些参观的人,来到院里,这些人都是傅老刚的旧相

英汉对照
English-Chinese
中国文学宝库
Gems of Chinese Literature
现代文学系列
Modern Literature

acquaintances of the blacksmith. They used to admire the combined skill of the two artisans. Now, they could see that there was a separation between Old Fu's art and Old Li's business. People no longer paid any attention to Old Li's carpentry. They were merely curious whether his new enterprise would prosper.

The two old friends plainly had developed two different standpoints. Old Li was entirely aware of this, and Old Fu quickly became aware of it also. That was at the root of the tragedy. It seemed to Old Fu that Old Li had now openly adopted the "bossy" attitude they had both despised and ridiculed for so many years and was directing it against him. Of course, this wasn't the fault of the new society. It was a hangover from the old days.

As the blacksmith's work was drawing to a close, one day when they were eating together, Old Li laughed and said: "I've been living more and more frugally, relative. You mustn't laugh at me. I'm saving to build some rooms for Six and his brothers. I'm sure you don't care about money."

Assuming he was going to talk about the marriage between Nine and Six, Old Fu raised his head and listened. To his surprise, Li's next remark was: "Why not just treat these days as if you were earning your keep in a famine period in your own village?"

This last sentence angered the blacksmith. He furiously pushed his bowl away and stood up. "Relative," he said, "I didn't come to you as a famine refugee!"

Old Fu called his daughter, brought a bucket of water and extinguished the fire, loaded his equipment on his barrow and pushed it to the street. Several people tried to pacify him, but the black-

识,老朋友。过去,他们来是同时观赏黎老东和傅老刚的手艺的;今天,在这些人的眼里,傅老刚的手艺,和黎老东的家业,被分别了出来。人们不再注意黎老东的木匠手艺,在新的形势下面,只在关心他的发家致富的前途。

两个老朋友,显然已经站在不同的地位上。黎老东完全觉到了这一点,傅老刚很快也完全觉到了,这就是我们的悲剧产生的根源。傅老刚感到,过去多年来,他和黎老东共同厌恶、共同嘲笑过的那种"主人"态度,现在是由他的老朋友不加掩饰地施展起来了,而对象就是自己。这当然不是新的社会制度的过错,而是传统习惯的过错。

当铁工也接近完成,一次吃饭的时候,黎老东忽然笑着说:

"亲家,我过日子越来越细了,你不要笑话我,我要积些钱给六儿他们把房子盖好。我想,你是不争这些的。"傅老刚以为他要提说九儿和六儿的事了,抬起头来听着,谁知道下文却是这么一句:"这些日了,就当你们是在老家度荒午吧!"

最后一句话,十分激怒了傅老刚,他把饭碗一推,立起身来,说:

"亲家,我不是到你这里来逃荒呀!"

他叫出女儿来,提起水桶,泼灭了炉灶。他打整好小车,推到了街上来。很多人来劝说,老

英汉对照
English-Chinese
中国文学宝库
Gems of Chinese Literature
现代文学系列
Modern Literature

smith flatly refused to go back.

None of the villagers knew the real reason for the split between the two old friends. Neither Four nor Nine, both young and inexperienced, had ever suffered so painful a blow. Old Fu was miserable. He took Four aside and asked:

"Tell me, child. Whose fault do you think it is?"

"It happened at just the right time. Now you can help us solve a big problem."

"What problem? Are you laughing at us two old men, child?"

"We young people want to organize a well-drilling brigade. This winter we want to sink pipes into all the usable wells in the village. We've already borrowed a borer, and we've got a lot of tools that need repair. We've been wanting to ask you to help, but we were afraid my pa wouldn't agree. Now that you've quarrelled with him, you can work with us."

"Have you got iron and steel?"

"We'll each contribute some. There'll be enough. We'll take your equipment to the Youth League compound."

When the blacksmith arrived, the youngsters welcomed him ecstatically.

"You don't know how we need you, Uncle! You must never leave. We've got it all arranged with the village authorities. You can have the east wing. We'll repair it nicely and paper the windows for you. You can live here as long as you like. In the evenings we'll bring brushwood and heat your platform bed."

13

Alone in his courtyard, Old Li sat on a log thinking dully.

头儿说什么也不回去。

两位老朋友的决裂,村里人都说不出那真正的道理。在四儿和九儿那经历较少的身世里,也还没有体验过这样伤心的事情。傅老刚是感到十分痛苦的,他把四儿叫到一边说:

"孩子,你看,这到底是怨谁呢?"

"这样正好。"四儿说,"你给我们解决了难题。"

"什么难题?"傅老刚问,"你这小子倒要看我们两个老头子的哈哈笑吗?"

"我们青年要组织一个钻井队。"四儿说,"在今年冬天,把我们村里能利用的水井都钻好下管。我们已经借到一杆锥。很多工具需要修理,我们想请你帮忙,又怕我爹不让。这样一闹,你就可以去帮助我们了。"

"你们有钢有铁?"傅老刚问。

"我们每人捐献一些,就够用了。"四儿说,"我们把小车,拉到青年团办公的大院里去吧。"

到了那里,青年们对老人说:

"大伯,我们是多么需要你啊!你再不要回山东老家。我们和村干部商量好了,把这院里的东屋给你拾掇出来,把窗子糊好。你就在这里常住吧,晚上我们抱柴来给你烧炕。"

13

黎老东一个人呆呆地坐在院里一截木头

The Blacksmith and the Carpenter

When Old Fu had walked out on him, he had said to himself: "That kind of friendship is just as well ended. He can't hurt me. I can get someone else to finish his work. He's not the only blacksmith under the sun." Li had picked up his axe and, with the hammer, had angrily driven big nails into the cart's rear boards.

But gradually the carpenter cooled down. The hammering of the nails rang hollowly in the empty courtyard. Without the friendly accompaniment of the blacksmith's clanging hammer, Li suddenly found himself unable to work. Flinging his axe aside, he sat down. His friendship with Old Fu had been years in the building, it had stood the test of many an adversity. Old Li rubbed his left foot. Once, when he and Old Fu were working on a job in another village, Li was unhappy and his axe had slipped, putting a nasty gash in his foot. He was far from home, with no relatives to help him, and had little money. In the several months needed to recuperate, it was Old Fu who got the doctor, paid for the medicines, carried Li on his back to the latrine, fetched him water and brought him food. Of course, Old Li had reciprocated. That same summer, Old Fu had been scalded by molten metal. Old Li had looked after him just as faithfully.

The carpenter felt quite badly. "Why, after all, should Old Fu break off our friendship so abruptly? Is he jealous because I'm doing well?" But Old Li knew the blacksmith wasn't that sort of person. "Have I changed? Do I scorn the poor and love the rich? Have I treated my old friend shabbily?" The carpenter thought back on his words and behaviour since Old Fu had returned, and his misery grew weighted with shame.

上。当傅老刚决绝地推车出门的时候,他心里也曾经想:这样的交情,断绝了也好。你晒不了我黎老东的干ןj,剩下的活,我会找别人来帮助,天下又不是只有一个铁匠。他拿起斧头来,气愤地锤击着车尾板上的大钉。但是,当他渐渐平静下来,听到只有他的斧头声音,在空旷的院落里回响,失去了亲切的钢铁的伴奏的时候,他忽然不能工作了,把斧头放在一边,坐了下来。他想,同傅老刚的交情,不是一年二年建立起来的,而且经过多次患难的考验。他用手抚摸着左边这一只脚。有一年,他同傅老刚给一家做活,他心情不好,一时失手,这只脚被锛砍伤了。那时离家在外,举目无亲,手里没有多少钱。在自己养伤的几个月的时间里,是傅老刚请医生,花药钱,背出背进,给水给饭。当然,这也报答过他了。同一年热天,傅老刚被热铁烫伤,自己曾经服侍过他。

他难过的是,究竟为了什么,傅老刚这样决绝?是他看我过得好些了,心里嫉恨?但想来想去,傅老刚从来也不是这样的人。是我变得嫌贫爱富,慢待了多年的朋友?他回忆着在这一段日子里,自己的言谈举动,他的痛苦就被惭愧的心情搅扰,变得更加沉重了。

英汉对照
English-Chinese
中国文学宝库
Gems of Chinese Literature
现代文学系列
Modern Literature

As Old Li sat brooding, Six came in. The carpenter looked at his son, the boy's body, his face. He could see there nothing but dissolute failure. "I've thought only of constructing a cart and building rooms these past two years, all for him," Li said to himself. "Offending my friend was because of him too! The boy lives for pleasure. He never gives a thought to his father's feelings."

"Is the food ready yet, Pa?" Six asked lazily, standing beside the window in the sunlight.

"Ready. Just waiting for you!" Old Li jumped up, grabbed his axe and charged.

Six had a quick eye. He turned and ran. Shortly before he had had another quarrel with Yang Mao on the street. Yang had learned that the male pigeon was dead, and was determined to go to Old Li and protest. Now, Six bumped into him at the compound gate. Clasping hands together in a respectful greeting, Six pleaded:

"Let's not fight over that pigeon, Brother Mao. Go in and soothe my father, quick! He wants to kill me!"

Yang Mao could never resist flattery and soft words. He at once undertook the mission and rushed inside. Spreading his arms, he halted Old Li at the door.

"For my sake, Uncle, let's go back. We can talk this over calmly."

He shunted Old Li back into the courtyard, brought him a stool, handed him a cigarette. Squatting down beside him, Yang Mao urged:

"Get the cart finished soon. Don't miss the winter season.

这时六儿走了进来。黎老东抬头望着自己的儿子,在儿子的身上脸上,只能看见一层不成材的灰败的气象。他一时想到:自己这二年,一心要打车,要盖房,得罪亲友,都为的是他!而这个孩子,只知道自己玩乐,从来也没有想想当父亲的心情。

"做熟饭了,爹?"六儿站在窗台下太阳地里,懒洋洋地问。

"做熟了,就等你了!"老头儿跳了起来,抢着斧子赶过去。

六儿眼快,回头就跑。他刚才在街上又和杨卯儿争吵了一次,杨卯儿知道了那只雄鸽的死亡,要找黎老东来说理。六儿在门口碰上他,向他作个揖说:

"卯儿哥,咱们的事儿别闹了。你快去劝劝我爹,他要打死我哩。"

杨卯儿生来经不住别人半点奉承,一句好话。仓促之间,他把这个委托应承下来,他快步向前,在梢门洞里,举起胳膊拦住了黎老东:

"看在侄儿面上。"杨卯儿说,"回家去,有话慢慢说。"

他把黎老东推进院里,给他找了一个坐物,又递给他一支香烟,自己蹲在一边,慢慢劝说着:

"快把车装制起来,别错过这个冬季,正是

The Blacksmith and the Carpenter

That's when the money is made! Look at Li the Seventh. One trip to Dingzhou earns him scores of yuan. In three trips he gets enough to build a big brick house, even after deducting the cost of his meals and the horse's feed. There's a house like that for sale in the western part of the village, Uncle Li. The price is reasonable. Are you interested?"

"No," said the carpenter. "My heart is cold."

"All elderly people are the same," said Yang. "They hate to see their youngsters going wrong. When my pa was alive, you two were good friends. You know how strict he was with me, how much trouble he took. Of course, I can't say I ever earned him much glory, but, in all fairness, I never made him lose face! I'm an honest fellow who's been around a lot. I'm always fighting against injustice, and I'd do anything for a friend. Money is no object. It's true I haven't got anywhere till now, but that's because I was fated to hardship, not that I'm incapable. Brother Six isn't a bad sort, it seems to me. He's intelligent and sensible. A bit wild, perhaps, but all young fellows go through that period. You get the cart finished and give it to him. Once he has a legitimate job to do, he'll settle down. Don't you agree?"

Old Li's anger gradually abated as Yang Mao led him back to his original line of thinking. About that time, Four returned. Without a word, he went to feed the horse. He had something in his hand, partly concealed by his padded robe. He did his best to keep it out of his father's sight as he neared the door.

"What have you got there?" Old Li demanded.

"An old spade head." Four halted and showed it to the carpen-

赚好钱的时候啊！你看见黎七儿了，一趟定州就是几十万，除去人吃马喂，三趟就可以盖座大砖房。老东叔，西村有座砖房要卖，价钱公道，你倒是有意思没有？"

"没有意思。"黎老东说，"我的心凉了。"

"谁家的老人也是这样，"杨卯儿说，"最恨小人儿不争气。我爹活着时，你们交情好，是知道的，管我管得多么紧？在我身上费了多大力？我当然不能说给他老人家挣来了多少光荣，平心而论，一辈子也没有给他老人家丢过什么脸面呀！咱是个正直人，从小儿走南着闯北，打抱不平，为朋友两肋插刀，花钱从不分你我。到老来没落下什么，不是我不能干，是命里穷苦。六儿兄弟，我看不错，为人聪明懂事，就是荒唐点儿，这也是年轻人必经之路，你快把车打整起来，交给他，一有正经事儿，他也就不胡跑了，你说是不是？"

黎老东的气渐渐消了，杨卯儿又把他引到原来的思路上。这时四儿回来了，他一声不言语，到屋里给牲口筛了两底儿草，手里提着一件什么东西，叫棉袍掩盖着，躲躲闪闪地又要出去。

"你手里提的什么？"黎老东问。

"一把破铁锹。"四儿只好站住，把东西亮出来。

英汉对照
English-Chinese
中国文学宝库
Gems of Chinese Literature
现代文学系列
Modern Literature

ter.

"Where did you get it? I've been looking all over for scrap. Why didn't you tell me?" Old Li asked angrily.

"I picked it up that year we dismantled the Japanese gun tower. It wasn't any use then, so I put it aside. Now, our superiors are calling on us to dig wells, and I'm thinking of repairing it."

The old man swore, "The whole damned family is turning against me!" He stood up. "Put that back where you found it. Your superiors call on you to dig wells; I call on you to build that cart! No one's going to do it for me. You hurry and cook some food; after you're full, you're going to help me drive nails!" Again, Yang Mao hastened to intervene. Four had no choice but to make the meal. Later, he would find some way to get the old spade head out of the house.

14

Drawing Six into study and work, as Nine had proposed, was proving extremely difficult. He rarely would join in meetings or other activities. When cadres tried to get him to take part, he would insist that at the moment production was of primary importance. Making a great show of diligence, he would take a basket and trot off into the hills on the pretext of gathering brushwood.

The village authorities discussed the matter. Some thought they ought to try to reform Man'er first. Approaching Man'er was easy enough. Although the young men wouldn't go near her — either because they were timid, or afraid of becoming suspect — the girls

"哪里来的这个,我这些日子到处找烂铁,你怎么不言语?"黎老东又挂了火。

"这是那年拆日本炮楼,我捡来的,因为没有用,就扔在一边了。"四儿说,"现在上级号召打井,我想去修理修理它。"

"他妈的,整个儿的六国反叛!"黎老东说着站起来,"从哪里拿的,还给我放回哪里去。上级号召打井,我号召打车!人家不给我干了,你快去做饭,吃饱了帮我上钉子!"

杨卯儿又赶过来劝解,四儿只好先去抱柴做饭,再慢慢想法把铁锹运出去。

14

九儿所想的,吸收六儿参加学习或是参加工作,都是很困难的事。他轻易不接近这些集会和活动。干部去找他,他会说现在是生产第一,装模作样地背上一副柴禾筐,遛遛跶跶到地里去了。干部们也曾讨论先从改造小满儿入手。接近小满儿是容易的,但男青年们不愿意去,有的是胆怯,有的是避嫌疑。当然,女同志

certainly could talk with her.

Man'er would warmly greet any young woman who called on her. If she brought a baby, Man'er would feed it goodies, hold it in her arms and smother it with kisses. Even the shyest child became happy, snuggled against Man'er's bosom. And Man'er's lovely young visage glowing with warmth would add colour to the baby's face. Laughing, Man'er would talk vivaciously, as if her lips were oiled. Her caller would warm to Man'er in spite of herself, and when she criticized Man'er, her tone would automatically soften.

"A clever girl like you ought to study, Man'er," the woman might urge. "I'll call for you tonight, and we'll attend class in the night school together."

"Fine," Man'er would retort smilingly. "I've always wanted a chance to study. But you needn't call for me, Sister. The streets are dark and you're carrying a baby. What if you should fall? I'll go myself. I know my way around this village perfectly."

"You'll be sure to go, then?"

"Definitely." Man'er would see her guest to the door and smile and wave at the baby. But after her visitor had turned the corner, Man'er's face would darken and she would think a moment. Then she would enter the house, change her clothes and go to her mother's place in the county town.

If any political campaign was going on in the village, and frequent meetings were being held, Man'er wouldn't show her face for days. Once in a while, she would put in an appearance at the night school. She always sat far from the lamp, in a dark corner of the room. After the lesson started and everyone was settling down,

们也可以和她去谈。女同志去了,小满儿总是热情地招待着,如果抱着小孩,她总得给孩子弄些好吃的东西来,并且要接到怀里,不停地在孩子的脸上亲亲吻吻。任何认生或是任性的孩子,到了小满儿的怀里,也会高兴起来的,孩子的脸也会叫她的充满青春热情的面孔,陪衬得更为出色。她会说,说笑起来,嘴上像撩上油儿似的。在这种场合,女同志们都是有些喜欢她,在批评上,那口气就自然软和多了。

"小满儿,拿着你这样聪明伶俐的人儿,好好学习学习吧;晚上,我来叫你,我们一块到民校听课去。"女同志热心地说服着。

"那很好,"小满儿笑着说,"我盼不能得儿愿意去学习呢。不用大姐来叫,黑灯瞎火,道路又不好走,你抱着个孩子,跌倒怎么办?我自己去吧,这个村子,街道都叫我磨平了,谁家我不认识呀!"

"你可一定去。"女同志又叮咛一句。

"一定。"小满儿把她送到门口,又和孩子招手耍笑着。等到女同志一拐弯儿,她把脸一沉,想了想,到家里换上件衣服,就进城回娘家去了。如果村里有什么运动,连续开会,她会几天几夜不露面儿。有时,她也到民校晃晃。她总是坐在灯光不亮的地方,在讲课刚开始,人们安

英汉对照
English-Chinese
中国文学宝库
Gems of Chinese Literature
现代文学系列
Modern Literature

she would pretend to listen also. But when the other students grew absorbed, she would quietly slip away.

Whether living with her mother or with her sister, Man'er loved to go walking outside the village, alone. She was a night bird, revelling in the darkness. On hot summer evenings she flitted about like a firefly, engaging in wild flights of fancy. Intoxicated with nature, she would wander over the brambly dunes far from the village walls. She was quite fearless at night. Marauding foxes would run past her, insects would knock against her face or crawl over her body, but she would sit happily on a dark sand dune, letting the cool breezes caress her while the sun-baked sand warmed her beneath. In winter, the savage winds excited her. Whirling snowflakes, landing on her face, melted as if they had fallen on a slab of red hot metal.

Every night she came home very late, when all was still. With skilful familiarity, she would round the wall, hop over the fence and slip into bed so softly that no one was aware of her return. She would rise early the next morning and light the stove and cook breakfast, full of energy. There seemed no limit to her youthful vigour. Wasting her precious youth, she teetered constantly on the edge of a precipice.

Man'er was a girl of many talents. Everyone knew that if planted in suitable soil, she would bear rich fruit. No matter how intricate the pattern of a length of cloth, or how new the fashion of a pair of cloth shoes, she needed only a glance to be able to duplicate them, quickly and well. She had a sharp intellect. A thing had only to be pointed out to her and her mind penetrated it immediate-

静不下来的时候,她装做安静的听讲。当人们渐渐入神的时候,她就偷偷溜出来了。

无论在娘家或是在姐姐家,她好一个人绕到村外去。夜晚,对于她,像对于那些喜欢在夜晚出来活动的飞禽走兽一样。炎夏的夜晚,她像萤火虫儿一样四处飘荡着,难以抑止那时时腾起的幻想和冲动。她拖着沉醉的身子在村庄的围墙外面,在离村很远的沙岗上的丛林里徘徊着。在夜里,她的胆子变得很大,常常有到沙岗上来觅食的狐狸,在她身边跑过,常常有小虫子扑到她的脸上,爬到她的身上,她还是很喜欢地坐在那里,叫凉风吹抚着,叫身子下面的热沙熨贴着。在冬天,狂暴的风,鼓舞着她的奔流的感情,雪片飘落在她的脸上,就像是飘落在烧热烧红的铁片上。

每天,她在夜深人静的时候,才回到家里去。她熟练敏捷地绕过围墙,跳过篱笆,使门窗没有一点儿响动,不惊动家里任何人,回到自己炕上。天明了,她很早就起来,精神饱满地去抱柴做饭,不误工作。她的青春是无限的,抛费着这样宝贵的年华,她在危险的崖岸上回荡着。

而且,她的才能是多方面的,谁都相信,如果是种植在适当的土壤里,她可以结下丰盛的果实。不管多么复杂的花布,多么新鲜的鞋样,她从来一看就会,织做起来又快又好。她的聪

英汉对照
English-Chinese
中国文学宝库
Gems of Chinese Literature
现代文学系列
Modern Literature

ly, like a finger poking through thin spring ice or a flimsy paper window.

When the whim took her, she would carry buckets to the garden to water the vegetables. She was a match for the strongest young man. In one morning, she could scoop a well dry. And it was nothing for her to walk a dozen or more *li* to market with eighty catties of beans in baskets suspended from the ends of her shoulder pole. At such times, even many of the old folks in the village praised her. They hoped that some force could be found to pull her back on the right track.

That year, the new *Marriage Law* was proclaimed, and Man'er suddenly began to take an active part in public affairs. She voluntarily attended meetings, asked people to read the newspaper to her, grew quiet and thoughtful. The articles said that women and men were equal, that the women had already done a great deal of work and that in the future they would make an even larger and more important contribution to the country.

But then Man'er heard some people propose an investigation of illicit relations between men and women in the village, and she stopped going to meetings and returned to her free and easy way of life. That was why the vice-chairman brought the provincial offcial to live in the home of Stupid Li.

The same day, Man'er's mother arrived. Though over fifty, she still dressed very flashily. It was obvious she had made herself up carefully in preparation for this exploratory call.

"Man'er," she said, "your husband will be coming home soon. Your mother-in-law came to see me. It's almost New Year's time.

明,像春天的薄冰,薄薄的窗纸,一指点就透。高兴的时候,她到菜园里生产,浇起园来,可以和最壮实的小伙子竞赛,一个早晨把井水浇干。她可以担八十斤的豆角儿走出十里去上市。在这个时候,连村里一些老年人,都称赞她,希望有一种力量,能把她引纳到人生的正轨上来。今年,村里宣传婚姻法的时候,这女孩子忽然积极起来。她自动地到会,请人读报给她听,正正经经地沉默着,思想着。在那些文件上说明:女人和男人是平等的,她们已经做了很多工作,将来还会对国家有更大更多的贡献。但后来听到有些人,想把问题引到检查村里的男女关系,她就退了出来,恢复了自己的放荡的生活方式。因此,副村长向青年们提议,把那位高级干部带到黎大傻的家里。

　　这一天,她的母亲来了。这是一位到了五十多岁年纪、还在热心打扮的女人。可以看出在探看女儿的这次行动上,她曾经在头面上做了很细致的准备。她见到小满儿,就说:

　　"满儿,你男人快回来了,你婆婆找到咱家

You ought to go back and live there a while."

"I won't," said Man'er. "You and sister picked him without consulting me. Since you two have taken over my marriage, you're the ones who should receive him when he comes back!"

"How dare you speak to me like that, you little snip! There's a lot of idle talk about the way you're running around here!"

Man'er sat down on the edge of the platform bed and toyed with her shoes and socks. "Why should I pay any attention to it if it's only idle talk? Some people have nothing better to do than gossip!"

"It's giving you a bad name, pet," the mother retorted, clapping her hands together fretfully.

Man'er walked over to the mirror and combed her hair. "If I'm getting a bad name it's only because I'm following the example you two have set!"

"Who set you any examples?" her sister demanded, Man'er's quarrelling with her mother irritated her. "You're not fit to be my pupil. Just look at you. You've been sweet on Six all winter and he hasn't even given you a pair of new padded trousers. And you have the nerve to criticize!"

"You go earn a pair for me then!" Having finished making up, Man'er flipped aside the door curtain and walked out.

Man'er wandered into her sister's vegetable garden. It was near the big sand dune west of the village. Because Stupid Li and his wife were lazy and did nothing to stop it, over the years the dune had encroached into half the garden. A young peach tree was bent almost to the ground by the weight of the shifting sand. Man'er dug the sand away and straightened the tree, then wrapped the trunk

去,眼下就过年,你该到人家那里去住些时候了。"

"我不去。"小满儿说,"婚姻是你和姐姐包办的,你们应该包办到底,男人既然要回来,你们就快拾掇拾掇上车走吧。"

"你他妈的说的这是什么话?"母亲说,"你在这村里疯跑,人家有闲话哩!"

"既是闲话,"小满儿坐在炕沿上低着头整理着鞋袜说,"我管它干什么?叫他们吃了饭没事,瞎嚼去吧!"

"名声不好听哩,"母亲拍着巴掌,"我的小祖宗。"

"名声不好听,"小满儿跳下炕来对着镜子梳理着头发,直眉立眼地说,"也不是从我开始,是你们留给我的好榜样呀!"

她这样和母亲冲突,使得姐姐也不高兴了,姐姐说:

"小满儿,你不要胡说八道,谁给你留下的榜样?你够得上当我的徒弟吗?看你和小六儿,恋了一冬天,连条新棉裤也穿不上,还有脸强嘴哩!"

"你先去挣一条来给我穿吧!"小满儿打整好,一摔门帘出去了。

她一个人走到她姐姐家的菜园子里,这个菜园子紧靠村西的大沙岗,因为黎大傻一家人懒惰,年久失修,那沙岗已经侵占了菜园的一半,园子里有一棵小桃树,也叫流沙压得弯弯地倒在地上。小满儿用手刨了刨沙土,叫小桃树直起腰来,然后找了些干草,把树身包裹起来。

英汉对照
English-Chinese
中国文学宝库
Gems of Chinese Literature
现代文学系列
Modern Literature

with straw.

She sat down on the sheltered side of the dune, out of the wind. A large rooster atop the dune crowed shrilly. A dry poplar leaf fell upon her breast. Suddenly Man'er felt miserable; she covered her face and wept. At that moment, she understood herself, pitied herself, hated herself. She had always been unloved, she was always travelling alone. But had she chosen the right road? Man'er began thinking back on the criticism and advice people had given her.

15

When her sister left to escort her mother to the edge of the village, Man'er returned home by another route. She found Stupid Li helping a government officer put a room in order. Man'er was surprised. She knew that because her sister's family was backward, dirty and had an unsavoury reputation, no cadre had ever lived there before. The place they were readying, a room in the east wing, was full of rubbish. In the room next door, a little donkey was quartered.

Man'er observed that her brother-in-law seemed both respectful and uneasy in the presence of his guest. Stupid couldn't understand why, of all the people in the village, the authorities should have come to him with such a high-ranking individual. As he clumsily helped with the moving, Stupid kept asking the guest for his instructions.

Judging by his dress and manner, it seemed to Man'er that the

她在沙岗的避风处坐了下来,有一只大公鸡在沙岗上高声啼叫,干枯的白杨叶子,落到她的怀里。她忽然觉得很难过,一个人掩着脸,啼哭起来。在这一时刻,她了解自己,可怜自己,也痛恨自己。她明白自己的身世:她是没有亲人的,她是要自己走路的。过去的路,是走错了吧?她开始回味着人们对她的批评和劝告。

15

她看见姐姐送着母亲走出村来,她才绕道儿回到家里去;到家里,看见黎大傻正帮着一个干部收拾屋子,小满儿惊奇了,她知道姐姐家因为落后、肮脏和名声不好,是从来没住过干部的。他们收拾的是东房的里间,这间屋里堆着一些烂七八糟的东西,外间,喂着一匹很小的毛驴。

她看见姐夫在这位干部面前,表现了很大的敬畏和不安,他好像不明白为什么村干部忽然领了这样一位上级来在他的家里下榻。他不断向干部请示,手足不知所措地搬运着东西。

小满儿看来,这位干部的穿着和举止,都和

comrade was out of harmony with the room being given him. His clothing showed that he was of provincial government rank, at least. Insisting on absolute cleanliness, he wielded the broom and swept out places that hadn't been touched in ages. For some reason, Man'er suddenly wanted to help him. She filled her own pretty basin with water and sprinkled the room to settle the dust.

"Who are you?" the cadre asked her.

"She's my sister-in-law," said Stupid with some pride, yet slightly fearful.

"Oh, you must be Comrade Man'er, then," said the newcomer, looking at her intently. "The village authorities just told me about you."

"What did they say?" asked the girl, her head bent as she swept the floor.

"A few words can't tell a person's whole story. Living here in the same house, we'll be like one family. We'll gradually get to understand each other."

The comrade placed his luggage on the platform bed. Man'er brought some kindling, scraped the top of the stove, scrubbed the pot, filled it with water and said:

"This room was empty for a long time. It's cold. I'll heat the platform bed for you."

"I'll do it," said Stupid, who was standing beside her.

The girl ignored him. When the water was hot, she poured it into her basin, then went out and brought her own soap in a container. Handing it to the comrade, she said:

"You can wash your face. Have you any towels?"

他要住的这间屋子不相称。从他的服装看来,至少是从保定下来的。他对清洁卫生要求很严格,自己弯腰搜索着扫除那万年没人动过的地方。小满儿不知道为什么忽然愿意帮帮他的忙,她用自己的花洗脸盆打来水,用手在那尘土飞扬的地上泼洒。

"你是这家的什么人?"那位干部直起身来问。

"她是我的小姨子。"黎大傻站在一边有些得意又有些害怕地说。

"啊,你就是小满同志。"干部注视着她说,"村干部刚才向我介绍过了。"

"他们怎样介绍我?"小满儿低头扫着地问。

"简单的介绍,还不能全面地说明一个人。"干部说,"我住在这里,我们就成了一家人,慢慢会互相了解的。"

干部在炕上铺好行李,小满儿抱来茅柴,把锅台扫净,把锅刷好,然后添上水,说:

"这屋里长年不住人,很冷。我给你烧烧炕吧。"

"我来烧。"黎大傻站在她身边说。

小满儿没有理他。她把水烧热了,掏在洗脸盆里,又到北屋里取来自己的胰子,送进里间:

"洗脸,你自己带着毛巾吧?"

英汉对照
English-Chinese
中国文学宝库
Gems of Chinese Literature
现代文学系列
Modern Literature

That evening, the comrade went out to a meeting. It was quite late by the time he returned. On the platform bed now stood a short-legged table that had been rubbed very clean. There was a thermos flask filled with boiled water on the table, and a brightly polished kerosene lamp, its flame turned low. He touched the platform bed; it was warm, heated by flues underneath.

The door of the north wing squeaked. Soon Stupid's wife, covering her bosom, entered.

"Comrade," she said, "if you have more meetings in the future, you'd better get back earlier. We've always barred our compound gate. If we have to leave it open for you, I'll be afraid to sleep."

She shut the door forcefully and departed.

Making use of the table and the lamplight, the comrade wrote something in his notebook. As he was preparing for bed, Man'er glided into the room noiselessly. A flowery towel kerchief covered her hair, the design of a large peony directly above her forehead. She looked pale in the lamplight and seemed very tired. Sitting down on the end of the platform bed, she leaned against the wall and smiled.

"Comrade, pour me a drink of water."

"It's late. Why aren't you asleep?" The cadre handed her a filled bowl.

Man'er smiled. "I wanted to ask you. What's your job? Do you look after production?"

"I've come to learn about the people here."

"That's rich," Man'er laughed. "Government production administrators are coming to our village all the time. They only examine

晚上,干部出去开会,回来已经夜深了,进屋看见,小小的擦抹得很干净的炕桌上面,放着灌得满满的一个热水瓶;一盏洋油灯,罩子擦得很亮,捻小了灯头。摸了摸炕,也很暖和。

他听见北屋的房门在响。黎大傻的老婆,掩着怀走进屋来。她说:

"同志,以后出去开会,要早些回来才好。我们家的门子向来严紧,给你留着门儿,我不敢放心睡觉。"

说完,就用力带上门子走了。

干部利用小桌和油灯,在本子上记了些什么。他正要安排着睡觉,小满儿没有一点儿响动地来到屋里。她头上箍着一块新花毛巾,一朵大牡丹花正罩在她的前额上。在灯光下,她的脸色有些苍白,她好像很疲乏,靠着隔扇墙坐在炕沿上,笑着说:

"同志,倒给我一碗水。"

"这样晚,你还没有睡?"干部倒了一碗水递过去说。

"没有。"小满儿笑着说,"我想问问你,你是做什么工作的?是领导生产的吗?"

"我是来了解人的。"干部说。

"这很新鲜。"小满儿笑着说,"领导生产的干部,到村里来,整年价像走马灯一样。他们要

英汉对照
English-Chinese
中国文学宝库
Gems of Chinese Literature
现代文学系列
Modern Literature

our millet and wheat. What do you want to see?"

The comrade smiled but didn't answer. He looked at the young woman. Although it was late and they were alone together under circumstances that might easily be misunderstood, her expression was quite innocent. There wasn't even a hint of anything improper in her manner. It's not easy to know a person, he thought. So far, I can't quite figure her out.

"Finish the water and go to bed," he said. "Your sister must be waiting for you."

"She blew out the lamp and went to sleep long ago," said Man'er. "I'm very tired and your platform bed is warm. Let me sit a while."

The provincial officer picked up a newspaper and began to read. Was the girl as loose and shameless as the villagers said? Was this a device of hers to get on the good side of him so that he wouldn't criticize her? Or was she just a naive, curious girl trying to be helpful?

"If you want to learn about the people here," said Man'er, bowl in hand, "why don't you go to some activists' home instead of coming to a rowdy place like this?"

"Rowdy?"

"Living here, you're like a snare set beside a pile of grain. The birds all give us a wide berth. It's not usually so quiet here. Usually, my sister's room is jammed every night."

"In that case, I'm interfering with your social life. I'll move tomorrow."

"That's up to you. I'm not Yang Mao. I'm not driving you

看谷子和麦子的产量,你要看些什么呢?"

干部笑了笑没有讲话。他望着这位青年女人,在这样夜深人静,男女相处,普通人会引为重大嫌疑的时候,她的脸上的表情是纯洁的,眼睛是天真的,在她的身上看不出一点儿邪恶。他想:了解一个人是困难的,至少现在,他就不能完全猜出这位女人的心情。

"喝完水去睡觉吧!"他说,"你姐姐还在等你哩。"

"她们早吹灯睡了。"小满儿说,"我很累,你这炕头儿上暖和,我要多坐一会儿。"

干部拿起一张报纸,在灯下阅读着。他不知道,这位女人是像村里人所说的那样,随随便便,不顾羞耻,用一种手段在他面前讨好,避免批评呢? 还是出于幼年好奇和乐于帮助别人的无私的心。

"你来了解人,"小满儿托着水碗说,"怎么不到那些积极分子和模范们的家里,反倒来在这样一个混乱地方?"

"怎样混乱?"干部问。

"你住在这里,就像在粮堆草垛旁边安上了一只夹子,那些鸟儿们都飞开,不敢到这里来吃食儿了。"小满儿说,"平日这里可没有这样安静。平日,每到晚上,我姐姐的屋里,是挤倒屋子压塌炕的。"

"这样说,是我妨碍了你们的生活。"干部说,"明天我搬家吧。"

"随便。"小满儿说,"我不是杨卯儿,并没有

英汉对照
English-Chinese
中国文学宝库
Gems of Chinese Literature
现代文学系列
Modern Literature

away. What I mean is learning about people isn't like looking at a picture. You can't do it just sitting here, or in a short time either. Some people know how to put on an act; to your face they'll say all sorts of fine-sounding things. Others won't say a word; they'll just wait and see what kind of subjective judgment you'll make."

At first though her voice trembled she restrained her tears. Finally, she broke into sobs. Tears ran down her face on to her tunic.

Startled, the provincial officer put his newspaper aside. But Man'er said no more. She removed her head kerchief and wiped her eyes with it. Gravely, she put down the bowl, turned and left.

Stupid didn't feed the little donkey all night. It brayed and kicked in the room next door and gnawed its trough. Rats, either because the room was warm or because it contained a newcomer, grew lively. They scampered squeaking over the table, the platform bed and the window sills.

For a long time the provincial officer was unable to fall asleep. He awoke very early the next morning. Man'er came running in, dressed in a red woollen jersey. Her collar was open and her sleeves were pushed up; her face and neck were wet. Evidently, she had just been washing. Looking for something on the end of the platform bed, she leaned over the provincial officer. Her breasts brushed against his face. He could smell her warm fragrance. Finally, she found the soap container which she had loaned him the night before and hurried with it from the room.

16

The blacksmith's forge was set up in a new location.

撑你的意思。我是说，你了解人不能像看画儿一样，只是坐在这里。短时间也是不行的。有些人，他们可以装扮起来，可以在你的面前说得很好听；有些人，他就什么也可以不讲，听候你来主观的判断。"

她先是声音颤抖着，忍着眼泪，终于抽咽着，哭了起来，泪珠接连落在她的袄襟上。

干部惊异地放下报纸。但是小满儿再也没讲什么，扯下毛巾擦干了眼泪，稳重地放下水碗，转身走了。

整个夜里，黎大傻并不来给小毛驴添草，小毛驴饿了，号叫着，踢着墙角，龈着槽帮。耗子们因为屋里暖和了还是因为添了新的客人，也活动起来，在箱子上，桌面上，炕头和窗台上吱叫着游行。

干部长久失眠。醒来的时候，天还很早，小满儿跑了进来。她好像正在洗脸，只穿一件红毛线衣，挽着领子和袖口，脸上脖子上都带着水珠，她俯着身子在干部头起翻腾着，她的胸部时时摩贴在干部的脸上，一阵阵发散着温暖的香气。然后抓起她那胰子盒儿跑出去了。

16

铁匠炉在新的场所生起来。

英汉对照
English-Chinese
中国文学宝库
Gems of Chinese Literature
现代文学系列
Modern Literature

"This time, I'm going to take charge," Nine told the young people. "We're the Well-Diggers Youth Brigade!"

"We're with you," the youngsters said. "We'll take turns swinging the big hammer and pulling the piston bellows. Old uncle won't have to do a thing except stand on the side and supervise."

The metal they contributed was broken old scraps buried over the years beneath the earth and in various corners. Now these pieces would be melted down and forged together. They would be made into a sharp steel bit that could bore into the ground and bring up the spring waters. To the youngsters it was as if the mounting enthusiasm of each of them was being forged into a single powerful force for building up the nation.

Nine's face reflected the red flames of the forge. The small hammer in her hand beat out a clanging tattoo on the anvil. The sound had a competent ring to it, for she was no longer a beginner at this heavy work. When still a little girl she had helped her father make horseshoes and bits for the mounts of innumerable cavalrymen. Now the sharp raps of the hammer ringing in her ears recalled memories of her childhood: During those years of warfare, echoing in the hoofbeats of the battle chargers on the paths that crisscrossed the plain was the heart, pure as gold, of a little girl making her first contribution to her country!

Of course, she could remember an even earlier period. Today's work could serve as a memorial to her mother, who had been poor all her life and died middle-aged. When Nine was born, her mother had placed her on a small platform bed near the forge. Day and night, Nine had heard the sounds of this type of labour. Her moth-

"这回,我要当掌作的。"九儿对青年们说,"我们是青年钻井队么!"

"拥护你。"青年们说,"我们轮流抡大锤、拉风箱,叫大伯站在一边指点着就行。"

青年们捐献来的钢铁是零碎的、破旧的,它们曾经多年埋没在角落里、泥土里,现在要经过锻炼,铸接在一起,形成一杆尖利的,能钻探地下,引出泉水来的铁钻钢锥。在青年们看来,这就像要把他们各人的高涨的热情,铸炼成一股共同建设国家的力量一样。

九儿的脸,被炉火烘照着,手里的小锤,叮当地响在铁砧上。这声音,听来是熟悉的。因为,她已经不是初次接触这种沉重的劳动了。在她的幼年,她就曾经帮助父亲,为无数的战士们的马匹,打制过铁掌和嚼环。现在,当这清脆的锤声,又在她的耳边响起的时候,她可以联想:在她的童年,在战争的岁月里,在平原纵横的道路上,响起的大队战马的铿锵的蹄声里,也曾经包含着一个少女最初向国家献出的,金石一般的忠贞的心意!

当然,她可以想到更早一些的日子,她可以用今天的工作来纪念她那贫苦终身、中年丧命的母亲。当母亲生下她来,把她放在炉边的一条小炕上,她就昼夜听到这种劳动的声响了,母

英汉对照
English-Chinese
中国文学宝库
Gems of Chinese Literature
现代文学系列
Modern Literature

er had plied the piston bellows while singing the lullabies that put her to sleep. Even when Nine was still being carried within her mother's body, her mother had engaged in this heavy work.

Now, in the bitterly cold morning, warm perspiration soared through Nine's thin clothing. It was the first time she had ever worked together with her own companions according to a plan that had been discussed collectively. These young people virtually fought for the jobs, snatched at them, yet were concerned about and co-operated with one another. This, to Nine, was particularly new and exciting. It seemed to her that her father was stimulated too. In his long years of hardship and wandering from place to place, he had never dreamed that a worksite could present such a scene!

The first snow of the year had already fallen upon the plain when the young people began labouring out in the open. At noon, the snow glittering on the nearby sand dunes gradually melted. Most of the fields had been given their autumn ploughing, and the soft turned earth was moist. But the weather was already quite cold. The soil would freeze again in the mornings and in the evenings.

They set up high treadle wheels. Rising one after another on the vast plain, the tall structures were a new element on the scene, arousing longings and stirring the imagination. They made you think of fluttering banners, of windmills in foreign stories, of water towers at railway stations, of the towers above mine shafts, of the wooden scaffolding for the large buildings being erected in the cities. As the young people laboured diligently to tap water sources, their songs whirled through the air like the treadle wheel

亲站在风箱前面,给她哼着催眠歌曲。或者说,当她还同母亲是一个躯体的时候,母亲就带着她从事这种沉重的工作了。

现在,热汗在严寒的早晨,透过了她单薄的衣服。这种同自己的伙伴们在一起,按照集体讨论的计划来工作,对她来说,还是第一次。这些青年伙伴们,在工作面前是争着做,抢着做的,是互相关怀和协同动作的。因此,九儿感到特别振奋和新鲜。据她看来,父亲也是振奋的,在他那漫长的劳苦和跋涉的一生里,现在的工作场景是做梦也不曾梦见过的啊!

当青年们在田野里工作的时候,平原上已经降过了初雪。中午,雪在附近的沙岗上闪烁着,慢慢融化着。在普遍秋耕过的土地上,泛起一层潮湿的松土。但是天气已经大冷了,大地在早上和晚上都要封冻。

青年钻井队的高大的滑车,在平原上接二连三地树立起来了。它们给漠漠的平原,添上了一种新的使人向往并能诱发幻想的景色。它们使人想起飘扬的旗帜,使人想起外国故事里的风车,使人想起车站的水塔,矿山的竖井,都市里高大建筑的木架。青年人为开发水源,勤奋地工作着,他们的歌声和空中的滑车一同旋转飞扬着。

英汉对照
English-Chinese
中国文学宝库
Gems of Chinese Literature
现代文学系列
Modern Literature

on high.

Four, Kitchen Stove and Nine were on the same team. They brought their own dry rations and millet, and cooked them together at noon beside the well shaft, burning fallen branches and dry reeds they cut in the overgrown cemetery.

"As you know," Four said to Nine, "we're on the plain here. But the village has sand dunes on three sides. The ones to the west have come down from the mountains. Their flow does more damage than the river's floods. When the spring winds blow, the sky is covered all day with flying yellow sand. It leaps over walls and fences, it rolls into the fields and vegetable gardens. It smothers the young garlic and scallion sprouts, fills the furrows of the wheat fields and buries young trees. After every big spring wind, we have to sweep the sand from the fields. We even have to get down on the ground and blow it from the tender sprouts that are pale and bent by the weight of it, and let them see the sun again. The big winds blow so much sand into the streets you feel like you're walking on the beach by the river, it's that deep. The sand gets under the doors and breaks the paper windowpanes. Every day the women sweep from the room a couple of dustpans full. That's the kind of natural surroundings we live in. This call the authorities have put out for everybody to dig wells and plant trees — nothing could be more ideal for us here."

"We lived in the mountains," said Nine, "but we also had drought year after year. As long as I can remember, hot sandy winds blew in from the northwest every spring and beat for all they were worth against our little house. There used to be a stream in

四儿、锅灶和九儿是一个小组,他们带来些干粮、小米,中午从坟地里砍些蒿草,捡些树枝,在井边烧起饭来。

"你是知道的,"四儿对九儿说,"我们这里是平原,可是村子的三面,都叫沙岗包围起来了。西边这条沙岗,从山地流过来,它的流沙比河水泛滥还厉害。每到春天,整天刮着遮天盖地的黄风,黄沙会滚滚地跳过墙头篱笆,灌到地里来,灌到菜园子里来。黄沙盖住刚出土的蒜苗、韭菜芽,封住麦垄,埋住小树。每年春季,大风过后,我们就不得不到地里去用笤帚扫,甚至伏在地下用口吹,使得那被沙子压得发弯发白的嫩芽儿,重见天日。大风把沙子灌进街里,使人像在河滩走路,一陷多深。沙子灌进房门,打破窗户,妇女们每天要从屋里打扫出几簸箕土来。这就是我们的自然环境。上级号召打井栽树,是最适合我们这一带的情况不过了。"

"我们那里是山地,"九儿说,"也是荒旱连年。从我记事起,每年春天,干热的风沙就从西北山谷里吹过来,拚命吹打我们的小屋。我们

front of our door. In winter we could hear the water gurgling under the ice. But when spring came, it was gone. In our place we had to live on chaff and leaves every spring."

They talked and dreamed about the future. If, starting with their generation, nature could be transformed, if they could change the bitter road people had been travelling for so long, if they could bring in bumper harvests, raise forests of trees, make the springs gush and crisscross the land with irrigation canals — what a happy world it would be.

On the sand dune to the south a tableau formed that was very much out of keeping with what they were talking about. Six, a hunting falcon on his right arm, led the way up the dune. Behind came Stupid Li and his wife, like a pair of attendants, each carrying a dead rabbit. They stood beside Six, one to his left and one to his right, and gazed and pointed at something in the distance. And behind the dune, like a faint sprig of peach blossom, appeared Man'er's lustrous head.

"Your kid brother gets more complicated by the day, Four," said Kitchen Stove. "He's playing with falcons now."

"I can't make head or tail of those people," said Four. "Six and Yang Mao had a big fight over pigeons. The hatred between them was something enormous. But then Li the Seventh hauled the three of them into town for a meal. The two became good friends again, and Yang Mao loaned Six his falcon."

"What do you mean the three of them?" queried Kitchen Stove.

"Man'er went too," said Four. "She's their focal point, their organizational centre, the guide of all their actions. They can't do a

门前有一条小河,冬天,水还在冰下哗哗地叫,到春天就干得没有了。我们那里,到春天靠榆皮树叶过日子。"

他们交谈着,向往着,如果能从他们这一代,改变了自然环境,改变了人们长久走过的苦难的路程,使庄稼丰收,树木成林,泉水涌注,水渠纵横,那对他们是太幸福了。

这时,在南面沙岗上出现了一幅和他们的谈话非常不相称的景象。六儿右胳膊上架着一只秃鹰,第一个走上沙岗来。随后而来的是黎大傻和他的老婆,夫妇两个每人手里提着一只死兔子,像侍卫一样,一左一右,站在了六儿的身旁,向远处张望着指点着。而在沙岗背后,像隐约的桃枝一样,出现了小满儿的光耀的头面。

"老四,你弟弟越发的不简单,玩起鹰来了。"锅灶说。

"这些人的事,咱弄不清。"四儿说,"和杨卯儿为鸽子吵了架,仇大得不得了。经黎七儿把三个人拉到城里吃了一顿饭,两个人又成了好朋友,把鹰借给六儿了。"

"怎么是三个人呢?"锅灶问。

"小满儿也去了。"四儿说,"那是他们的主心骨,组织中心,行动的指南。离了她是不行

英汉对照
English-Chinese
中国文学宝库
Gems of Chinese Literature
现代文学系列
Modern Literature

thing without her. I've also heard that Yang Mao has become the best customer of Stupid Li's dumpling shop. He goes there every night and fills up. Stupid's wife told him: You only eat well and dress well. Your new life still can't be considered complete. I'm going to introduce you to a nice girl, but you have to treat me to a meal first.... So Yang Mao invited her to a restaurant in town."

"Why not call him over and ask him to help us bore this well?" Kitchen Stove urged.

While Four hesitated, Six and his entire retinue left the sand dune and disappeared in the opposite direction.

People usually comment upon passing incidents only casually. They don't always notice what a depressing effect they may have on those concerned. Nine sat gazing abstracted at the bare sand dune. She was still thinking of her childhood at home. After her mother died, Nine had frequently sat alone by her small window. Outside the window was a date tree where little birds gathered to enjoy the sun and avoid the wind. There they played, obviously very affectionate. Several, perching on a branch together, chirruped with perhaps the greatest fondness of all. Soon, one of them flew to another branch. Then, a sudden gust of wind, and all flew their separate ways. In front of Nine's door, there also had been a tiny cove of reeds. When the river was low, little fish used to gather there and frolic around a weed growing in the water. But in summer, when the river rose, each went off on his own, no one knows where!

Such memories are painful, enervating. Nine stood up and said:

"We've had plenty to eat and enough to drink. Let's get to

会儿滑车。"

"小心掉在井里呀!"锅灶笑着说,"你们猜我在想什么?我想六儿的包子不能吃了,净是兔子肉!"

九儿上到滑车上,用力攀登着,像一个勤奋的小昆虫在清晨和黄昏的时候工作。滑车滚动着,四儿从井底望着她,一时感到这是一个奇异的动人的少女图像。

她的工作越来越熟练从容,太阳从她的前方,慢慢向西移动。她可以看得很远,可以看到县城南关药王庙前面的两根高矗的旗杆。可以望见旷野里送粪的,捡柴的,放牧牛羊的和整理园地的人。她看见六儿正和小满儿在田野里追逐,听到黎大傻和他老婆的喊叫声音。

在下面工作的锅灶和四儿,也在谈论这件事。

"老四,你的理论高,你给我解释,我们在这里受累受冷的工作,你的老弟在那里带着女人玩耍。在人生这条道路上,是我们走对了哩,还是他们走对了?"锅灶冲着井底喊叫着。

"你提出的这个问题很重要,这是个人生观的问题。"从井里冒出四儿的声音,"你羡慕他们的生活吗?"

英汉对照
English-Chinese
中国文学宝库
Gems of Chinese Literature
现代文学系列
Modern Literature

"Sometimes they make me sick. But sometimes I'm a little envious too."

"The way they look at things, they're sure they're right. But I don't envy them in the least. Sometimes they must feel ashamed of the way they live. Otherwise, when they saw us why did they sneak away?"

"But there's another old question: Why hasn't he ever been able to reform?"

"I've been thinking about that myself these past couple of days. If we rely only on the strength of us few, it isn't going to be easy to get results. How does a fellow become politically conscious? Study is important. A person's experience is important. But more important is the influence of society. I think we can compare Six's mind with this parched land we're changing. If we do our work well, we can tap water on it, make it able to bear crops, even bumper crops. But all around are dust-laden winds and shifting sands that can close it off, bury it, turn it into an eternal desert where not an inch of grass will grow. We've got to strengthen the positive influences in our society. That means increasing the number of irrigated fields, cutting down the dry patches, tapping more and more sources of water until we've wiped out the sandstorms."

"Yes, it can be done," Nine said to herself on the treadle wheel. As she paced on, the scoops brought up earth and sand from the shaft bottom. She looked down. Fresh clean water had begun to seep through. But what about love? It was different from the companionship of childhood, she thought gravely. Only a love that had a common revolutionary goal, a love formed in the course

"有时候觉得他们讨厌,有时候,也有点羡慕。"锅灶说。

"在他们看来,一定是他们走对了。但是,我一点儿也不羡慕他们。"四儿说,"他们这样生活,有时候,自己也会感到羞耻的,不然,为什么望见我们就躲开了呢?"

"可是,还有一个老问题,他为什么一直不能改变过来呢?"锅灶说。

"这两天,我又把这个问题想了一下,"四儿说,"只凭我们几个人的力量去改造人,是不容易收到效果的。人怎样才能觉悟呢,学习是重要的,个人经历也是重要的,但更重要的是社会的影响。我有这样一个比方,六儿的心,就像我们正在改造的旱地。我们工作得好,可以在这块地上开发出水泉,使它有收成,甚至变成丰产地;可是,四外的黄风流沙,也还可以把它封闭,把它埋没,使它永远荒废,寸草不长。我们要在社会上,加强积极的影响。这就是扩大水浇地,缩小旱地;开发水源,一直到消灭风沙。"

"是的,这是可能的。"九儿在滑车上想,她攀登着,一斗子一斗子的淤沙积泥,从井底提上来,她望望井底,新的清澈的水,开始翻冒出来。但是爱情呢? 她严肃地思考:它的结合,和童年的伴侣,并不一样。只有在共同的革命目标上,

英汉对照
English-Chinese
中国文学宝库
Gems of Chinese Literature
现代文学系列
Modern Literature

of long and co-operative hard work, could endure the many trials of life, could be truly firm and everlasting. Of course, love could be born during serious work, or it could be born in the midst of childish laughter. But those loves were as different from each other as flowers that bloom on the unruffled surface of a placid lake and those which grow atop a mountain cliff — digging deep tenacious roots into the soil, able to withstand drought and wind and rain.

17

The provincial officer naturally hadn't come to the village for the sole purpose of learning about the local residents. But he had developed a warmth during his years of work that made him want to help somebody. He hoped that with his aid Man'er would change. And he knew that it was only through study and work that she could change. Of course it would be very difficult, for he realized that he didn't really understand her yet.

That evening when Man'er returned victorious from her hunt, the provincial officer was standing in the courtyard. Stupid Li's family lived in a broken-down compound. In the northwest corner of the crumbling compound wall, beside an old storage cellar for cabbages, was a half-dead elm tree. Extremely ugly, it was withered on top, and its trunk was split and warped. A big branch which should have been chopped up for firewood long ago hung over into the neighbouring courtyard, where it served as a roost for the neighbour's chickens. Several of the birds had already flown up on

在长期协同的辛勤工作里结合起来的爱情,才能经受得起人生历程的万水千山的考验,才能真正巩固和永久吧。当然,爱情,可以在庄严的工作里形成,也可以在童年式的嬉笑里形成。那分别就像有的花可以开在风平浪静的水面上,有的花却可以开在山顶的岩石上,它深深地坚韧地扎根在土壤里,忍耐得过干旱,并经受得起风雨。

17

那位干部当然不是专为了解人们的生活,才跑到乡下来的。他也抱着一种多年工作积累的热情,愿意帮助一个人。他希望小满儿能在他帮助下面,有所改变。他并且想到,只有在学习和工作里,小满儿才能改变。这当然是很困难的,因为他明白,他还没有真正了解她。

这天晚上,就是当小满儿行围射猎胜利归来的时候,干部站在院里。黎大傻家是个破大院,西北角破围墙下面,有一个荒废的白菜窖,旁边有一棵半死的老榆树,这棵树长得十分丑陋,它的头顶干枯,树身破裂歪斜,一枝早可以拉下来做柴烧的大横干,垂到邻舍的院里,成了邻家的鸡窠,有几只鸡已经飞到上面,准备过夜了。

it, preparing to retire for the night.

When Man'er came home, she bore no traces of her wild running, her exultation or her weariness, in the fields. She returned after her sister and brother-in-law. Each bearing a dead rabbit, they were covered with dust, and bone-tired. But Man'er seemed to have made some preparations before entering the door. Neat and clean, her hair smoothly combed, she strolled past the provincial cadre with her usual easy step.

"Doing anything after dinner?" he asked her.

"Not a thing," Man'er replied with a smile. "What's up?"

"The Youth Leaguers are having a study class tonight. Why don't you go and listen in?"

"Will they let me?" Man'er asked with a sly laugh. "A backward character like me!"

"Of course. First cook dinner. Afterwards, we'll go together."

Man'er nodded. She made no reply, but the cadre could see from the face that she turned away how displeased she was. As she carried in an armful of brushwood and sat down before the stove and lit the fire, she kept shooting glances out of the corner of her eye. The cadre remained standing by the door.

"Aren't you going out to eat, comrade?" Man'er asked.

"Put some more rice in the pot," the cadre smiled. "I'll have a meal with your family."

"Our food's no good," said Man'er. "You won't be able to eat it."

"Good or bad, I'll pay for my share," the cadre laughed. He stood in the courtyard until Man'er finished cooking.

小满儿回到家来,一点儿也没有带着在野地里奔跑、狂欢、疲累的痕迹。她是在姐姐和姐夫回家以后才回来的,姐夫和姐姐,一人提回来一只死兔子,两个人浑身是土,疲累不堪,而小满儿好像在进门之前就作了准备,她的身上整齐干净,头发也梳理过了,她用那惯常的轻捷悠闲的步伐,走过干部的面前。

"小满同志。"干部叫住她。"你吃过饭有事情吗?"

"没有,我是个大贤(闲)人。"小满儿笑着说,"干什么吧?"

"今天晚上,青年团员们学习,你也去听听吧。"

"人家叫我听吗?"小满儿狡猾地笑着,"我这个落后分子儿!"

"当然可以听,你先做饭,回头我们一块儿去。"干部说。

小满儿点点头,没有说什么。但是干部可以从她扭转过去的脸上看出,她是如何的不高兴。她抱柴做饭,坐在灶前烧火,不住地用眼角溜撒着,干部一直站在门口。

"同志,你不出去吃饭吗?"小满儿说。

"你多添点米,"干部笑着,"我在你家吃一顿吧。"

"我们家的饭不好。"小满儿说,"你吃不下。"

"不好也一样给粮票。"干部说。他在院里一直站到小满儿把饭做熟。

小满儿这一顿饭,磨磨蹭蹭,费了有两顿饭

英汉对照
English-Chinese
中国文学宝库
Gems of Chinese Literature
现代文学系列
Modern Literature

Man'er dawdled. She spent long enough to cook two meals. Several times she thought of running away from the house. But her intelligence told her the provincial officer intended to prevent her from doing that very thing — that was why he was watching her. And she knew his intentions were good. Assuming a completely peaceful air, she sat down and had dinner with him.

Her brother-in-law ate his meal in the next room. Her sister, sensing that something had come up between Man'er and the cadre, stayed out of the way and didn't speak.

It was already quite dark by the time dinner was over. Man'er switched from the defensive to the offensive. Putting down her bowl, she said:

"Let's go, comrade."

When they left the compound gate, Man'er ran on ahead, a small flashlight in her hand.

"You've got one of those gadgets," said the cadre. "That's fine."

"I'll show you the way," she said. "We'll go round the outside of the village. It's shorter that way."

From the small lane she turned north and proceeded to the outskirts. Since she walked quickly and kept darting the flashlight, which wasn't very bright, in every direction, the cadre, who was following behind, couldn't see a thing. He was only conscious that the path was extremely bumpy.

Man'er flew down from a small sand dune, then turned east, hugging the old village wall. This stretch was all soft sand, and was pitted with holes of uprooted trees. Stumbling and staggering

的工夫。她几次想从家里跑出去,但凭她的聪明,她知道干部正是防备她逃跑,才在那里监视她,她并且了解到这是一种好意,她装作十分安静地同干部吃了晚饭。

这一顿饭,她的姐夫蹲在外间没进屋,她的姐姐不明白这个干部和小满儿之间,发生了什么问题,也一直在避讳着什么,没有讲话。

吃过晚饭,天已经很黑了。小满儿从被动转为主动,首先放下饭碗说:

"同志,我们走吧。"

走出大门来,小满儿跑在前面,手里拿着一个小手电。

"你有这个家当。"干部说,"太好了。"

"我给你带路,"小满儿说,"我们从村外走,可以近一些。"

她从小胡同里往北转到村外来,因为她走的太快,那个手电的光亮太小,加上一闪一晃,干部跟在后面,反而什么也看不见了,只感到脚下绊绊磕磕。

小满儿飞快地跳过一个矮沙岗,贴着寨墙里面往东走,这一带都是软沙,有很多刨了树的大坑,干部深一脚,浅一脚,跌跌撞撞,只好慢

英汉对照
English-Chinese
中国文学宝库
Gems of Chinese Literature
现代文学系列
Modern Literature

on the uneven ground, the cadre had to go slowly, depriving himself of her leadership and wildly darting flashlight.

"Walk a little faster," Man'er urged. "They must be starting class. We don't want to be late."

"Where are you taking me?" the cadre asked, half in jest. "This isn't the right path."

"What is the right path?" Man'er countered. "As long as it gets you there a little faster, it's good. Be careful. There's a well here. Don't fall in whatever you do."

Cautiously feeling the windlass, he skirted around the well. Beyond was a sharp incline, which Man'er leaped down. The provincial officer very nearly skidded to the bottom.

"Watch out. Fence." Man'er edged between some clumps of brambles. The brambles caught on the cadre's clothing.

"Take this." Man'er turned and handed him the flashlight. She continued to walk ahead. Along a rubble-strewn path, she led him to the rear gate of a large temple compound. The cadre had visited here before. As they walked through the main temple building, he played his flashlight on the idols lining the aisle. Grotesquely askew, they were missing arms or legs; some had lost their eyes. Man'er nonchalantly slowed her pace.

"Ever go to any of our spring temple fairs, comrade?" she asked. "They were very exciting. When the wheat was half as high as a man, old ladies used to come from all over to pray, bringing their daughters with them. The village boys would lure the girls to the wheat fields outside the village. If you took a walk through there at night, you'd flush them out like birds. They rose up out of

走,以便脱离她的领导,并避免了她那手电的扰乱。

"走快点儿啊!"小满儿说,"人家一定上课了,我们不要迟到。"

"你带的这是什么路?"干部半开玩笑地说,"这不是正路。"

"什么是正路?"小满儿说,"只要抄近儿就好。小心,这里有一眼井,你可千万别掉下去。"

干部小心地扶住辘轳架,从井边沿过,然后是一陡坡,小满儿跳了下去,干部差不多是滑了下去。

"小心,篱笆。"小满儿侧着身子从荆棘之间闪过去,荆棘挂住了干部的衣服。

"给你吧。"小满儿回头把手电交给干部。她仍然在前面走着,从堆着很多破砖乱瓦的道路上,走进了一座大庙的后门。这座大庙,干部是参观过的,当他们在大殿中间走过时,干部用手电照了照那站在两旁的,歪歪斜斜,缺胳膊少腿或是失去了眼珠的罗汉们,小满儿毫不在意地走过去,她的脚步放慢了。她说:

"同志,你没有赴过四月初八的庙会吧?这个庙会太热闹了。那时候,小麦长得有半人高,各地来的老太太们坐在庙里念佛,她们带来的那些姑娘们,却叫村里的小伙子们勾引到村外边的麦地里去了。半夜的时候,你到地里去走一趟吧,那些小伙子和姑娘们就会像鸟儿一样,一对儿一对儿的从麦垄儿里飞出来,好玩极了。"

英汉对照
English-Chinese
中国文学宝库
Gems of Chinese Literature
现代文学系列
Modern Literature

the wheat, pair after pair, and flew away. It was very funny."

"What was so comical about it?" the cadre demanded.

"I've only heard people talk," said Man'er. "I was never there when all the fun was on. During the war of resistance, the guerrillas in this village were very brave. They held out in the third temple building. Some of them sat on the idols' heads to keep watch for the enemy sweeping in this direction and fight them off. The temple nuns carried ammunition for the guerrillas. Now all the nuns have gone back to ordinary life. The youngest and most beautiful one married the son of the village vice-chairman."

"Those war stories are fine," the cadre said.

Man'er halted. "Let's not go to the meeting then. Let's go home, and I'll tell you stories all night."

The provincial officer shook his head.

"They won't attack me at the meeting?" she asked in a small voice as they emerged from the main building.

"Certainly not," the cadre said. "What ever are you thinking?"

"A nun hung herself here." Man'er pointed to a large tree in front of the temple. "Because they wouldn't let her marry the one she loved. I saw her when she was alive. She knew how to play the *Sheng* pipes. She was very good-looking."

The cadre didn't say anything. A wind scraped the treetops and the roofs.

"I'm afraid." Man'er whirled and virtually threw herself on his chest. Her voice trembled. He could hear her teeth chattering. Supporting her, he switched on the flashlight. Her face was deathly pale, her eyeballs turned up. She was muttering something he

"那有什么好玩的?"干部说。

"我也是听人说的,"小满儿说,"那么热闹的时候,我并没有赶上。抗日的时候,这村的游击队很英勇,他们站到第三层大殿上,有的就坐在神像的头顶上,放哨和阻击向这里扫荡的敌人。庙里的尼姑替他们搬运子弹,现在她们都还俗了,有一个最年轻最漂亮的,是副村长的儿媳妇。"

"这些抗日的故事很好。"干部说。

"那么,"小满儿停下来,转回身说,"我们不要去开会了,回到家里去,我给你讲一晚上故事吧!"

干部摇了摇头。

"他们不会斗争我吧?"走出大殿,小满儿小声问。

"绝对不会的。"干部说,"你想到哪里去了?"

"有一个尼姑,曾经吊死在这里。"小满儿指着大殿前面的一棵大树说,"因为恋爱不自由。活着的时候,我见过她,她会吹笙,长得也很好。"

干部没有说话,有一阵风扫过树尖和屋顶。

"我害怕。"小满儿忽然转回身来,几乎扑到干部的怀里,她的声音抖颤着,干部听到她的牙齿发出"得得"的打击声音,他扶住她,用手电一照,她的脸色苍白,眼睛往上翻着。她说着听不明白的话,眼里流出泪来。

英汉对照
English-Chinese
中国文学宝库
Gems of Chinese Literature
现代文学系列
Modern Literature

couldn't understand, and tears rolled from her eyes.

"What's the matter?" he exclaimed in agitation.

"I saw her! I saw her!" Man'er shouted.

"Hysteria!" the cadre said to himself. "I'd never have thought she was the type."

The first one Man'er's cries brought running in from the street was Six. He had just sent Yang Mao a rabbit and was on his way home. Only when Six entered did it occur to the cadre that he was in quite a compromising situation. A dark night, a deserted spot, and alone with a girl having hysterics. He explained to Six how he and Man'er had happened to come here.

"Save me! Carry me home on your back!" Man'er groaned when she heard Six's voice.

"A good idea," said the cadre. "Lend a hand and carry her. Do you know where she lives?"

"Yes," said Six. He squatted down and pulled Man'er's arms over his shoulders. Man'er was still crying, her tears falling on his neck. When he reached the street she grew quiet. Pursing her lips, she blew a silent puff on the back of his neck. At first, Six had been rather worried. But when Man'er stealthily placed her mouth against his cheek and kissed him ardently, he knew that there was nothing really wrong with her.

18

To Old Li the carpenter, Six's first day out with the new cart was a matter of the greatest importance. When the cart was finished,

"怎么回事?"干部慌了手脚。

"我看见了她,我看见了她!"小满儿大声喊叫。

"歇斯底里!"干部心里说,"没想到她有这种病症!"

听到喊声,第一个从街上跑到大庙里来的是六儿,他给杨卯儿送了一只兔子去,回来路过这里。直到六儿进来,干部才感觉到,他现在的处境,很容易引起别人的怀疑。在这样黑的夜晚,在这样荒无人烟的地方,在他的身边,一个女人发生了这种情景。他向六儿说明他同小满儿来到这里的经过。

"你救救我!你背我家去!"小满儿听到六儿说话,发出了这样的呻吟。

"好,"干部说,"你帮忙背背她吧,你知道她的住处吗?"

"知道。"六儿说着蹲下来,拉起小满儿的两只手,放到肩上。小满儿仍然在哭泣,眼泪滴在六儿的脖子里。走到街上,她安静了,她撮起嘴来轻轻地无声地吹嘘着六儿的脖子后面。起初,六儿也有些害怕,但等到她偷偷地把嘴唇伸到他的脸上,热烈地吻着的时候,六儿才知道她并没有发生什么意外。

18

六儿出车,黎老东看成是一件头等隆重的事件。自从把车打成,他运用毕生的工作经验,

英汉对照
English-Chinese
中国文学宝库
Gems of Chinese Literature
现代文学系列
Modern Literature

he used his lifelong experience to see to it that the paint dried quickly in spite of the winter cold. That evening, he prepared some wine and tidbits and invited Li the Seventh to his home.

"Brother Seventh," he said, "I entrust my boy Six and my new cart to you. Teach him well, give him the benefit of your half a lifetime's experience as a carter. Teach him to follow the right road, and not tumble and turn over."

Li the Seventh readily agreed. "Don't worry, Brother," he said, "I won't let him lose out. We're planning to go to Stonegate, this trip. What sort of merchandise do you want to bring back?"

"Whatever earns the biggest profit, naturally. You decide. But since it's a new cart, don't carry coal the first trip."

Li the Seventh laughed. "It's coal that earns the biggest profit in winter. Well, I'll see when we get there. Maybe I'll load you with an assortment of mixed goods."

When they were both half-drunk the carpenter said to Li the Seventh:

"I know there were some differences between us, Brother, during the land-reform days. But I never really considered you a rich peasant. I always thought of you as an upper-middle peasant. Of course your grandfather and your father were rich peasants, both generations. But even after you and your brothers divided up the family property, you were mainly a carter, and you didn't hire much help. Tho classify you as a rich peasant I thought was going a bit too far. Yet I didn't think you should be called an ordinary middle peasant — it seemed to me you were a little over the line. That was what the argument was about, at the time."

使油漆在冬季提前干好。晚上,他特备了酒菜,把黎七儿请来,对他说:

"七兄弟,我把六儿和这辆新车交给你,你要好好带动他,把你半辈子跑车的经验教给他,叫他在正道上走,不要翻车跌脚。"

黎七儿一口答应,并且说:

"不用大哥挂念,我不能眼看着叫他吃亏。我们这次打算到石门,大叔,你看拉些什么货物回来?"

"自然是拉什么利大,就拉什么。"黎老东说,"你看着吧。可是,因为是新打的车,头一趟可不要拉煤。"

"可是,"黎七儿笑着说,"冬季还就是拉煤利钱大。到那里看吧,要不就装点儿杂货。"

酒喝到半醉的时候,黎老东又向黎七儿说了这些话:

"七兄弟,我知道,在土改的那段日子里,你和我们有些隔膜。可是,我一直并不认为你是一个富农,我一直评你是个上中农。你爷爷,你父亲那两辈,当然是富农。可是自从你弟兄们分了家,你主要是跑车,雇人不多,要评成富农,我觉得有点够不上,要说是中农,好像又冒点尖儿,当时的争论,就在这上面。"

"过去的事情了。"黎七儿说,"当时,我就是

"That's all past now," said Li the Seventh. "What hurt me most was losing that mule of mine. Later on, I sold a few things and bought him back. I've got a bad status here, I don't like meeting people from my own village. Now that I'm a carter I'm getting along all right, as you can see. To tell you the truth, as long as a man's got ability and ideas he can eat and drink well even if he doesn's farm. I neither save nor stint. When I'm home, as you know, I eat whatever Stupid Li's dumpling shop has to sell. When I'm on the road and stop at an inn, my food is nothing but the best. And when I set out again, I've a bottle of good grog in my tunic. Whenever I feel thirsty I've only to bend my head to take a swig."

"I admire you," said the carpenter. "Those other families all remained collapsed. You were the only one to recover fast."

The carpenter got up several times in the night to feed his horse after Li the Seventh left. At the first cock's crow, he awakened Six and loaded the feed. When the beast was being hitched, he helped with the harnessing, tightened the belly band and greased the axles. They finished breakfast before daylight, and Six drove the cart into the street. People who were up early all praised the new vehicle. The carpenter walked backwards before it, smoothing out ruts with his feet and giving Six continual directions.

Outside the village, Li the Seventh's big cart, pulled by a smart pair, took the lead. Yang Mao, going to Stonegate to buy some things for the New Year holiday, was riding with him. As they rolled out of the old stockade gate, Li the Seventh flourished his whip to rouse his pair, ran a few steps beside them, then jumped

心疼我那匹骡子。后来,我变卖些东西,又把它买回来了。咱成份不好,就不愿在村里见人。现在跑着车,我的生活,你看见了,也还过得去。坦白地说,人只要有能力办法,不种园子地,也能吃香喝辣!我不省着细着。平日在家,你知道,黎大傻家卖什么我吃什么。出门打尖下店,不是焖饼就是炸酱面;出店上车,整瓶子好酒在怀里一掖,什么时候想喝了,就低头来一口。"

"我就是佩服你。"黎老东说,"那些别的户都倒下了,就是你站起来得快。"

黎七儿走了以后,黎老东几次起来喂牲口。鸡叫头遍,他就叫醒六儿,装好草料。套车时,他帮着摆正辕鞍,结好肚带,抹足车油。天不明吃了早饭,六儿把车赶到街上来。早起站在街上的人,都称赞这辆新车。黎老东在车的前面倒着走,有时用脚填平道辙,不断地指挥着六儿。

出村,黎七儿的双套大车,赶在前面。杨卯儿要到石门去办年货,坐在他的车上。出了寨墙口,黎七儿摇动鞭子,把车轰开,跟着跑了几步,然后一蹿身,坐了上去。他回头望望六儿,

英汉对照
English-Chinese
中国文学宝库
Gems of Chinese Literature
现代文学系列
Modern Literature

up and sat sideways on one of the shafts. He looked back. Six, imitating him, leaped up and sat on a shaft of his own cart. The old carpenter, at the edge of the village, was gazing after them. Only after Six's cart rounded a big sand dune did he turn and go back.

The village chairman stopped Old Li at the crossroad and said he wished the carpenter would join the agricultural co-op. To ease his doubts, the chairman told him enthusiastically how other villages were also forming co-ops, and what they were paying to people who let the co-ops use their animals and carts. Old Li seemed not to hear any of this. As he headed home, people got the impression that his walk, which had been so satisfied and full of verve right along, suddenly became anxious and uneasy.

After rounding the big sand dune, the carts halted abruptly. Man'er, hugging a small package, sat waiting beneath an old poplar tree. Now she rose and climbed on to Six's cart.

Talking and laughing boisterously, Li the Seventh swung his whip. Behind the two carts rose swirling columns of dust.

19

Every day, when Nine returned home, Old Fu had dinner ready for her. He knew his daughter was doing heavy work. Just as when they were blacksmithing, he cooked up millet and served it thick. Every day, father and daughter sat on the platform bed beside a small kerosene lamp and ate their evening meal.

He noticed that she spoke little the past couple of days. Think-

六儿也照黎七儿的样子蹿上了车。黎老东在村边望着,望着六儿的车转过大沙岗,才转回身来。

在十字街口,村长拦住了他,和他说了希望他加入合作社的事。为了打破他的顾虑,村长还热心地向他介绍了别的村庄办社,对于牲口车辆的折价办法。这些话,黎老东好像全然没有听进去,他往家里走,从别人看来,他那一直兴奋得意的步伐,忽然变得焦躁和不安了。

车辆转过大沙岗,突然停下来。小满儿怀里抱着一个小包裹,坐在一棵老杨树下面等候着。她站起来,爬到六儿的车上去了。

然后,黎七儿大声说笑着,摇动长鞭。两辆大车的后面,扬起了滚滚的尘土。

19

每天,九儿回到家里,傅老刚已经做好了饭。知道女儿做的是重活,老人还是按照打铁时的习惯,做小米干饭。每天,父女两个坐在里间炕上,守着一盏小煤油灯吃着晚饭。

这两天,父亲注意到女儿很少说话,他以为她是太疲累了。他说:

ing she was overtired, he said:

"Some mutual-aid teams gave me money today. I helped them recently on a few odd jobs. I didn't want it, but they said that since we were away from home and couldn't earn an income from our land, our living depended on my blacksmithing. They insisted that I take it. I thought: New Year is coming; you ought to have some new clothes."

"I can get along without them." The girl lowered her head. "I can mend and wash my old clothes for the New Year. But your padded robe is too ragged, Pa, you need a new one."

"I'm an old man. There's no reason for me to dress up," said the father. "The chairman told me that some of the mutual-aid teams here are going to combine into a co-op next year. He hopes we'll join. He says a co-op always has blacksmithing to be done. I said I'd talk it over with you when you got home. Help me decide. Is it better to join, or not?"

"I'm for joining." The daughter smiled. "There's nothing I'd like better."

"That's how I feel too," the father said excitedly. "Of course we could go home and join there. But they're a step further advanced here, and we have a lot of feeling for this village. It's just as well to join here. The chairman said he hopes Six's family will also join. Then, the co-op will have both a blacksmith and a carpenter. That will be much more convenient for the work. But Old Li is so enchanted with carting, he doesn't want to join. I haven't seen Six around these last few days. Have you?"

The girl didn't answer.

"今天,有几个互助组,给我们拿来一些工钱,这些日子,我帮他们拾掇了一些零碎活儿。我不要,他们说我们出门在外,又没有园子地里的收成,只凭着手艺生活,一定要我收下。我想眼下就要过年了,你也该添些衣裳。"

"不添也可以。"女儿低着头说,"过年,我把旧衣裳拆洗拆洗就行了。爹的棉袄太破了,应该换一件。"

"我老了,更不要好看。"父亲说,"村长和我说,他们几个互助组,明年就要合并成合作社。村长愿意我们也加入,说是社里短不了铁匠活儿。我说等你回来商量商量,你帮我想想,是加入好,还是不加入好。"

"我愿意加入。"女儿笑着说,"这是最好不过的事。"

"我也是这么想。"父亲兴奋地说,"当然我们可以回老家去参加。可是,这里的工作更靠前一步,我们和这个村子又有感情,就在这里参加也好。村长还说,他们也希望六儿家参加,那样,社里有铁匠也有木匠,工作方便得多。可是黎老东正迷着赶大车,不乐意参加。这些日子,我总见不到六儿,你见到他了吗?"

女儿没有说话。

英汉对照
English-Chinese
中国文学宝库
Gems of Chinese Literature
现代文学系列
Modern Literature

"Aren't you feeling well?" Her father looked at her attentively. "You don't seem to have any appetite."

"I'm all right," the girl said. "Just a little tired."

She went into the next room and began to clean the pot and bowls.

"My quarrel with Old Li," her father called through the door, "is just between him and me, just a tiff between two old men. It doesn't amount to anything. You shouldn't take it to heart."

"I haven't taken it to heart," said Nine. "Your health hasn't been so good this winter, Pa. I wish you'd get more rest."

"Don't worry about me," the old man laughed. "I'll be all right when spring comes. There are no meetings tonight. After you've straightened things up, go to bed a bit earlier."

Nine spread her father's quilts on the platform bed. Closing the door of the room, she left for the home of the girls she was staying with.

The sky was very beautiful that night, and the moon was very round, very bright. Nine paused in the courtyard and listened. After her father blew out the lamp and lay down, he didn't cough nearly so much as he used to. Her heart lightened and eased. She felt that her emotions now were worthy of this clear winter's night, worthy of the bright moon overhead. Fixing her eyes on the round moon, it seemed to her that for the first time she could see clearly the adorable lively little rabbit outlined there.

20

Ah, childhood, from beginning to end beyond any doubt you are

"你不舒服吗?"父亲注意地问,"怎么看你吃不下?"

"不。"女儿说,"我只是有点儿累。"

她到外间去收拾锅碗。

"我和黎老东吵翻了。"父亲在里间说,"这只是一人一家的问题,只是两个老头子的问题,算不了什么。你不要把这件事情放在心上。"

"我没有放在心上。"九儿说,"今年冬天,我看着爹的身体不大结实,我希望爹多休息休息。"

"你不要惦记我。"老人笑着说,"我这病到春天就会好起来的。今天晚上不开会,收拾好了,你早点睡觉去吧!"

九儿给父亲铺好炕,带上屋门,到女伴们那里去。

夜里,天晴得很好,月亮很圆,很明净,九儿在院里停站了一会儿,听了听,父亲在吹灯躺下以后,并没有像往常那样咳嗽。她的心情也明快平静下来,她觉得她现在的心境,无愧于这冬夜的晴空,也无愧于当头的明月。她定睛观望,好像是第一次看清了圆月里那只小兔儿的可爱的活泼的姿态。

20

童年啊,你的整个经历,毫无疑问,像航行在春水涨满的河流里的一只小船。回忆起来,

like a small boat navigating the swollen waters of a river in spring. In retrospect, people's emotions always appear to have been happy. But can it be that wind and rain left no scars on your billowing white sail? Or that your prow, surging forward, met with no adverse currents or interfering rocks? Memories of you, like the load you bore, are sometimes light, sometimes oh so heavy!

But in youth your fiery power has no limit. Your hand on the tiller grows more and more experienced. Full of confidence, bearing a thousand-catty load, you sail swiftly on a journey of ten thousand *li*! Not for smooth sailing with the wind should you wish, but for the kind of strength that smashes through the mightiest waves, a strength that keeps you steady on the course no matter what the difficulties.

1956
Translated by Sidney Shapiro

人们的心情永远是畅快活泼的。然而,在你那鼓胀的白帆上,就没有经过风雨冲击的痕迹?或是你那昂奋前进的船头,就没有遇到过逆流礁石的阻碍吗?有关你的回忆,就像你的负载一样,有时是轻松的,有时也是沉重的啊!

但是,你的青春的火力是无穷无尽的,你的舵手的经验也越来越丰富了,你正在满有信心地,负载着千斤的重量,奔赴万里的途程!你希望的不应该只是一帆风顺,你希望的是要具备了冲破惊涛骇浪、在任何艰难的情况下也不会迷失方向的那一种力量。

1956年初夏